Worth the Wait

Synithia Williams

Crimson Romance
New York London Toronto Sydney New Delhi

CRIMSON
ROMANCE
Crimson Romance
An Imprint of Simon & Schuster, Inc.
1230 Avenue of the Americas
New York, NY 10020

ISBN 978-1-4405-6183-2
ISBN 978-1-4405-6184-9 (ebook)

This is a work of fiction. Names, characters, corporations, institutions, organizations, events, or locales in this novel are either the product of the author's imagination or, if real, used fictitiously. The resemblance of any character to actual persons (living or dead) is entirely coincidental.

Acknowledgments

Thanks to T.J. Proofs for helping me find my writing flow over virtual mugs of coffee. Big thanks to my trainer, Kelley Blashka for taking the time to provide insight in the life of a personal trainer. Finally, once again, thanks to my wonderful husband for supporting me and my writing career.

CHAPTER 1

"Look, Tasha, it's been fun going out with you, but unless we have sex tonight this needs to end right now."

Tasha Smith's jaw dropped. She stepped back from her date, clenching her keys in her hand. She was at the end of what was previously a nice dinner and movie date with Charles Worthington, a software developer her sister had introduced to her weeks before. It'd been so nice that she had planned to invite him in for coffee, and only coffee, but apparently he wanted more.

She raised an eyebrow as her eyes narrowed in on him. "Excuse me?"

He tugged at the corner of his shirt and shifted slightly, his caramel skin and hazel eyes quickly losing their appeal. He stopped fidgeting and stood straighter, his stance becoming defensive, and she glared back.

"Look, it's commendable that you're a virgin, but I'm a man with needs. If you can't satisfy those needs, then it's best we move on."

She looked away from Charles's face to the silent street before her home. There were a few lights on in the other single family houses. Ten minutes earlier the cool night air and faint scent from the roses along her porch would have been romantic. But now they set the scene for another disappointing date. She'd hoped—in vain—that Charles would be different.

Her internal warning bells had gone off about Charles when he'd hinted around about spending the night after a heated kiss on their third date and then didn't bother to hide his disappointment when she informed him of her virginal status. Of course he'd gone on to say it wasn't a big deal, and previous experience should have

5

reminded her that she'd heard it all before. His good job, good looks, and winning personality had muffled those bells. But once again, dating a woman who was saving herself for marriage had put too much commitment pressure on a member of the male species. She knew only one way to deal with Charles.

She relaxed her stance and smiled at him. "You're right. You do have needs and I shouldn't have ignored them."

His face brightened. "I'm glad you said that. I'm willing to wait a little bit longer. I mean, you are fine as hell." His gaze swept over her body. "If you want to hook a brother up with a blow job, that's cool."

She fought the urge to roll her eyes and leaned closer. "You'd like that, wouldn't you?"

He took a step closer. "Hell yeah."

She reached out and put her hands on his shoulders. "Then you know what you can do? You can go suck your own damn dick," she snapped as she shoved him to the ground ass first. "When I do give it up you'll be the last person to get it."

She turned and stormed into her house.

Once inside, she wanted to scream. The routine was beyond annoying. Every guy she dated was either overly fascinated to find a grown woman who was still a virgin, or ran away as if she carried the plague.

She was tired of the novelty of it. It had been easier to save herself when she was younger with hopes of meeting prince charming. But at twenty-nine, she didn't feel the same satisfaction from being different from the girls in high school and college who'd slept with any guy who looked their way. As her thirtieth birthday approached, with no marriage prospects in sight, being a virgin wasn't much fun, it was a burden.

She picked up her phone and called the person who was partly responsible for this latest disappointment: her sister. Angie was happily married with two little girls and made it her life's mission to ensure everyone was as happy as she. She grabbed a discarded hair band from her coffee table and swept her shoulder-length natural curls into a ponytail while waiting. At least she hadn't wasted time flat ironing her hair for this disappointment.

Angie picked up the phone on the third ring. "Hello?"

Her sister's hoarse voice gave Tasha only a passing second of guilt for waking her. Angie deserved to know she had set her sister up with an idiot.

"Never hook me up again, Angie," she said, kicking off her heeled sandals and rubbing her feet.

"Tasha? What are you talking about?" Angie's voice became more alert.

"I just pushed Charles off my front porch."

"What? Why would you do that?"

"According to him, if we're not having sex we don't need to see each other."

"I don't believe it."

Tasha fell back onto her sofa and sighed. "It's true. I'm so sick of this. It's the same thing with every guy I date."

"It's not every guy. You just have to find the right one."

Tasha leaned her head back on the couch and stared at her ceiling. "When am I going to find the right one, Angie? Men our age aren't looking for a virgin wife anymore."

"You're being silly. Men appreciate virgins. You just haven't found the one who appreciates you waiting on him."

Tasha rolled her eyes. Her sister was the last person who would understand. They'd both taken to heart the teachings of their father, a Baptist minister, and abstained from sex. But Angie found her husband in college and married him before the ink was dry on her degree. She'd never come close to going through the hell of post-college dating.

"Angie, you're living in a fairy tale. Guys aren't trying to wait around. The minute I tell them I'm saving myself for marriage, they run off as if I'd said I was a homicidal maniac."

She heard Angie chuckle. "You're a fool."

"No, I'm not, I'm serious. I'm tired of the whole thing."

"Dating?"

"No, being a virgin. I just want to get rid of it. Maybe then I can move forward with a guy without him feeling as if dating me means I expect us to get married."

"You can't be serious. Losing your virginity is a sacred, beautiful—"

"Can it, Angie, Mom and Dad aren't on the phone. Maybe it was beautiful and sacred in nineteen sixty, but today it's a liability. I need to get rid of it."

"You talk about it as if it were an old purse."

Tasha frowned. "I feel as if it is an old purse. One that's full of baggage and weighing me down."

"You're so dramatic." Tasha could imagine her sister rolling her eyes.

"Well, dramatic or not, I want to lose it before my birthday."

"Tasha, your birthday is next weekend. You've broken up with Charles, for a good reason, but now you're single. How are you going to lose your virginity?"

"I can find someone to take it."

Angie laughed. "Are you crazy? You can't just get some random guy to sleep with you. Okay, let me rephrase that. You don't *need* to find some random guy to sleep with you."

Tasha laughed. "It won't be random. I'll find someone I know."

When Angie spoke again all humor was out of her voice. "Tasha, I'm serious. Don't even consider doing that. It's stupid and you're upset about Charles. You want your first time to be special. It should be with the man you marry."

Tasha thought about her last few dates. All were smart, successful, and generally nice guys—Charles excluded. But they hadn't been ready for the commitment that came with dating a woman who was saving herself for marriage.

"Angie, I know you're trying to help, but I think I'm serious. I can't have this hanging over me anymore. It's got to go."

There was a pause before Angie continued. "Look, it's getting late and you're upset. Will you promise not to do anything rash and come see me tomorrow? We can talk about it then." The rumbling of her brother-in-law's voice echoed in the background. It was time to end the call before he chimed in.

"I can't come by tomorrow. The center is having its Senior Olympics. I have to be there all day."

As the program coordinator for the Central Midlands Recreation Commission she'd be spending the day making sure the annual sporting event went off without a hitch.

"Can you come by afterwards?"

"I'll see how I feel. It'll be a long day. Look, Angie, I'm sorry for waking you guys up. I'll call you tomorrow."

"Okay, but I'm serious. Don't do anything you'll regret later. Too many of our friends regret their first time. Don't make any quick decisions."

"I hear you, Angie. Bye," she said in a rush.

She tossed the phone on the couch beside her. She understood Angie's concerns. They both had witnessed friends sleep with idiots in high school and college, mainly because they fancied themselves in love, or they thought the guy they slept with was interested in a long-term relationship. But if she took matters into her own hands and picked a guy with no foolish expectations, she wouldn't fall into the same trap. She only wanted someone who would rid her of the nuisance, and that only required one sexual encounter.

If she did this, it would have to be someone who was good in bed. She didn't want her first time to be with someone who didn't know how to make it enjoyable for her—at least to some extent. It would also have to be someone she had no intention of falling in love with because emotions had no place in the situation. It would just be a simple transaction. She frowned. That made it sound horrible. It would just be casual, one-time-only sex. That's all.

Feeling better with that clarification, she returned to her list of characteristics. He would have to be discreet. She didn't want everyone to know she was looking for someone to take her virginity. She wasn't ashamed of being a virgin, but she didn't want to flaunt it either. He would also have to understand this was a one-time deal. She wasn't trying to become some guy's booty call. A guy who expected a steady series of hook ups was out of the question.

Tasha sighed and mentally went through the list of men she knew. Where would she find a discreet, non-committal guy who was good in bed and she respected enough to give her virginity to? Who was someone with whom she could never, *ever* fall in love?

She sat up suddenly. "Yes. He would be perfect!"

CHAPTER 2

Jared Patterson stepped out of his shower with a smile. He was usually antsy when he missed a morning workout, but today's miss was for a good reason. He still couldn't believe he'd let Tasha talk him in to serving as a celebrity judge for the Central Midlands Recreation Commission's Senior Olympics. It would be just another day of signing autographs and dishing out fitness advice. He'd thought moving from Los Angeles to Columbia, South Carolina three years ago would give him a reprieve from the attention. Instead, people were just as anxious to work out with the guy from the infomercial who'd helped so many stars lose weight.

Not that he minded the attention. He thought about the other reason he was missing his workout—the woman lying in his bed at that very moment—and his smiled widened. His recognition kept new chicks in his bed. He grabbed a towel from the chrome rack in his bathroom and dried off. After wiping the condensation from the mirror, he grabbed his toothbrush and stepped back to check out his profile, flexing his biceps and chest. He nodded with satisfaction.

Leaning in toward the mirror, his smile faded when he saw the dark purple hickey on his neck. "What the hell?"

He leaned in closer and swore under his breath. *That damn Monica!* It wasn't a secret he slept around, but he also didn't flaunt it. That hickey meant she would be crossed off his list of future hook ups. He didn't date women who tried to mark their territory.

He brushed his teeth quickly and walked into his bedroom where a shapely brown ass awaited him, seemingly floating in mid-air. His raised bed was the focus of the room, and the sight of

Monica, head down over the side of the bed, enticed him instantly. Maybe she could go on the reserve list.

He walked over to the bed and frowned. She was rummaging through his nightstand. "Are you looking for something?"

Monica froze before sliding back slowly. He had a generous view of the goodies between her legs before she turned to face him. She held up a condom. "Let's get one more in before you leave."

Jared walked to the other side of the bed and pushed the nightstand drawer closed. He mentally scratched her from his reserve list. Going through his things was an automatic dismissal.

Slipping the condom from her fingers, Jared said, "I don't think so. It was fun, Monica, but I've got to go. The housekeeping staff will be here in twenty minutes. Make sure you're gone before they arrive. I will ask them if you were here."

Monica pouted prettily. "You're not kicking me out. I thought I'd stay around until you get back." She flipped her legs toward him and spread her knees. "It was fun."

Jared ignored her. He didn't have time for women who didn't know their boundaries. He stepped away and swore as a sharp pain pierced his foot. "What the hell?" He lifted his foot and pulled out the small safety pin stuck in his heel. Snatching it out, he glared at Monica.

She blanched, guilt flashing on her face before she hid it behind a shrug and small smile. "Sorry, it must've come off my dress."

Something about the way she smiled nagged at him, but instead of arguing with her he threw the pin on the nightstand and turned away. "Just be gone, Monica."

He ignored her angry expression as he went into his closet and slipped on a Recreation Commission t-shirt and a pair of basketball shorts before sliding his feet into a pair of sneakers. When he came out of the bedroom Monica was still sprawled across his bed.

"You can't really want me to leave?" she said.

Jared shook his head. He picked her clothes off the floor and tossed them to her. "Just get out." He walked out of his bedroom without a second thought. He wasn't concerned about her staying too long. Housekeeping would arrive in fifteen minutes instead of the twenty he told her.

She would be his last quick pick up. The thrill of a new woman was easily washed away when she didn't understand the rules of a one-night stand. To make it worse, she had his phone number—she'd insisted on having it in case she got lost when following him home the night before. A dumb excuse, but that's what happens when he listened to the head between his legs instead of the one on his shoulders.

He called the housekeeping service as he entered his garage and got into his silver convertible BMW 650 CI. "This is Jared Patterson. If there's a woman in my house when your crew arrives, call the police."

The woman on the other end chuckled. "Yes, Mr. Patterson. We understand."

Jared ended the call and sped out of his garage and down his curving driveway. Twenty-five minutes later he swung his car into the side lot of the Central Midlands Rec Commission. The building used to be a school, but was converted into the offices for the Commission. It worked well, with classrooms used for adult and child programs, a gymnasium, and an outdoor running track where the Senior Olympics were taking place.

He glanced at the clock on his dash. He was a few minutes early, which meant he'd have time to figure out where he was supposed to be. He checked his reflection in the visor mirror, scowled at the visible hickey, and got out of the car.

He smiled and nodded at the group of people who'd stopped when they recognized his car before approaching a young man directing traffic in the parking area. He asked the guy where the judges were supposed to register and was directed to the stage set up on the old playground.

People repeatedly stopped him along the way. He appreciated that people who purchased his fitness DVDs and followed his nutrition regimen saw results. Sometimes the best feedback he received came from impromptu testimonials when he was out and about. He answered questions and signed a few autographs, taking extra time to appreciate the ladies who happily flaunted new and improved figures.

Breaking away from the crowd he strode to the stage. The area was bustling with Rec Commission staff, volunteers, and seniors arriving for the games. He stopped mid-step to watch Tasha Smith tottering on a stepladder trying to hang a banner along the back of the stage, and changed direction to help her.

Back when he was starting his personal training career, he'd worked part-time at the Rec Commission while Tasha was in charge of afterschool programs. She'd never ratted him out to the administration when he sold his homemade protein bars to clients and he'd always appreciated that. Years later, after he'd returned to South Carolina, it was a shock to learn she had become the deputy director—not because she didn't work hard, but because he'd assumed she would have already been married with dozens of babies. She had never made it a secret that she wanted a family and word on the street was she was saving herself for marriage; it was precisely how she had wound up in his "run far, far away from this chick" category in the first place.

He still couldn't understand why some fool hadn't married her yet. She wasn't his type—not enough height or breasts in his opinion—but she wasn't hard on the eyes. The Rec Commission polo shirts and khaki shorts she always wore didn't hide her nicely shaped figure. Her hair wasn't relaxed; instead, she pulled the curly, light brown tresses into a ponytail at the base of her neck. If she wore something other than a ponytail and showed off her figure, someone at her dad's church was bound to take notice.

He sprinted up the few stairs onto the stage and sauntered over. Her back was to him and he smiled when she cursed after one side of the banner fell. *Who'd have thought Tasha had a potty mouth?* She stood on her tiptoes and the edges of her khaki shorts rose up to reveal a smooth expanse of toned, caramel thighs. He whistled in his head. Tasha did have some nice legs.

Shaking that thought out of his head, he reached around her to help with the banner. "It looks as if you could use a hand."

She squealed before falling. Jared easily caught her in his arms. As a man used to holding women, he couldn't help but notice she weighed next to nothing. He also realized he'd never been so close to her before. She smelled good. Not like flowers or perfume, but a clean, soapy smell. Her honey-colored eyes were wide with surprise, and her lips formed a delicate "O." Just the perfect shape to wrap around his… *Damn, where the hell did that come from?*

Annoyed that she'd enticed him, even if unwittingly, he lashed out, "Tasha, what the hell are you doing?"

She scowled. "Why are you yelling at me? If you wouldn't have scared the crap out of me I wouldn't have tripped."

"I didn't mean to scare you, I only wanted to help."

"Well, announce yourself the next time." There was a breathless quality to her voice. It would sound delicious after a round of sex.

He cleared his throat. "Get someone else to hang the banners next time."

"I'm sorry, in the future I'll put you on the banner hanging committee. Then maybe you'd show up at the same time as the other judges instead of waltzing in late."

He raised a brow. "Are you trying to be funny?"

She tilted her head to the side. "Did I say something funny?"

He considered his response before glaring at her. She glared back, before smiling. *Damn, she was beautiful when she smiled.* Why hadn't he noticed that before? His gaze fell to her mouth.

Maybe he'd overlooked a lot of good things about Tasha. Like how juicy her lower lip was. She gasped once again, her lips parting to reveal the pink tip of her tongue. His eyes met hers and damn if she didn't have the "kiss me" look. His lips curled into a smile as he wondered what kissing her might be like?

Her eyes widened as if she'd read his thoughts. "Are you going to hold me all day?" Her voice trembled.

The hunter in him took notice. She was aroused. He winked as he put her down. "I'll finish hanging the banner."

She took a few steps backward and watched as it only took a few minutes for him to finish the job. When he stepped down she appeared calm. Too bad. He liked her breathless, kissable look.

"Thanks for doing that. Is there anything I can do for you?" She held her arms behind her back, causing her breasts to press against her shirt.

Hell yeah, you can help me, he wanted to say. Instead, he shook his head. She was a good girl. "Nah, I just need to register."

Another volunteer called her name and Tasha turned and motioned that she heard and was coming before turning back to Jared. "I have to go get things started. You'll be judging the hammer throw. Register over at that table." She pointed to a table beside the stage.

"Cool, thanks," he said flatly, fighting the urge to call her back as she turned toward the volunteer.

She paused at the top of the stairs and turned, as if she'd read his mind again. "Can you stick around until the end of the day? I need to ask you for a favor."

"What kind of favor?"

"Something I think you'll enjoy." She frowned. "Or at least I hope you'll enjoy."

He watched her walk away and reminded himself that despite the moment of attraction, she wasn't his type of girl. Unfortunately, the switch in his brain that caused his dick to get hard was firmly flipped in the "on" position. He knew she was still looking for a husband, and he'd rather break both legs than get married—he had enough proof marriage was a fool's contract—but there was no reason why he couldn't enjoy a quick fantasy of her mouth on his body. With a smile, he strolled toward the register.

CHAPTER 3

By the end of the Olympics Tasha was a ball of nerves. She decided against watching any of the interviews she'd done for the local news later that night. She'd floundered like an idiot with simple questions every time she'd noticed Jared watching her, and he'd only made it worse by smiling like he knew some secret. It was sexy and distracting.

Just that morning she'd realized she was making a knee-jerk decision to ask Jared to take her virginity after her bad date with Charles. But a few seconds in Jared's arms proved her idea had its merits. He had held her as if she weighed nothing. She'd known he was strong, but his body was as solid as a rock. When he looked at her as if he wanted to kiss her, it ignited something within her so hot and delicious it was almost scary.

Her stomach tied in knots and she secretly hoped he would forget her impulsive request for a favor. But he helped break down equipment after the Olympics and waited patiently for her to finish. Two hours after the official ending of the games, she walked over to him and the handful of volunteers remaining at the registration table.

"Do you need us to do anything else?" one of the volunteers asked.

She set a box of equipment on the table and looked around. "No, most of the items I brought I've gotten back and the rental company should be here in a few minutes with the truck for the larger items." Just as she said that, the truck pulled up behind the stage.

"There they are. They'll handle the rest. Thanks, everybody."

The guys in the truck walked over and Tasha gave them directions for packing up the bigger equipment. As they left to begin she turned to Jared. "I didn't realize it would take so long to break down this year. You didn't have to wait."

He shrugged. "It's no big deal. I didn't have anything pressing this afternoon."

Her lips curved into a teasing smile. "I don't believe that. Friday night isn't booked up already for Mr. Jared Patterson?"

He laughed. "Let's just say I shuffled my schedule a bit for you."

His low voice sent flutters across her spine and her heartbeat sped up as the breeze carried his scent over. She shoved the box in his hands. "Can you help me put this in the gym?"

He took the box from her and followed her into the back of the building. On the way she gave herself a pep talk. This wasn't a dumb idea. Remember all of the bad dates running for the hills. This would make her life easier.

He put the box in the storage room in the gym then sat on one of the bleachers. "So what is the favor you needed?"

She froze for a second before shuffling from foot to foot. *God, forgive me for what I'm about to do.*

She twisted her hands in front of her. "Well, I don't know the best way to ask. It's a personal favor."

Surprise flashed in his dark eyes before he gave her a reassuring smile. "We've known each other for years, so I guess it's okay to ask a personal favor. Do you need a reference or something?"

Heat crept up her face. How sophisticated, she was blushing. "Not quite. I need you to…relieve me of something."

He blinked and cleared his throat. "What is it?"

She took a deep breath and looked him in the eye. "I need you to take my virginity."

A range of emotions ran across Jared's face: confusion, disbelief, irritation, and desire. None of his expressions provided a clue to what his answer would be. Sure, he was her most logical choice, but it didn't mean he was interested in sleeping with her. They had a limited acquaintance, nothing more.

His features finally settled into an impassive expression before he spoke. "What are you talking about?"

She sighed with relief. At least he hadn't flat out refused. "Look, Jared, I know it sounds like a lot. But really it isn't."

He looked doubtful. "Taking your virginity isn't a lot?"

"No, not really. It's a nuisance for me. Whenever I meet a guy and tell him I'm saving myself for marriage he either dumps me outright or tries to seduce me just for the fun of it. I'm tired of the whole process. Men today aren't looking for a virgin bride and I'm tired of my virginity scaring them off. I need to get rid of it and you made the most sense to take it." She said everything in a rush out of fear she'd chicken out altogether.

He pointed to his chest, confusion clear in his eyes. "How in the hell do I make the most sense?"

She held up her hand and ticked off her reasons. "I respect you and what you've done with your life. I couldn't lose it to someone I didn't like. You aren't looking for a relationship and are used to casual affairs, so a one-night thing with me wouldn't be a big deal to you. You're discreet, although I'm surprised about the hickey today. Usually you don't flaunt your affairs."

He covered the hickey with his hand. "That was a mistake that won't be repeated. Go on."

"Well, you're also…I mean I assume…since you've had so many lovers and whatnot…" Her face burned. "I assume you're good in bed. I need someone who could at least make it decent. I know the first time hurts and isn't always the best, but I figured you could make it bearable."

"I can't believe this," he mumbled and lowered his head in his hands.

She went on. "Plus, there is no chance I would ever fall in love with you."

His head snapped up. "What the hell is that supposed to mean?"

She gave him a sheepish smile. "No offense, but except for respecting what you've done with your professional life, you're not exactly my type."

He frowned. "Why is that?"

"I mean really, Jared. You're a whore. No offense, but you do sleep around, and you've made it no secret you don't plan to ever get married. You're not exactly good husband material. I plan to marry someone who is more responsible—with women, I mean."

"So you think losing your virginity will help you find this pillar of responsibility?"

She ignored his sarcasm. "Yes, I do. It won't be there hanging over my head. The next guy I meet won't have to think that dating me means we're automatically getting married. Since the pressure is off, he's more likely to stay around."

"Why don't you just keep the fact that you're a virgin to yourself?"

She crossed her arms. "Because after about two weeks of dating, men start hinting around about having sex, and then I have to tell them why I'm not going to sleep with them."

"So when your virginity is gone, do you plan to start sleeping with them?"

She hadn't thought that far ahead. She didn't plan to sleep with every guy she dated, but maybe if she met someone she really liked it might be easier to move forward to a sexual relationship once her virginity was gone. "Not all of them, but maybe someone else in the future. I'll worry about that later. I just need to get rid of my virginity."

Jared stood up and shook his head. "Tasha, this is a big deal. Maybe you should wait—"

"No, I'm sick of waiting. I've been waiting for twenty-nine damn years and I'm through. I need someone to help me and I'd like it to be you."

He took a few deep breaths. "I need to think about it."

She squared her shoulders. "I need an answer before next week."

His eyebrows shot up. "Why so soon?"

"It's my birthday. I'd like to lose it before I turn thirty."

"So you want to do it this week?"

Her heart lurched, but she tried to go for nonchalant and shrugged. "It's not a big deal. I'll follow you to your house and we can take care of it tonight." Her voice shook.

Desire flashed in his eyes before he hid it and slowly shook his head. She'd seen guys look at her with desire before. He was tempted.

"We are not doing this tonight," he said.

She stepped closer. "But we are going to do this?"

His eyes traveled from hers to her lips. She'd never noticed how dark they were, like melted chocolate. She licked her lips and his eyes grew darker. It was suddenly hard to breathe. Feeling a surge of confidence, she licked her lips again and he stepped closer. Her heart pounded, her breasts ached, and an unfamiliar tingling trickled between her legs as she breathed in the spicy mixture of cologne and Jared.

She was heated from inside out. It was heavy, sensuous, and left her euphoric. She leaned up, hoping he would kiss her. He lowered his head and her breathing shallowed. With a curse, he quickly pulled back and turned away. Disappointment hit her like a tidal wave. She'd never anticipated a kiss that much before, never wanted a kiss that much. The knowledge was exciting and terrifying.

Hesitantly, she reached out and placed her hands on his arms. He stiffened but didn't pull away. Slowly, she leaned her body against his. The top of her head barely touched his shoulder. She took a second to get used to the feel of him against her. The softness of her breasts pressing against the hard muscles of his back caused a tremor to go through her. His body shivered in return. It was brief and so slight she only noticed because she was pressed against him so firmly.

"Are we going to do this?" Her voice was soft, throaty. The sound of her desire surprised her.

He took her hand and pressed it against the thick bulge in his pants. "You really want to handle this?"

Heat shot through her body and her panties liquefied. If any other man had done that she'd have cursed him out, but she welcomed his challenge. If she shied away from his boldness, then he'd say no. So with another prayer, and her face flaming, she softly squeezed his length. It got harder and her panties got wetter.

It was thrilling. It was frightening.

"Yes," she whispered.

He groaned before pulling away. "Dammit, Tasha, I'm not doing this tonight. I need to think about it."

She wanted to stamp her foot in frustration. It wasn't supposed to be this hard to get Jared Patterson in bed. "For how long?"

His eyes traveled the length of her body and she felt as if fire burned her everywhere his gaze landed. If desire made you feel this wild and reckless, it was no wonder some considered it a sin.

"Come to my house tomorrow night. We'll talk about it then."

She hid her disappointment with a nod. Even though her body was on fire for something she'd never had before, she understood why he would want to think about it. This was out of left field to him. Hell, it was an impulsive decision on her part, one she'd talk herself out of again if she thought about it too much longer. She'd let him consider it overnight, and hopefully he would agree to take it tomorrow before she reconsidered. She wasn't sure how it worked, but hopefully once they had sex the fire she felt for him would go out.

She smiled and nodded. "Okay, I'll come by at seven."

He nodded and took a step back from her, giving her one last heated look before marching out.

CHAPTER 4

The next morning, Jared was running at full speed on his treadmill when the doorbell rang. He cursed at the interruption and jumped off without stopping. He'd barely slept the night before, yet he'd woken up full of energy. He'd spent the morning doing every energy sucking workout he could think of, but exercise wasn't helping—at least not the type of exercise he was doing.

He'd been rock hard and aching after leaving Tasha the day before. He'd flipped through the names on his phone, but with each name he passed his frustration grew. He didn't want any of them. There was only one set of thighs he wanted to get between: Tasha's.

She was last person he needed to sleep with, but he'd known his answer before leaving. He was going to do it. Her favor was the last thing he'd ever expected, but he was flattered she'd chosen him. Even with the male whore comment. He wasn't a saint. Maybe it was male pride and barbaric, but the thought of being her first excited him. He'd never slept with a virgin. It would be a welcome change from the usual chicks he dealt with. Plus, she would remember him for the rest of her life. He couldn't deny the satisfaction of knowing she would never be able to forget their time together.

The problem was when. A part of him wanted to have sex with her tonight when she came over, but, surprisingly, a bigger part rejected that idea. It was her virginity and regardless of her eagerness, losing it should be special. They'd only discuss the details tonight, and then he'd plan for a night she'd never forget. *Thank goodness her birthday is soon*, he thought. He couldn't live with this frustration for long.

He jogged up the stairs from his home gym. He jumped up and down to get rid of some restless energy before opening the door to where his older brother Malcolm stood with a grin on his face that could only be described as goofy.

With a raised eyebrow, he eyed his brother. "What's wrong with you?"

Malcolm kept smiling. "Man, nothing's wrong. I'm just the happiest man on earth right now."

Jared laughed. "Okay, why are you so happy?" He stood aside and let Malcolm in. They walked into the kitchen and he pulled a bottled water out of the refrigerator. When he turned around Malcolm was still grinning.

"Kenyatta finally said yes. We're getting married."

Jared choked on his water and coughed.

Malcolm came over and hit him on his back. "Are you okay?"

Jared nodded and stepped to the side. "Yeah, yeah, I'm cool. So you really want to marry her?"

Kenyatta was Malcolm's girlfriend of two years. Although he liked Kenyatta and was happy his brother finally hooked up with her after lusting for her for so long, he couldn't believe Malcolm wanted to get married. Then again, Malcolm didn't know how fickle married women were.

Malcolm continued to smile like a lovesick puppy. "Yes. I've known ever since that crazy crap with Brad. After thinking I'd never see her again, I knew I wanted her in my life forever."

Malcolm had worked with Kenyatta for years, but had never acted on his desire for her. It wasn't until she'd agreed to marry someone else that he finally made a play for her and won. Unfortunately her fiancé at the time was a psycho who tried to kill her when he found out, but he was killed by an ex-lover after kidnapping both her and Kenyatta. Two years had passed and Malcolm and Kenyatta had remained inseparable. It shouldn't have been a surprise for his brother to marry her, but Jared was still upset. He knew firsthand how unfaithful married women were. Malcolm would do better keeping things as they were.

"Can't you two just live together or something? You know once you marry them everything changes. Kenyatta might not be so wonderful once you put that ring on her finger." It was the first thing that came to his mind.

Malcolm's smile fell. "C'mon man. I thought you would be happy for me. Just because you never want to get married doesn't mean you have to rain on my parade."

Jared shrugged. "I'm not trying to do that, I'm just pointing out the facts. Once women get married they become bored. Before you know it she'll be tired of you and out trying to find some other man to keep her happy."

Malcolm stiffened and pointed at Jared. "Kenyatta's not like that."

Jared scoffed. "That's what you think."

Malcolm frowned and took a step toward him. "Hey, man, watch yourself. I'm in a good mood today, but if you say anything else about Kenyatta I'll knock the shit out of you."

Jared held up his hands. "My bad, I meant no disrespect to Kenyatta. Hey, maybe she is different."

Malcolm threatening to knock sense into him was nothing new. Although they hadn't fought since they were young boys, it wasn't unusual for them to disagree on things. Not only were their personalities different—he considered Malcolm a choir boy and Malcolm considered Jared a playboy—but they looked different too. Malcolm had the darker, more rugged looks of their father while Jared shared the lighter, more refined features of their mother, a resemblance Jared secretly hated.

Malcolm pushed away from the counter with a curse. "Damn, man, I should have known not to tell you first."

Jared plastered a smile on his face. Today wasn't the day to talk some sense into his brother. "I'm just messing with you, man. Truly, I'm happy for you. When is the big day?"

Malcolm looked skeptical but the goofy grin resurfaced. "We're thinking a fall wedding. September or October."

Jared put his water bottle on the counter with a loud thud. "That's only a few months away."

Malcolm shrugged. "We've been together for two years, there's no need for a long engagement."

Jared shook his head. "All right, man. Just let me know when and I'll be there to stand beside you." *And I'll be there when she breaks your heart later,* he thought.

"Thanks, man, I'm glad to hear that." Malcolm narrowed his eyes and studied Jared. "Are you training for something? You haven't stopped sweating since you came to the door."

Jared used his shirt to wipe the sweat off his brow. "No, why would you say that?"

"'Cause it looks like you're working your ass off. What's up?"

Jared sucked down the rest of the water. "Just trying to work off some excess energy."

Malcolm scoffed. "You usually say that when you've got some woman around. Since I don't think anyone is here, she must have turned you down?"

Jared sucked his teeth. "Never that. She's coming over tonight."

Malcolm laughed. "At the rate you're going you won't be any use to her tonight."

Jared blew air through his lips. "You forget who you're talking about. Besides we're not sleeping together tonight. I'm trying to wait."

Malcolm's head snapped back. "You're trying to wait? Hell must be freezing over."

"Man, I can wait, when it's worth it."

Malcolm raised an eyebrow. "Someone who's worth the wait? Damn, man, I never thought I'd hear you say that. Who is she?"

"It doesn't matter who she is, and I'm not waiting long. I just need to find the right place."

Malcolm laughed. "What's wrong with down the hall in that massive bed you've got?"

Jared shook his head and frowned. "Nah, she deserves better than that for her first time. I'm not going to treat her like any other chick."

Malcolm stopped laughing and held up his hands. "Wait, wait, wait. Did I hear you right? Her first time? What, you're playing with virgins now?"

Jared cursed. Malcolm didn't need to know what he was doing. His brother was such a moral high roller he wouldn't approve, but Jared didn't turn down beautiful women, and since Tasha offered, he wasn't about to pass up the chance to be her first.

"It's not like that. She asked me to be her first, so I agreed."

Malcolm crossed his arms and scowled. "What the hell is wrong with you? You don't F around with virgins, man."

Jared laughed at Malcolm's shortening of the curse word. "I'm not *fucking* around with a virgin. She's almost thirty and wants to lose it before her birthday. I was her choice, so why deny her?"

"Because her first time should be special. You're the last man to make something special with a woman."

"Whatever. I know how to make a lady feel special."

"It's more than that."

Jared lifted a shoulder and held his hands out. "Since when do I need your permission to sleep with someone? She's a grown woman and knows what she wants. Besides, the way she was palming my dick yesterday lets me know that she's more than ready."

Malcolm shook his head. "Man, you're something else. You're right, it's your business. I'm just saying this whole situation may blow up in your face."

"I doubt that. I'm going to take my time with her and make it good. It'll just be this one-time thing, and then we'll move on."

"Sure, I'll believe that when I see it."

Jared was tired of the conversation. "Look, man, I've got to get back to my workout. Did you want anything else?"

Malcolm sighed nodded. "Mom's birthday is coming up. I wanted to rent out the community center in the old neighborhood and have a party for her. Sixty-five is a big deal."

Jared smiled tightly while inwardly he cringed. Pretending an interest in their mom was nothing new. Malcolm never questioned why he always had to relay messages between the two, and Jared had no plans to change that. He'd rather let Malcolm assume he was a less than stellar son than reveal they had a less than stellar mom.

"Sure, man, that's a good idea. Just let me know what you need."

Malcolm nodded and headed toward the door. "Don't work out too hard. You might tire yourself out before you can deflower your virgin."

"Ha ha, very funny."

"I'll holla at you later."

Jared waved his brother out the door before going back down to his gym, but he no longer felt like working out. Malcolm's announcement had killed his energy. His brother was getting married. It felt like it came from nowhere, but he should have known. They did seem perfect for each other, so maybe it could work. But his parents had seemed perfect for each other too, and he knew that had been a damn lie. Hopefully Malcolm would be luckier.

His cell phone rang and he walked over to pick it up. Monica's number popped on screen under a new name: Clingy Snoop. He ignored the call, noting that it had been her fourth call for the day.

He crossed the gym to his home office. He needed a distraction, and the work on his desk would do. He was finishing up a fitness manual based on his exercise philosophy, and he needed to call Cassandra, his public relations manager in Los Angeles, for an update on her trip to his production facility.

After work he would decide how to handle Tasha's first time. He meant what he'd said to Malcolm—she did deserve better than just one night in his bed. Even though they wouldn't be together afterwards, he wanted her to look back with a smile for the rest of her life.

CHAPTER 5

Tasha parked in the circular drive of Jared's California style home at 6:59. She sat in the car taking several deep breaths as she stared at his door. Her body hummed with desire after leaving him yesterday. It was a new experience that thrilled and frightened her. Although she'd been attracted to men in the past, she'd never experienced it at this magnitude. He made it too easy to forget why she'd been a virgin for so long.

Feeling this way thrilled her, but the fact that it was for Jared worried her. Even though they'd worked together, she only knew him superficially. How could she desire him so much after one encounter? Why did his slight tremble at her touch yesterday keep her awake for hours? And why, when she had slept, she'd dreamt about feeling his erection without his pants in the way.

She would have to tread carefully to make sure she remained in control of the situation. She couldn't afford to lose herself, and if she forgot the reason for sleeping with him, Jared could make her lose all thoughts of self-preservation.

She got out of the car and went to his door. With a reassuring breath, she rang the bell. She'd never been to Jared's house before, but hadn't had trouble finding it. She'd gotten his address from the Rec Commission files before leaving the day before. She'd been nervous that if she called him for the address he would tell her over the phone he wasn't going to grant her favor.

Jared opened the door and Tasha's mouth went dry. He wore nothing but basketball shorts low on his hips. Her eyes ran over his body, taking in the broad shoulders, well-toned chest, and rock hard abs. His sinewy biceps gleamed in the late afternoon sun. A tattoo of an eagle with its talons out was on his left one. Her eyes followed the light sprinkling of hair covering his chest down his abs to where they disappeared in the waistband of his shorts. She skipped the shorts to take in thighs and calves that looked as if they were carved from granite. Even his feet were sexy.

When she finally dragged her eyes back up to his, he smiled as if he knew his body was an awesome sight to behold. He flexed his pecs and winked at her. Desire shivered through her and she squeezed the muscles between her legs.

"Like what you see?"

She cleared her throat and tried to appear calm. Control, she had to and maintain control. "Do you always answer the door undressed?"

"I'm perfectly decent...for now." He flexed his pecs again and Tasha wanted to run in the opposite direction. This was too much for her. A smart woman would turn around, go home, and forget the whole damn thing. But at the moment she didn't feel very smart. She only felt hot and horny. She hoped his words meant he was accepting her offer.

"Does that mean you're going to relieve me of my problem—tonight?"

He reached out, took her hand, and drew her into the house. "We'll talk about that in a second. Come in and make yourself comfortable."

Tasha took her eyes off of his body to look around. White marble floors in the foyer opened up to a sunken living area bathed with sunlight from large French doors connected to a patio. Sunlight sparkled on the surface of a pond visible through the doors. The living area was surrounded by four white pillars connected by wrought iron railing. A marble and wrought iron staircase led to the second floor. Neutral colors, yellows and greens adorned the walls and furnishing which combined with the windows and view of the lake to give it an open feel.

"You have a beautiful home," she said.

He smiled, drawing her eyes to his sensuous lips. "Thanks, it was already decorated when I bought it. I thought it made the place feel open so I left it the way it was. Come on around to the kitchen."

He took her hand in his and led her to a spacious kitchen with granite countertops and stainless steel appliances. It looked like a kitchen from Food Network and her fingers itched to use the commercial grade stove. The small kitchen in her home was pitiful compared to his.

"Do you cook?" she asked.

He shook his head. "Not often. I have someone come in and prepare my meals for the week. Why?"

"The kitchen is beautiful. It looks like it was made for cooking meals for a large family."

He laughed. The sound sent an unfamiliar shiver down her spine. "Not here. Fortunately, I don't have to make up my protein bars and shakes anymore. There's an entire production facility for that. Do you want something to drink?" He let go of her hand and she clenched her fist to hold onto the warmth.

"Yes, thank you."

He reached under the cabinet into a wine cooler and pulled out a bottle of wine. "I hope you like Chardonnay." He took two glasses out of the rack above the bar.

"I just want water."

"It's no problem. I was going to open this anyway." He opened the wine and poured her a glass.

"What if I don't like white?"

He rubbed his jaw and grinned. "I have red, if you prefer."

She did prefer white, but she didn't like that he'd ignored her request for water. "I'd prefer water."

His smile remained as he turned to get a bottle of water out of his fridge. When he came over, he stood so close she was engulfed by his spicy scent. That combined with his near nakedness, made her skin tingle with anticipation.

"Your water." His eyes bore into hers, desire and amusement rolling in the chocolate centers.

She cleared her throat and took a step back. "Do you plan to put on some clothes?"

He took a step forward. "Do I really need to get dressed?"

She blushed. It was true, if he agreed to her favor then he really didn't need clothes. Something about the idea that it could happen so soon caused her stomach to flutter. She fought the urge to wipe her now clammy hands on her pants. Instead she opened the bottle and gulped. "So you're ready to do it now? Okay, just give me a…second to, you know, get used to the idea."

He chuckled and stepped back. "I'm not going to take your virginity on my kitchen floor, Tasha. Although once it's gone I might make love to you on the counter."

She swallowed loudly. A picture of him lifting her up onto his counter filled her head. As erotic as the thought was, she pushed it aside. Once her virginity was gone there wouldn't be another time. It was a one-time deal and that was all. For her sanity she would have to stick with that.

He grinned. "I'm teasing you, Tasha. You actually caught me as I got out of the shower. I lost track of time and didn't realize it was so close to seven. If you give me a second I'll change and we can talk."

She gave him what she hoped was an impassive look before nodding. "I'll wait for you here."

"You can follow me to my room. If you'd like." There was a teasing glint in his eye, which only made him sexier.

She may be less sophisticated than the women he usually dealt with, but that didn't mean she couldn't handle his game. *Actually, you can't handle it, but you're going to pretend that you can.*

She raised her chin. "I need to see it sooner or later."

If he was surprised by her answer he hid it well. "Follow me."

With another reassuring breath, she walked behind him and froze at the door of his bedroom. In the middle of his room was a mahogany four poster bed. It was raised at least two feet from the floor. A black satin comforter and sheets gleamed in the recessed lighting that shined down as if it were a monument.

If Jared noticed she'd stopped at the door he didn't acknowledge it. He disappeared into his walk in closet. Blinking her eyes rapidly she looked around his room. He had a large flat screen television on one wall with a small sitting area around it. A matching mahogany dresser and chest of drawers took up the other wall. There were a few black and white landscape portraits on chocolate colored walls.

Her attention went back to the bed. It couldn't be ignored. She walked over to it. At five feet four inches she considered herself average height, but she would need a stepstool to get on it. How many women had he slept with in that bed? Probably dozens. The thought excited her. She wanted to experience what other women had with him, and she wanted it in that bed. She ran her hands along the smooth comforter and closed her eyes, imagining herself naked, sliding on the sheets.

"Do you like my bed?"

She snatched her hands away as if she'd been burned. She turned to the closet where Jared stood, watching her. He'd put on a loose fitting pair of jeans and a black shirt he hadn't buttoned. His feet were still bare. She definitely liked what she saw.

"It's a nice bed. Is this where we'll…" Although she knew what she asked she couldn't say the words.

He walked over, placing his hands on the bed, trapping her between it and him. The heat from his body radiated toward her. Time seemed to freeze as the force of her attraction buzzed within her. If she was going to do this she couldn't be a ninny. She hesitated, before lifting her hands and placing them on his chest. His skin was surprisingly soft over the hard muscles underneath. He flexed his pecs and she jerked. Her pinky finger accidentally flicking over his flat nipple and his breathing pick up.

He lightly ran a finger down her cheek. "My plan was to wait, but you're making it very difficult."

Tasha shivered as he gently traced her earlobe. "How?"

"Because right now all I want to do is take your clothes off, throw you on that bed, and get deep inside you."

Oh, God, what am I doing? Despite her fear she said, "Then... then do it."

He stared at her for what felt like hours before he closed the distance between them and kissed her. Fire spread throughout her body, so hot she was sure he could feel it. His lips were firm and demanding against hers. When his tongue reached out for entrance into her mouth she quickly obliged. He immediately filled her mouth with his tongue and Tasha's hands clenched against his chest. He groaned, kissing her harder.

His hand came up to caress her breast through her shirt, softly massaging her aching flesh. When his thumb brushed across her nipple she trembled as liquid heat replaced her bones. His other hand clutched her waist, pulling her against him. He reached around to cup her behind as he pressed his erection against her.

His mouth left hers, leisurely kissing his way to her ear. "I'm going to touch you," he said, his hand leaving her butt to pop open the button of her shorts. Excitement and fear trembled within her. It was happening to fast.

His tongue played with the curve of her ear. "Tell me to touch you." Her zipper released, and his hands skimmed along the waistband of her panties. All reasoning left.

"Touch me."

She felt his smile against the side of her neck before his lips returned to hers. At the same time his hand broke the barrier of her underwear. His fingers gently played with the hairs covering her sex, each pull sending a shockwave of desire through her. She knew she was soaking wet, and was almost embarrassed by it until he finally slid his finger against her clit. She gasped, pulling away from his kiss to drop her head back. He groaned and kissed the side of her neck.

He was devouring her. She could hardly breathe she was so engulfed by his passion. It was raw, hot, and overpowering. It was actually about to happen. She was going to lose her virginity.

But she wasn't in control. He was making her feel out of control, and very unsure. This was happening too fast.

The doorbell rang, bringing reality back to her. She pushed against his chest. "Jared, someone's at your door."

His head jerked up. He stared at her, searching her eyes for something while his hand slowly slipped out of her underwear. Her body thrummed and she fought between asking him to continue and thinking she needed to escape. Bewilderment and passion swirled within his eyes. Had he noticed her panic?

The doorbell rang again. He slowly stepped back, took a deep breath, and buttoned his shirt.

"I ordered dinner. That's probably it. We can eat in another part of the house," his eyes flicked to the bed and back to her, "where it's less volatile."

He strolled out of the bedroom and didn't wait for her to follow. She was making a mistake. Jared had awakened an inferno of desire within her she didn't know how to control. Even now, with him out of the room, the wetness continued to flow between her thighs and her breathing was ragged. She couldn't go through with this. It was too much. *He* was too much. She would have to find someone else to take her virginity. Someone who didn't make her feel as if she were riding a roller coaster of desire.

With shaky hands she buttoned and zipped her shorts. Her face burned as she remembered his hands against her. She wanted it again. Okay, so sex with Jared wouldn't be bad. In fact, it would probably be awesome. But could she really do it without losing herself?

She rushed out of his bedroom to the front door. Jared's back was to her and she could hear a woman's voice on the other side.

She couldn't make out what the woman said. Jared's shoulders were tense. He glanced over his shoulder, saw her, and cursed.

"Not today, Monica," he said and slammed the door.

When he turned to face her he at least had the decency to look guilty. "Sorry about that."

She held up a hand. "Don't be. No need to apologize for who you are." Her words were strong, but inside she was embarrassed. Common sense would have told her he was seeing someone else, but it didn't ease the pain of having another woman show up at his door while they were pressed against his bed. "I think I should go. This was a bad idea."

He frowned and took a step toward her. "Because of that?" He pointed to the door. "That was nothing."

She shook her head. "No, that's the reason I chose you. No commitments, no chance of love. But you're too much, what happened in your bedroom was too much. I thought I could handle it, but I'm not sure anymore."

He relaxed and smiled. "Tasha, what happened in my bedroom was normal. You want to feel that type of passion with whoever you have sex with."

"Does it always feel that...overwhelming?"

He walked over and took her head in his hands. "With the right person." He kissed the side of her mouth.

She froze. "But you're not the right person."

He rolled his eyes. "The right person in bed isn't always the right person to marry."

"But—" she started, but he interrupted her with a kiss. She forgot what she was about to say when his arms encircled her. With a sigh she wrapped her arms around his neck and let him deepen the kiss.

When he pulled away he smiled at her. "I want to take you to Charleston for your birthday."

It took a second for his words to penetrate her brain. "You want to spend the weekend with me in Charleston?"

"It's not very far so we can get there in a day, and we don't have to worry about people we know seeing us together. You mentioned that you wanted discretion."

She frowned. "But my family and I get together for my birthday."

"You'll be thirty, Tasha. They will be okay if you miss a year."

She tried to pull away. "That's too much. I can't do that."

"Can't or won't?"

"I won't."

"Why?"

"Because…it's not what I wanted. I don't want a romantic getaway with you. I just want you to take my virginity as quickly as possible."

"Romance isn't a part of this, Tasha. I'm not taking you away in order to woo you. I'm taking you away so that we can be discreet."

She looked around. "What's wrong with your house?"

"Too many people know me and watch my house. Do you really want to be linked as my latest fling?"

"No, but…"

"Do you really want to lose your virginity, or was all this just some type of game?"

She thought about Charles and every other man either afraid of commitment or looking for a conquest when they realized she was a virgin. Did she really want to do that for another ten years?

Her eyes met Jared's. His arms were still wrapped around her waist, and even now she wanted to lean up and kiss him. It was much easier to remain a virgin when she wasn't burning with desire. If she were really going to do this, it made more sense to do it with a man who turned her on than one who didn't.

"I'll go to Charleston." Triumph filled his eyes. Feeling like his conquest, instead of the other way around, she pulled out of his embrace and he let her. "Don't look so damn cocky. I still might change my mind."

"I know," he said, smiling. "Let's get something to drink while we wait on the food."

He held out his hand and she took it while trying to ignore the feeling that she'd made a life changing decision with a man who would trample her heart.

CHAPTER 6

"I asked Jared Patterson to take my virginity," Tasha said to her sister the next morning. Not a second later, she was hit with the mist of sweet tea Angie spit out of her mouth.

"You what!" Angie yelled, wiping her mouth.

Tasha grabbed the towel hanging on her parents' stove and wiped her face. She cut her eyes at her sister the entire time. "Was that really necessary?"

Angie snatched the towel from her. "Yes, when you say dumb stuff like that."

"Girls, is everything all right?" their mom called from the dining room.

Tasha looked at Angie and mouthed the word *please*. Angie scowled but yelled back, "It's fine, Mom. Tasha almost dropped the macaroni."

Their mom started muttering, probably about how silly they were, but thankfully she didn't come in the kitchen. Tasha got the macaroni out of the stove and placed it on the counter.

"Why would you ask him something like that?" Angie whispered.

"Because I need it gone and he's the best person to do it."

Angie put her hand on her hip. "I thought you were joking when you said that the other night. Did Shayla put you up to this? That girl is a straight up ho."

Tasha rolled her eyes. Angie had never liked her friend Shayla. "Shayla is not a ho, and no, she didn't put me up to this. I haven't even told her about this. It was all my idea."

Angie didn't look convinced. "Well, it sounds like something she would support. I know Charles turned out to be an asshole, but that doesn't mean you need to go out and sleep with Jared Patterson." Angie wrinkled her nose when she said his name.

"He's Malcolm's brother, so he can't be all bad."

"Kenyatta got lucky with Malcolm. Jared is no good," Angie replied. Angie and Kenyatta had been best friends since college.

"Jared isn't no good. So he sleeps with a lot of women. He's successful, good looking, and single. There's nothing wrong with that." She thought of the faceless woman he'd slammed the door on the day before and changed direction. "Look at the business he's built with his gyms and health food line. You can't deny the man is smart."

Angie walked over to the stove and checked the collard greens. She stirred them before turning off the stove and turning back to Tasha. "Your first time is special. You don't want to lose it to some guy who doesn't give a damn about you."

"That's easy for you to say, Angie. You met Jonathan in college, and married him two weeks after graduation. You were lucky to find someone worth waiting for. I'll be thirty next week. What if I never meet someone? I'll die a virgin."

"Better to die a virgin than burn in hell," their mom's voice cut in. She narrowed her eyes as she looked from one daughter to the other. "What are you talking about? You'd better not let your father know."

Tasha sighed. Her parents would have simultaneous massive heart attacks if they knew her plans.

"I was just telling Angie she was lucky to find Jonathan and that I might die a virgin," Tasha said with a frown.

Virginia Smith's plump cheeks widened as she smiled at her oldest daughter. "Waiting to give herself to Jonathan on her wedding night was the most precious gift Angie could give him. We're very proud of her." Angie looked away guiltily and Tasha frowned. What was that look for? Virginia didn't notice Angie's guilt as her gaze drifted to Tasha. "Don't go to your husband's bed as damaged goods. Believe me, he'll love you more for it."

Tasha picked the macaroni from the counter with a pot holder and handed it to her mom. "I know, Mom. I'll remember that."

Virginia smiled. "Good girl. Your father should be finished with the deacon meeting by now. He'll be home in a few minutes, and we'll be ready to eat when he gets here."

When their mom walked out of the kitchen with the macaroni, Tasha rushed over to Angie. "What was that look for?"

Angie didn't meet her eye. "What look?"

"That guilty look. You're hiding something."

"No I'm not." Angie tapped her foot. A sure sign she was lying. "Tell me."

Angie sighed. "All right." She lowered her voice. "Jonathan wasn't my first."

It was Tasha's turn to yell. "What!"

Angie grabbed Tasha's hand and pulled her out the back door into their parents' sunroom. She lowered her voice so much that Tasha had to strain to hear. "I lost my virginity to this idiot in college who only wanted to sleep with virgins. It was devastating and I don't want the same thing to happen to you. Every day I wish I would have waited for Jonathan, and I can't take that back. He doesn't know. Nobody knows except Kenyatta and Carol, so please don't say anything."

Tasha hit Angie's shoulder. "How could you tell your friends and not tell me?"

Angie hit Tasha back. "It's a long story, all right? And not one I'm proud of. Just remember, once it's gone you can't get it back. Don't waste your first time on someone like Jared."

Tasha opened her mouth to reply when Jonathan came into the sunroom. He was holding the hand of their youngest daughter, Angela, who was dripping wet and looking at the floor. Knowing the eight-year-old, it was no telling what she'd gotten into.

"Angie, please come help me clean up the mess in the family room. It appears your daughter thought it would be fun to swim with your dad's fish."

Angie jaw dropped. "Not the fish tank?"

Jonathan nodded. "Exactly."

Angie rolled her eyes. "Angela, what were you thinking?"

"I didn't know it would fall," Angela answered, eyes still glued to the floor.

Angie went over and the trio walked from the sunroom. Tasha shook her head. Cleaning her daughter's mess would keep Angie from finishing her story for a while. At least now she knew why Angie always lectured her about waiting, but it didn't make her any less pissed. Angie had made a bad choice her first time, but that was her bad. Tasha was almost thirty, not nineteen. She knew where things stood with her and Jared, so she wouldn't get hurt. If anything, Angie's confession only proved she needed to lose her virginity on her own terms.

The front door opened and a second later, her dad's voice preached to Angela. It was the same thing every Sunday. One of Angie's kids would do something unexpected and damaging—which was odd for girls, according to their mother—and then their dad would preach to them for the remainder of the afternoon. She took a deep breath. Missing it next week may not be bad at all.

Later that evening Tasha picked up the phone and called Shayla. Angie was wrong about a multitude of things, including her opinion of Shayla. Despite the four-year age gap between her and Shayla, they'd clicked after meeting in high school at a cheerleading camp. Although they attended different schools, they'd kept in touch. Shayla often came to Tasha whenever she needed to escape the trials of her life. She wasn't a ho as Angie described, just really unlucky in love.

On the sixth ring Tasha prepared to hang up when Shayla's breathless voice answered. "Hello."

"Shayla, are you okay?"

"Oh, hey, Tasha. Yeah, I'm fine." Shayla giggled. "I'm finished what I was doing."

There was a man's voice in the background and she guessed what Shayla was doing. "I'll call you back."

"No, no, no. Don't go." There was shuffling in the background before it got quiet. "What's going on?" There was an echo to Shayla's voice.

"You're not about to use the bathroom are you?"

Shayla laughed. "No, I came in here for privacy. If you're calling me at ten on a Sunday night it must be important."

Tasha chuckled. "You've got that right."

"Okay, so tell me what's going on."

"I told you about my date from hell with that guy Charles."

"Yes. Damn, Tasha, I don't know how you always end up with these fools. It might be better for you to sleep with someone and get it over with. Then the novelty of dating a virgin won't plague you."

"I know, right? That's why I found someone to have sex with."

The line went silent. "Hello? Shayla? Are you still there?"

"Yeah, I just thought I heard Miss I'm Waiting for Prince Charming casually mention she's found a guy to sleep with."

"I did say that. I'm sick of guys either running for the hills or becoming fake Billy Dee Williams trying to seduce me into bed when they find out I'm a virgin. Angie thinks I'm stupid, but I'm ready to see what all the fuss is about."

Shayla laughed. "Angie would think it was stupid. She's a pure romantic. Who's the guy?"

"Jared Patterson."

"Wait, the guy from the infomercial?"

Tasha grinned. "I forgot he did that. Yes, that's him."

"Damn, Tasha! That brotha is fine. I went to his gym here in Atlanta for about a year. A picture of him was right near the treadmills. I damn near came just looking at his body every time I went for a run. How in the hell did you land him?"

"We worked together years ago, and he still mentors at the

Rec Commission. He's lived in Columbia since opening his production facility two years ago."

"If I would have known that I would have moved back home."

"Cool it. He's mine," Tasha told her friend. Jared wasn't really hers, but hearing Shayla go on about him was making her uncomfortable.

"Girl, please, you know I wouldn't go after your guy. I've got enough on my plate as it is."

"Yeah, I heard him earlier. When are you gonna tell me his name?"

Shayla laughed. "When he's all mine. Anyway, are you dating Jared?"

Tasha let her friend change the subject. When Shayla was ready to tell her who she was dating then she would. "No, we're not dating. It's just a one-time deal. I want to at least try to enjoy it this first time with someone who won't expect anything."

"I'm glad to hear you're not expecting too much from him. From what I've read online he's a true player. One blogger even said that he likes to eat downtown, if you know what I mean."

She knew exactly what Shayla meant and she squirmed in her seat. "How would they know?"

"Girl, nowadays no one's secrets are safe. If it's true, you will enjoy yourself. Just don't get caught up. Like I told you, once you start it's hard to stop. And if it's good, it's damn near impossible."

Tasha crinkled her nose. "Do you think I should pick someone less experienced?"

"Hell no! You know how awful my first time was. I hate to even think about it. You did right picking someone who knows what they're doing. Just don't get all caught up in him. Learn some tricks of your own so he's not always in control."

"How do I do that?"

"Read some erotica, watch some porn, get all baby oiled up and ready, I don't know. Whatever works for you."

Tasha smiled. She'd heard enough from Shayla to have an idea about what men liked. It wouldn't hurt to show Jared that she wasn't completely out of her league. "You've got a point. He's so full of himself. I don't want him to think I'm some sex puppet on a string."

"That's my girl. When is this going down?"

"We're going to Charleston next weekend for my birthday."

"Damn, he's taking you away. He must want this as much as you do."

"You think?"

"Why else would he take you out of town? No guy's gonna turn down sex. If it was a simple one time thing he would have just told you to come over and hit it once. If he's taking you out of town that means you'll have to spend the nights together as well as the days. He must like you a little bit."

"Not like that. We've always been cool—I think he's trying to be nice to a friend."

"Yeah, well he can be nice to you for twenty minutes in his bed at home. Taking you out of town is a bit more than nice."

There was a knock on the other side of the phone. "Look Shayla, go be with your guy. I'll call you later this week."

"All right, but call me before you leave and as soon as you get back. I need all the details."

"Why?"

"Because you've heard my sex stories for years, it's payback."

Tasha laughed. "My story may not be worth discussing."

"I doubt that. Bye, girl."

"Bye." Tasha hung up and stared at the phone. Why did Jared insist they leave town? He'd had other women in his bedroom at home whose names were unknown, so the discretion thing was just an excuse. He was happy when she'd said yes. It didn't mean he was interested in her outside of the bedroom, but he definitely wanted to sleep with her. Was it for the same reason as other guys, to say he deflowered a virgin? She knew he wasn't sleeping with her because he cared or anything.

Tasha stood and went to her bookshelf. She pulled down a book of erotica Shayla had given her last year in an effort to liberate her mind. It was wrapped in the cover of a cookbook so her parents wouldn't know she had it. She'd forgotten it was there until now. She may be a virgin, but she wasn't completely innocent. Admittedly, her limited experiments with her high school boyfriend paled in comparison to Jared's love life, but Shayla was right. If she wanted to keep some control then she'd need to be able to meet him step-by-step next weekend. Or at least put up a good show.

CHAPTER 7

"Another excellent inspection, Mr. Patterson. I wish all of the facilities I visited were as well organized as yours." The health inspector reached out a thin hand, which Jared happily shook.

"I appreciate that, Mr. Simmons, but it wouldn't be this way without the hard work of my superintendent." Jared turned to his plant superintendent Barry Jordan.

Barry's already massive chest puffed up with pride at Jared's compliment. "I appreciate that, Mr. Patterson."

Jared hated formalities, but Barry insisted on giving him respect when others were around.

Jared nodded. "I'm only speaking the truth."

Mr. Simmons turned back to Jared. "And you're very lucky to have such a diligent superintendent."

Barry continued to smile, but didn't say anything else. Jared would have to thank him again later. Barry's hard work allowed Jared the time he needed to focus on running the operations of his business and continue personal training for exclusive clients. Without Barry, Jared's dream of a production facility would've been harder to achieve.

Mr. Simmons looked at his watch. "I have another facility to inspect before lunch. I doubt their inspection will go as well as yours…" His voice trailed off and his jaw dropped.

Jared followed his line of sight as Cassandra Davenport, his public relations advisor, stepped into the lobby. He couldn't blame the guy, Cassandra was fine. Her exotic looks, courtesy of a black father and Korean mother, combined with dark hair that stopped mid-back, large breasts, and well-rounded backside were enough to stop any man in his tracks. She raised a brow, a knowing smile on her lips as she approached them.

Jared acknowledged Cassandra with a head nod. "Mr. Simmons, this is Cassandra Davenport. She handles my public relations."

Mr. Simmons's eyes were glued on the black camisole peeking out of Cassandra's red suit jacket. Jared cleared his throat.

Mr. Simmons shook his head, as if snapping himself out of a daze. "Um…yes. It's nice to meet you, Ms. Davenport. I was just leaving."

Cassandra gave him her most award winning smile as she reached out a manicured hand. "It's great to meet you, Mr. Simmons. I noticed you during the inspection."

Mr. Simmons face lit up like a light bulb. Barry looked at Jared and rolled his eyes. Cassandra had that effect on men. She'd once had that effect on Jared, but he'd known her for so long he now only saw her as a friend. And, she was too high maintenance.

Cassandra continued talking to Mr. Simmons. "I'm glad to hear you all are finished. I need Jared for a few minutes before catching my flight back to L.A." She turned to Jared. "Can we meet in your office?"

Jared reached out to shake Mr. Simmon's hand. "Mr. Simmons, thanks again. Barry, will you finish up with him?"

Barry nodded and Jared walked away with Cassandra. As soon as they were on the elevator Cassandra frowned.

"I can't wait to get back to L.A. The men in South Carolina behave as if they've never seen a woman."

Jared laughed. "You get the same reaction in L.A."

She smiled. "You're right. But if one more man calls me 'ma'am' I'm going to throw up." Her frown turned into one of her well-practiced pouts. "When are you going to move back to L.A., Jared? The facility is up and running perfectly. You don't have to stay here to oversee things, Barry is wonderful. I miss having my buddy around."

They got off the elevator and crossed the hall into the main office of the facility. One side was Plexiglas, allowing him to look out over the floor. Since Jared didn't work there daily, he'd assigned it to Barry, but used it whenever he came to the facility. Instead of sitting behind the desk he went to the couch near the window, pressed a button to lower a screen, and sat down. Cassandra slid in across from him.

"I'm not coming back to L.A., at least not anytime time soon. Like I told you before I left, I'm a southern boy at heart. I don't like the hustle and bustle of L.A."

Cassandra rolled her eyes. "Southern boy my ass. You love L.A. The women, the excitement, the celebrities paying too much money to work out with you. You'll be back."

Jared nodded and laughed. He did love the women in L.A., but the memory of Tasha's caramel skin, honey-colored eyes, and soft lips filled his head. L.A. women didn't compare to the sweetness of a Carolina girl. "Yeah, maybe. But for now, I'm staying here. My brother's here so that works. Now, did you really need to talk with me, or did you just want to badger me about moving back to L.A.?"

"Both," she said.

Jared could only laugh. He did miss Cassandra, his only female friend. He also appreciated she let one of the reasons for his hasty return to South Carolina slide: avoiding sleeping with her again.

He'd met Cassandra while working at a gym after moving to L.A. Every other male trainer worked overtime to land her as a client, including him. She'd denied him at first, but as usual his tenacity won out. It wasn't long before their workouts began taking place out of the gym. He'd turned her on to his line of health food products, which combined with his workout routines helped her get her already slim body down to Hollywood standards. After that she'd put all of her PR muscle into promoting him. She'd recommended him one of her clients, an R&B singer with roots in South Carolina who wanted to lose some baby weight. When that worked, his name was tossed around as a person who could make miracles in the gym. Before he knew it, he was the most preferred personal trainer in Hollywood. By then their sex life had run its course, but she'd stayed on to handle personal relations for his brand. She was the reason his products, gyms, and workouts received nationwide attention.

He reached over and squeezed her hand. He knew she wanted him back in L.A., but he meant what he said. He liked building his empire here, where things were more stable. Celebrities were fickle, and their love of him could be gone in a flash.

"Since you've already asked me to move back and I've said no, we can move on to your other reason for wanting to talk to me."

She squeezed his hand back before pulling away. "I'm not giving up on you, but I guess I'll move on. I think you should consider placing some of your organic products at the new State Farmers Market."

Jared sat back. He jerked at the tie he'd worn for the inspection and hastily untied it. "Really, why?"

"I've been working and I finally got the Department of Agriculture to award your products with the Certified South Carolina label. Since you use products grown in South Carolina, it was a no brainer. With that certification, placement at the Farmers Market will introduce you to a line of customers you haven't reached before."

Jared threw the tie over the back of the chair and relaxed as he undid the top buttons of his shirt while considering Cassandra's suggestion. Since his facility was in an agricultural county, he had insisted on using products grown locally whenever possible. It not only saved on shipping costs, but the quality was better. The fruits, vegetables, and other ingredients were fresher since they weren't shipped half way across the country. It was a smart move on Cassandra's part to get the certification. He wished he'd thought of it first.

He nodded. "That's a good idea, Cassandra. Now I know why I hired you for PR."

Cassandra sucked her teeth and flipped her hair over her shoulder. "Don't play. You know I'm great at what I do."

Jared reached over and playfully tapped her chin. "Yes, you are." He stood, walked to the desk, and pulled out his duffle bag. He'd missed his morning workout due to the inspection and was anxious to change and get to the gym. He preferred working out in his personal gym, but since he was making rounds, it wouldn't hurt to combine his visit to his local franchise with his workout.

He pulled his shirt out of his waistband and finished unbuttoning it. When Cassandra whistled appreciatively as he pulled it off he gave her a grin. "Cut that mess out, girl. I don't need your jolly green giant to come after me." Jared referred to Cassandra's boyfriend, a defensive end for the L.A. Raiders.

Cassandra stood. "Please, Ramon is the least of your worries."

"Why is that?"

"Because I'm finished with him. It was fun while it lasted, but I'd rather be with a man who can talk about something other than Saturday morning cartoons."

Jared laughed. "What, all muscle, no depth?"

"Exactly." She walked over and ran a hand over his arm. "I need beauty and brains." Her eyes hinted he could fit the bill.

A few years ago he would have accepted her invitation, but he knew Cassandra too well. Beneath all of her gloss and sophistication, she was a woman looking for a stable relationship. She was his friend and he wouldn't take her up on that offer. Besides, he still couldn't shake the feeling that no one other than Tasha would satisfy him right now. He didn't want to think about why.

When he didn't reply she smiled slightly and let her arm drop. "I better go and get ready to catch my flight. I can work on placing your products in the Farmers Market from L.A., but I'll call if I need you to do anything on this end."

Jared was glad she didn't say anything about his brush off. "I can handle that. Call me when you land."

"Will do. Bye, lova." She'd been calling him lova since their affair broke off years ago. She waved as she went out the door.

Jared hurried and changed, feeling much more relaxed and himself in basketball shorts and a cutoff t-shirt. He searched out Barry and thanked him for another job well done before going to his gym, Red Fitness.

When he'd first moved back to Columbia the local franchise was the first thing he'd overseen before plowing full steam on his production facility. Before Cassandra, his health food products were just a side hustle while he concentrated on building a name for himself as a personal trainer and fitness expert. He'd only been selling them to celebrities and a few health food stores, but she'd pushed to get them into Wal-Mart and Target. Once the big boxes placed his products, he'd quickly decided it would be smarter, and cheaper, to open a production facility in the south.

At Red Fitness he went straight to the general manager's office. The gym was busy for a Wednesday afternoon. He looked at his watch and saw it was lunchtime, which explained the crowd. He met briefly with the general manager before starting a circuit around the gym.

Halfway through, he noticed a middle-aged man struggling with the equipment. Jared stopped his workout and went over to assist. Someone struggling with a workout today was the same person who gave up working out tomorrow. After five minutes he'd introduced himself, learned the man was trying to lose the weight he'd put on after getting married a year ago, and hadn't worked out regularly since college. There was always an underlying reason why people either gained, or tried to lose, weight. Learning that reason was the key to ensuring his clients stuck to their goals.

Jared spent the rest of the hour working with him. During the course of the workout he'd discovered that the guy's wife had lost interest, something Jared wasn't surprised about. He hadn't come across a faithfully married woman in years. When they finished he offered the guy six weeks of free personal training. Despite his belief in the stupidity of marriage, the guy wanted his wife's attention again and Jared would help him try.

After he showered his phone rang. It was his friend Devin.

"What's going on, man?"

Devin groaned. "Nothing but a long day with no end in sight."

Jared laughed. "Why complain, doctor? Busy days mean more money."

"Easy for you to say. You don't have to see half the black population in this town." Devin was the only black doctor in Helena, a town on the outskirts of Kershaw County. It was where Devin had grown up, and he'd gone back to practice medicine after graduating from med school. Jared admired his friend for his dedication to his hometown, because he would avoid moving back home like the plague.

Jared waved bye to his general manager and headed for the front of the gym. "You chose to practice in Mayberry, so don't hate on the popularity."

Devin laughed. "Never that. Look, I only have a minute before my next patient, so I'll get to the point. I just found out about a basketball tournament in Columbia this weekend. One of my patients is trying to put together a team and I thought you, Malcolm, and I could play."

Jared rubbed his jaw. "I'm not sure about a team that one of your patients is putting together. Can the brotha even play?"

"He's not sick."

"Then why is he seeing you?"

Devin chuckled. "For reasons I can't say, but know this, I wouldn't be playing with him if I didn't think he could win. He played for Carolina back in the day. He's good."

Jared scoffed. "Now I know he's sorry." He was a strong Georgia Tech fan, having received his undergraduate degree from that very school.

"Blow that crap out your ass another day. You in?"

He would have usually jumped at the opportunity to play in a basketball tournament, but he didn't want to cancel his weekend with Tasha. He was looking forward to it too much.

"It sounds like fun, but I have plans this weekend. I'll have to catch y'all later."

"Okay, I get it. What's her name? Never mind, because I'll never even meet her. Just cancel and tell her you'll catch her after the tournament."

Jared smiled. "I can't cancel on this lady, Devin. It's going to be a special weekend I don't want to miss." He looked at his watch again. "In fact, I'm on my way to take her flowers now."

There was a silence on the other end of the phone and Jared called Devin's name to be sure the call wasn't dropped.

"Yeah, I'm still here," Devin answered. "I just thought you said you were taking a woman flowers."

Jared frowned. "It's not like I've never given a woman flowers."

"For as long as I've known you, you've never taken a woman flowers. You've already got a weekend lined up with this one, so why flowers? Are you getting serious?"

Jared laughed out loud. It drew the attention of a few people in the gym so he quickly exited and walked to his car. "Man, the day I get serious about a woman is the day you can call a psychiatrist to come and take me to the nut house. I'm just making it special for her."

"Why? You've never cared before."

Jared's laugh died and he frowned. It wasn't as if he'd been truly uncaring with the women he'd been with in the past he just made sure they understood he wasn't looking for any commitments. Devin talked as if he was cold blooded. He had been pretty cold to Monica, but she'd crossed the line. But he liked Tasha, and respected her. He couldn't treat her like any other chick off the street.

"Tasha's cool. She's not like the usual ladies I deal with, so she gets a bit more respect."

Devin didn't immediately respond, but Jared could picture his friend with his brow furled as the considered that. "This should be interesting to see pan out."

"Excuse me?" Jared asked.

There was rustling on the other end of the line. "Nothing, man. Handle your business. Look, my next patient has arrived. It seems like it'll just be me and Malcolm this weekend. Holla at me when you get time."

"No problem. Good luck this weekend, all right?"

"Cool. Peace." Devin hung up the phone.

Jared got into his car and sped out of the parking lot. He hadn't considered taking Tasha flowers until he'd said it to Devin. He wanted to see her. He still planned to wait for the weekend, but nothing could prevent him from trying for a kiss or something. He smiled as the thought of her lips on his. Yeah, it wouldn't hurt to go by her job and see her. Get her just as excited about their weekend as he was.

CHAPTER 8

"Excuse me, I'm looking for Tasha Smith."

Tasha froze in the middle of filing papers in her office. What was Jared doing here? It was too early for his mentoring session. That happened at six and it was barely three. Her excitement at seeing him was dampened by the thought that he'd changed his mind. She peeked around the corner as her high school intern, Latiffa, answered.

"Hello, Mr. Patterson. I mean Jared. Do you care if I call you Jared? I know you don't care, because you're cool like that. I heard you started out here at the Rec Commission, way back when. I mean…I don't mean that you are old or anything. Just that you started in the nineties and that was like a while ago. My bad. I mean, you're still fine as hell…how old are you, anyway?"

Jared chuckled. "Too old for you."

Latiffa leaned over the counter. "I'm old enough."

Tasha slammed her file cabinet closed and came out of her office. "That's enough, Latiffa." She glared at the young girl. "We didn't give you this job to hit on every man that comes in the door."

Latiffa lowered her eyes. "I know, but dang, Ms. Tasha. Look at him."

Tasha rolled her eyes and finally looked at Jared. Damn, why did he have to look so good? He licked his lips before they spread into a sexy smile. There was a promise in his eyes that left her breathless. Tasha cleared her throat and broke eye contact. "Jared Patterson knows how he looks. He doesn't need me, or you, telling him."

Jared leaned on the desk and winked at Latiffa. "I don't know, Tasha. I don't think you've ever told me your thoughts on my looks. Maybe I should take off my shirt, flex a few muscles, and you can give me thumbs up or down."

Latiffa's eyes sparkled like Christmas lights. "Oh, will you!"

"No, he won't." Tasha glared at Jared. "Did you have a reason for being here?"

He stood and nodded. "Yeah, I came to see you."

Her heart sped up. "Why?"

He glanced at Latiffa before answering. "I had a question about one of my mentees. Can we go in your office?"

She nodded. "Sure. Follow me."

Jared came around the desk but stopped at her door. He tapped the door's glass window, then glanced at her. "You know what? I haven't seen the renovations to the gym. Why don't you show me and we can talk on the way."

Tasha frowned and put a hand on her hip. "Jared, I have some stuff to put together for the budget hearing next week. We can talk here and then I'll get someone else to show you the gym."

He stepped closer and lowered his voice. "I would prefer talking to you alone." His eyes went back to her mouth before returning to her eyes. "I promised discretion, but if you don't come with me I'm going to kiss you right here in the middle of the office."

Her eyes widened and she took a quick step back. With just a few words, her annoyance melted into a delightful tingling. Humor reflected in his eyes. He was teasing her again. Her anger returned full force. She squared her shoulders and scowled. "Fine. Let's go." She brushed passed him, knocking him with her shoulder in order to push him out of the way.

As she hurried out of the office and down the hall toward the gym, she fought the urge to slap the smug smile from his face the moment they were alone. How dare he come to her job, in the middle of the day, and look at her as if he wanted to devour her. She'd picked him for his discretion, but apparently, he didn't care about showing the entire world they would be sleeping together.

It didn't help that he came here looking like he'd just tumbled out of bed. Did the man own anything other than basketball shorts and t-shirts? Just the sight of his well-formed biceps was enough to get her blood boiling.

"Why are you here?" she asked without turning to look at him.

When she didn't get an answer, she stopped and spun around. The hall was empty. She was about to call out his name when he came around the corner, grabbed her arm, and pulled her down the corridor they'd just passed.

"This isn't the way to the gym. What are you doing?"

He didn't say anything, just looked to see if they were being followed. She tried to dig in her heels and stop him, but it was no use. He just tugged on her arm and pulled her along as if she weighed nothing. He turned suddenly to the right and pulled her into an empty classroom. It was the room they used for the evening aerobics class.

Jared looked at the door and cursed. "I forgot every damn room in this building has a window."

Tasha tried to pull her hand free. "Why does it matter if we have windows on the doors?"

He pulled her to the left of the door and pressed her against the wall. As soon as she felt the heat from his body her protest died on her lips. It was as if the air had been sucked from the room. She knew he was only pursuing her as a favor, but when he looked at her as if she were the most desirable woman in the world common sense left.

Jared ran the back of his hand along the side of her face before using his thumb to trace her lower lip. Without thinking, she poked her tongue out to wet her lips. His eyes grew dark with desire and he brought his other hand up to run his fingers in her hair. It was in its usual ponytail and he made quick work of removing the clip holding it back. Tasha sighed with relief when the pressure from the clip was removed. He ran his fingers along her scalp, massaging with strong sure strokes. Tasha closed her eyes and let her head fall back.

When his lips touched hers, she didn't fight it. He kissed her softly before running his tongue along her lower lip. Without hesitation, she opened her mouth and granted him access. Passion erupted as he cupped her face in his hands and kissed her as if he couldn't get enough. He slowed down and pulled back, but she grabbed him by the waist and pulled him closer. His hands went back into her hair and he angled her head to kiss her again.

His desire pressed thickly against her belly. If they kept doing what they were doing, she'd be willing to drop her shorts and let him make short work of her virginity right here. But that wasn't what she wanted. He'd swept in and taken control. He was overwhelming her senses and she was being taken for a ride. Control, she had to reestablish control.

She abruptly broke off the kiss and turned her face to the side. Undeterred, Jared kissed her jaw, ear, and neck. His sensual assault was going full swing and she was about to be a causality of a war she didn't know how to fight.

"Jared, we've got to stop," she said between gasps.

"I know," he replied, but didn't stop kissing and sucking on her neck.

She reached up to place her hands on his chest to push him away, but he brought his lips back to her ear and traced his tongue around the sensitive edge. With a moan, she turned to kiss him again.

She was floating in a haze of desire and once again she was about to forget all of the reasons why she needed to stay in control. Why not let him take the lead? That was why she picked him, wasn't it? Why not lose herself in the experience of being with Jared Patterson? *Because once you're lost in him, you'll never find yourself. Or a husband.*

Tasha broke the kiss and pushed him away. When he groaned and reached for her she darted out of his reach and tried to catch her breath. He rested his head on the wall briefly before turning it to look at her from the corner of his eye. When he bit his lower lip and let his eyes travel the length of her body she thought she'd burst into flames.

"Stop it. You can't just show up here and kiss me senseless. This isn't what I asked for," she said.

He didn't lift his head from the wall. "You chose me for a reason."

"I know, but not for all of this. Just for one night, which you've turned into one weekend. I just need to lose my virginity, that's it." She couldn't believe she could say that with a straight face. Not when her breasts were aching, her nipples were tingling, and there was wetness between her legs.

He turned his body and rested his shoulder against the wall. "I came to bring you flowers."

She frowned and shook her head. "What? Why? There's no need for all of that."

He ran his hand over his face. "Don't ask why. I've never taken a woman flowers. I thought it would make...I don't know what I thought."

His discomfort was endearing. She'd never thought she'd see Jared unsure of himself. "Where are the flowers?"

"In the car."

She laughed. "Why are they in the car?"

He grinned at her. "I was trying to be discreet. Obviously, I'm not doing a good job at that."

She shook her head and combed her hair with her fingers. "Well. At least you picked an empty room."

He pushed away from the wall and brought her hair clip over. "Score one for me."

She snatched the clip from his hands. "This isn't a competition." She turned from him and put her hair back into a ponytail. She was being sensitive, but it felt like she was losing and she didn't want this to be a game.

He put his hands on her shoulders and pulled her against his chest. She held her body stiff until he kissed the top of her head. She relaxed into him.

"I know it's not a game, Tasha. That's why I'm trying to make it special. I'm sorry I showed up and attacked you in the aerobics room. I just wanted a taste of those lips."

It would be so easy to get used to this. Their bodies fit together too easily, as if they were made for each other. Where the hell had *that* come from? She wasn't made for Jared Patterson. She didn't even want a man like him. He was only good for one thing and that was taking her virginity.

She pulled away and turned to face him. "Is it true that you like to eat downtown?"

He frowned. "Downtown Columbia?"

"No, I mean, is it true that you like to eat…" Her voice trailed off and her face burned with embarrassment. Unable to finish, she pointed between her legs.

Comprehension dawned on his face and a sly grin split his full lips. "I do enjoy that, with the right woman. I don't eat at anyone's table. But I have a feeling I'm going to want a taste of everything you have to offer."

Her panties became wetter, but she straightened her spine. "Good. It'll be nice to have a comparison."

The smug smile dropped from his face. "Comparison to what?"

She lifted her chin and squared her shoulders. "I'm not as innocent as I look. I have had certain things done to me and I was…curious to see if…all men did it the same." She could barely meet his eye her embarrassment was so great, but it was worth the look on his face.

He stepped closer, his shoulders rigid. "What the hell are you talking about?"

It was her turn to smile slyly. "You'll be the first man inside of me, but you won't be the first man to pleasure me. Remember that when you think you can come around and play games. I'm not just some dumb virgin."

She left him with his mouth hanging open. It served him right. Just because he was going to be her first didn't mean she would let him treat her like a puppet on a string. She hadn't exactly lied. Her boyfriend in high school had tried that on her once as an alternative to sex. It had been awkward and uncomfortable, but Jared didn't need to know that. All he needed to know was that he wasn't the only man in the world who could pleasure her. And he damn sure wasn't going to be the last.

CHAPTER 9

Unsure of when Jared wanted to leave for Charleston, Tasha took Friday off. After she'd thrown her limited experience in his face, she wondered if he'd show up. She hadn't called him to confirm their plans, and neither had he. The bravado she felt after speaking to Shayla had vanished. She'd read all of the erotica in her library, which consisted of the one book from Shayla, but couldn't imagine doing those things with Jared. Getting Jared to take her virginity was one thing. Sharing all types of intimacies should be reserved for her husband. She doubted Jared would see it that way.

While Jared hadn't called, her mother had—constantly, since Tasha had told her she was going out of town this weekend. She wasn't foolish enough say she was going out of town with a man, opting instead to say she had to go to a conference in Charleston for work. It was hard to break her family's tradition of getting together for birthdays, but a part of her was happy for the excuse. It was bad enough she was turning thirty without a husband, but to bring in the next decade with cake and ice cream with her mom and dad was depressing.

After cleaning all morning with still no word from Jared, she was starting to think he had changed his mind when her cell phone vibrated, alerting her of a text.

I'll be there around 3. JP

She let out an unsteady breath. She had four hours to occupy herself before he showed up. She wrung her hands in front of her and chewed on her lip. This was a bad idea. She'd waited her entire life for the right man to give her virginity to, only to casually sleep with a known player over the weekend. It was reckless, stupid, and way too impulsive. If she met a man she wanted to marry later, what would she bring to the table now other than the fact that she was Jared Patterson's leftovers? Another notch on the belt of the fitness trainer and entrepreneur who slept with half of the women in South Carolina? What man would want those sloppy seconds?

Her finger hovered over the call back icon on her phone display. She would call Jared, tell him this was a mistake, and continue to wait.

She didn't press the button.

Wait for what? Wait for the next guy she dated to become excited with the thought of deflowering a virgin, or break things off as soon as he discovered she was saving herself for marriage? She'd done that for thirty years. Whomever she married didn't have to know who she'd slept with in the past. Jared promised discretion. Although he'd shown up at her job this week, she doubted he would do that again. He was only doing this as a favor to her, not because he was overcome with the urge to sleep with her. He was notorious for one-night stands. From what she'd heard, he rarely slept with the same woman for an extended period of time.

Her head cocked to the side as she considered that. Why did he switch from woman to woman so much? Could he really be that much of a lothario that he wanted to sleep with every woman he came in contact with?

Tasha shook her head. It didn't matter why he slept with the women he did, or why he stayed away from long-term relationships. His experience was the reason she'd chosen him. He knew what he was doing, would be discreet, and would make sure she enjoyed it.

Warmth spread through her body as she remembered the way he'd looked at her on Wednesday. He appeared as affected by the desire between them as she was. She agreed with Shayla he must want her a little bit. He may not have wanted her before, but he wanted her now. And if she didn't want the same situation her sister had, losing her virginity to a man who'd only pretended to care, then it made more sense to control the situation.

Feeling somewhat better, if not calmer, Tasha stood and went through her kitchen out the back door. Weeding her vegetable garden would distract her for an hour or two. She'd packed the night before, and really had nothing left to do to prepare for the weekend. A few hours tending her tomatoes, squash, and cucumbers would keep her from changing her mind yet again.

The outside air was warm without a trace of humidity as she walked into her backyard. The one tall oak tree in the middle of the yard cast shade on her porch, and the smell of the potted marigolds on her patio greeted her. Smiling, she walked to the garden along the privacy fence in her yard. These were the types of days when she preferred being at home instead of in her office. It was too beautiful outside to be stuck behind walls.

After getting her tools from the shed, she started pulling weeds from between the still growing plants. Before long, her mind began to clear as she focused on the joy of feeling dirt on her hands as she worked.

Shortly after she started a person's shadow covered her. She spun and held her trowel out in front of her, but the sudden movement from a crouched position caused her to fall awkwardly onto her ass. The sun behind him prevented her from seeing his face, but she knew it was Jared.

"You scared the crap out of me," she said with her hand over her pounding heart. "What are you doing here already? It's not three."

Jared reached down and pulled her up. A shot of electricity shot from where his hand clasped hers straight to her belly. She snatched it away and took a step back, only to step on one of her tomatoes.

If he felt it, he didn't show. He only stood there scowling at her. "Who are you comparing me to?"

Tasha returned his scowl. "What? You came here early and scared me half to death to ask who I'm comparing you to?"

He stepped closer. "Let's get one thing straight. You're not to compare me to anyone. When we're together, the only person you're supposed to think about is me. Don't bring up another guy's name when we're together."

Anger bubbled hot in Tasha's belly. She reached out and shoved his chest with every ounce of strength she had. Caught off balance, Jared fell backwards into a pile of weeds. She put one leg on either side of his hips, stood over him and pointed a finger in his face.

"*You* need to get a couple of things straight. Number one, I'm not one of your groupies, so don't talk to me like I should be privileged to sleep with you. Half of the women in South Carolina and California have slept with you so believe me, it's not like it's hard to do. Number two, stop trying to take advantage of the fact that I'm a virgin. My experience with men is limited, but I know enough to see that you want me. Badly. But I'm not going to let you take control of everything and get me all mixed up. Number three, there will be no more 'when I'm with you' after this weekend. I need a favor from you—that's it."

Jared stared at her for a few seconds before shaking his head and laughing. "I can't believe you pushed me down."

Tasha crossed her arms and tapped her foot. "Believe it. And if you come around making demands of me, or trying to kiss me senseless again, I'm going to do more than that."

He stopped laughing and looked at her seriously. "I'm sorry, Tasha. I didn't mean to try and take advantage of the situation." She raised an eyebrow, and he rubbed his jaw. "Okay, I did. You're right. I do want you, badly. And when I want a woman I let her know."

His voice rang with sincerity while desire crept into his dark eyes. Some of her anger subsided as her body heated in response. How did he make her go from boiling mad to lustful with just a look?

Her body relaxed slightly and he took advantage. He grabbed her arm and pulled her down on top of him before she could blink an eye. He didn't flinch when she landed heavily on top of him.

"You want me too, Tasha. Don't you?"

Get up and tell him that you've changed your mind, she thought. But the hardness of his body underneath hers, and the thickness of his erection rising against her stomach, chased that thought out of her head. She wanted him as much as he wanted her.

"Yes, I want you, Jared, but not like this."

He smiled. "I don't plan to fuck you on the ground in your backyard."

She rolled her eyes. "I'm not talking about on the ground. I need you to stop being Jared the playboy and just be the Jared I see on occasion at the Rec Commission."

"I thought you chose me for the playboy side," he said with a wink.

"I did, but it's too much for me. I like the Jared who teases me about being anal with the mentor attendance logs, or the Jared who lets me twist his arm into judging the senior Olympics. I've always respected that when we're together you don't treat me like one of your playthings. You treated me with respect. That mutual respect was why I chose you. I can't do this if you keep treating me like another woman off the street."

Jared closed his eyes before rolling to his side and lifting her up as he stood. When they were back on their feet, he stepped away from her. "In my life women fit into two distinct categories. The ones I'm fucking and the ones I'm not. I never thought you'd be in the former category, but once you were, a switch went off in my head. This is new to me. I don't sleep with female friends."

"It's new to me too. Brand new. I need my friend to do this… please."

She held her breath. He had the look of a toddler who'd just been told they couldn't have cookies before dinner. He may have known her words made sense, but she doubted he was happy with it.

"I don't know if I can do it," he held up his hand when she started to interrupt, "without ever slipping back into old habits. But I'll try." He reached over to hold her hand and pull her against him. "Now that I've gotten a taste, I don't want to mess things up and miss my chance. But if I make you uncomfortable, let me know."

Tasha stared into his eyes and her heart melted. He looked so sweet, and tempting as hell. It was easy to see why women fell at his feet.

"I'll let you know," she whispered.

"Good." He rubbed his erection against her. "Am I making you uncomfortable?"

She trembled, but shook her head.

He squeezed her hips. "Good. I came early because I had to kiss you."

This was going too far. They felt too familiar, too right. But it was only for one weekend. What would it hurt to indulge herself once? "Then do it."

Before the words finished leaving her mouth his lips met hers. It was just like before, an explosion of heat and electricity. She didn't hesitate to open her lips and grant his tongue entrance. He kissed her until her knees went weak. When she wrapped her arms around his neck and pulled him closer, a groan rumbled through his chest. He slowly broke the kiss, but didn't push her away.

"We can leave for Charleston, or go inside to your bedroom," he said. She tried to push away from him, but his arms tightened around her. "I'm only teasing, Tasha. We can leave whenever you're ready."

Heat filled her face but she smiled. "I need to take a shower, then we can go."

He nodded and finally let her go. "I'll wait in your living room."

Tasha ignored her disappointment when he didn't offer to join her. That would have only freaked her out, but she already missed his aggression. It was a definite turn on, but not what she needed. She just needed to get through this weekend with her sanity intact.

"I'll put these things up first." She motioned to her garden tools on the ground.

"I'll put them in your shed. You go take the shower. I'm anxious to get out of town." He winked at her.

Tasha's heart sped up. She hoped she could survive this weekend.

CHAPTER 10

While Tasha showered, Jared looked around her house. It could be considered snooping, but he didn't care. He wanted to know more about the personal side of Tasha. He'd always dealt with her professionally, and had intentionally never hit on her, so he knew little about what she liked outside of work. It was surprising that his professional treatment of her factored into her decision to sleep with him.

The moment he'd decided to sleep with her he'd begun treating her like any other woman he slept with. How was he to know she would view it as him not respecting her? It was true he had little respect for the women he slept with—they were always throwing themselves at him, going after his money, or were so easy to catch he treated them like the gold diggers they were. The only woman to ever go from lover to friend was Cassandra, and that was because she'd insisted on helping his career once their affair was over. Once she moved to the professional category, he no longer treated her like a conquest. But the sex also stopped, so there was no way to confuse the lines. Tasha asked him to blur his lines. He didn't respect his lovers, and he didn't sleep with friends or colleagues. He wasn't sure if he'd be able to respect Tasha's wishes, but he wanted her enough to try.

Her home was nicely decorated with a lived-in feel. The things there showed pieces of Tasha. The stack of books on her coffee table told him that she liked reading in front of the TV. A sweatshirt was tossed over the end of her sofa with a pair of reading glasses on them. Pictures of her family were all over the house—one shelf of her bookcase was dedicated to her sister's wedding and another shelf was filled with pictures of her nieces. Another sign she wanted a family.

He took his perusal into her kitchen. There was a teacup and saucer in the sink, and mail littered her kitchen table. He smiled when he saw the recycling bin next to the trashcan. Malcolm and Kenyatta would like her just because she recycled and grew her own vegetables.

Where did that come from? It didn't matter if his brother and his fiancée liked Tasha. Things wouldn't go so far she would be introduced to his family.

Shaking off that thought Jared turned to leave the kitchen and ran right into Tasha. He reached out to steady her but quickly pulled his hands away. Touching her did strange things to his body. If he was going to remember her request, he would have to limit touching her until they got to Charleston.

"That was a quick shower." His eyes assessed her. He'd only seen her dressed in Rec Commission uniforms or jeans. But today she wore a white and gold sundress. The thin material hung from her body, clinging to her curves in just the right places and stopped just above her feet. Her hair wasn't in the usual ponytail. Instead, the curls hung loosely around her shoulders. His groin tightened and he had to fight to breath. She looked beautiful.

"I didn't want to linger and give you a reason to come looking for me."

He cleared his throat. "Is there anything you needed to do before we leave?"

She shook her head. "No, I'm packed and ready to go."

They stood there looking at each other. Jared felt like a teenager on his first date. He still wanted her, but now that he was respecting her wish to not lump her in the category of the other women he slept with, he wasn't sure how to proceed.

Tasha smiled and pushed her hair behind her ears. "I'll get my bag." She turned and disappeared down the hall.

Feeling foolish, Jared ran his hand over his face. This wasn't a big deal. They were just going to go down to Charleston, sleep together, and come back. He'd taken plenty of women to his condo; this was no different. Except none of those women were virgins and none of those women drove him mad with desire.

He went into the living room just as Tasha came back down the hall rolling a small duffle bag behind her. It was a good thing she hadn't packed a lot of clothes because he planned on keeping her naked for most of the weekend. The thought sent his dick from half swollen to rock hard.

Tasha froze at the end of the hall. He continued to stare as he willed himself not to drag her back down the hall to her bedroom. She looked unsure for a second before dropping the bag and coming over to him. He held his breath as she reached up to pull his head down. Her eyes closed as she pressed her lips against his. Without a second thought, he squeezed her body and took over the kiss. He didn't know how long they were wrapped in each other, but she was the one to finally break the kiss.

"You looked as if you didn't know whether to devour me or run out the door," she said against his chest. "I thought I'd ease the tension a bit."

Jared smiled and kissed the top of her head. "You only created another type of tension." He pushed her away and walked over to pick up her duffle bag. "Lock up and I'll meet you at the car." He walked outside without touching her again.

Two minutes later Tasha came out. He'd already put her bag in the back of his car and was sitting in the driver's seat. When she got in, the fresh scent of whatever she'd used in the shower filled his car. Again, he appreciated it more than the fruit- or flower-scented perfumes most women wore. When she fastened her seatbelt, he pulled away from the curb and drove toward the interstate.

He didn't start a conversation, and she remained silent. The tension was so thick he was surprised it didn't smother them. Maybe this was a bad idea. He didn't know how to treat Tasha like a friend *and* lover. As much as he wanted to slide himself deep inside of her, he was beginning to doubt if he could do this.

He gripped the steering wheel and opened his mouth to tell her that when she reached over and punched his arm. "Red Volkswagen," she said with a smile.

He'd barely felt her punch, but he rubbed the spot. "You can't be serious."

Tasha laughed and the sound washed over him. He wanted to hear her laugh more. "You bet I am. And if I see another one, I'm gonna hit you again."

"Don't start a game you can't win. And don't think that I'll take it easy on you because you're a girl."

She cut her eyes at him. "Excuse me? I don't think you understand I hold the championship title in my family. By Sunday you'll be begging me to quit. I can spot a Volkswagen from a mile away."

"You may have held the title, but that was before you challenged me, sweetheart. You see, my brother had to get a sling for his arm after I tore him up on a trip to D.C. when we were kids."

Unfazed by his claim Tasha rolled her eyes. "We'll see who needs the sling." As if fated, a yellow Beetle glided into traffic. "Yellow!" Tasha reached over and hit his arm again before he could open his mouth.

Laughing, Jared shook his head. This weekend was going to be more interesting than he thought.

CHAPTER 11

Tasha loved Charleston. The smell of the harbor, the historic buildings, the epitome of Southern lifestyle all combined to make Charleston one of her favorite cities. Even though she was only a ninety-minute drive from the beautiful city, she hardly had time to visit. Charleston was a place for lovers, and being a single virgin made it hard for her to come alone. The last time she'd visited was two years ago for a family reunion. Although she'd loved walking through downtown with her family, she'd still felt a pang of longing as she watched all of the couples in her family hold hands and chase after their kids along those cobbled streets.

She'd imagined visiting here often when she was married, but never had she expected to be here with a man just to have sex. It was the total opposite of every daydream she'd had about coming here. Charleston wasn't a place for weekend flings or unattached sex. It wasn't Las Vegas. But Jared had chosen the city she associated with romance as the place for their encounter. She wasn't going to tell him how strongly her feelings were attached to the place and make a weird situation worse.

She'd done all she could to break the tension in the car. Playing travel games was something she'd done as a child to pass the time. It had seemed like the easiest thing to do to take both of their minds off why they were coming, as if that were possible. She didn't know why, but she could tell her request had rattled him. Jared treated most women as interchangeable playthings—she wasn't much better since she was using him for sex—but it was her first time and she wanted it to be somewhat special.

She hadn't expected him to take her to Motel 6, but she couldn't hide her surprise when he pulled into a garage for a condominium on Broad Street in Charleston's French Quarter.

"You rented a condo?"

He cut the engine and winked. "I bought this condo last year just for the view of the harbor at sunrise."

"I never would have thought you had a romantic streak."

His head snapped back. "What's romantic about that?"

She laughed. "Don't get all wrapped up about it. Just the fact that you bought this place so you can watch the sunrise over the harbor is almost poetic."

"Well, don't tell my brother or best friend. If they hear the word poetic and my name in the same sentence I'll never live it down."

They got out of the car and Jared grabbed their bags out of the back. The lobby had an elegant modern décor, with tall ceilings that filled the area with light.

He punched in a code for the elevator and Tasha's heart did a tap dance in her chest as they rode to the top floor. It was time. They were finally here. He was going to officially deflower her. Her palms grew sweaty with anxiety and excitement. She did want this, there was no use denying it, but was she really ready for it?

Jared turned and squeezed her hand. "Let's go."

She nodded stiffly and followed him off the elevator. Her stomach was tied in so many knots she couldn't appreciate the panoramic views of downtown Charleston and the Cooper River. Her feet carried her through the tastefully furnished living room to the bedroom. A massive king bed sat in the middle of the room facing large windows that overlooked the harbor. She swallowed hard. Another altar for the god of sex where she would be sacrificed. Would he want to do it immediately? The way he'd looked at her at her house, as if he wanted to pounce on her, flashed through her mind. He'd almost sexed her in the middle of her vegetable garden. There was no denying he'd want to do it as soon as possible.

Her hands trembled and her breath came in short pants. She took a step backward and collided with his chest. Her body jerked and she tried to move away but his hands came up instantly to grab her forearms and pull her against his body. His erection pressed against her buttocks and despite her anxiety, desire languidly slid throughout her. It was time to get it over with. She reached up to the straps of her dress and began to push it off her shoulders.

Jared's hands came up to stop her and she stiffened in his arms. Why drag this out? Why increase her anxiety? She wanted to lose her virginity and she wanted to lose it now.

He moved a hand from her shoulder and placed it against her chest, right above her breasts, before leaning over to kiss her ear. "Your heart is pounding."

Still breathing as if she'd run a marathon, Tasha opened her mouth to answer but nothing came out.

"I'm not going to pounce on you, Tasha. I told you I wanted to make this special for you and jumping you the minute we enter my condo is not the way to do that."

She swallowed loudly and took a few more breaths before she could talk. "Why keep waiting? It's obvious we both want this, we're here, the bed's ready, let's get it over with."

The rumble of his laugh against her back caused her to stiffen. "There are many things I want you to say before we have sex, but *let's get it over with* isn't one of them." He kissed her ear again before slowly trailing kisses down the side of her neck. When he softly sucked on the sensitive spot where her neck and shoulders met her tension evaporated. His hand slid beneath her dress to cup her breast, which was bare beneath the v-neck. Her knees buckled when he took the nipple between his forefinger and thumb and squeezed gently. His other hand shot around her waist to hold her against him. "This is your weekend, Tasha. You asked me here as a friend, so I'm treating you like a friend and will let you decide when the time is right. If you hadn't dragged that promise out of me, I'd have you naked and on top of that bed right now. So when you're ready just tell me. Today or Sunday, it doesn't matter. Okay?"

She nodded and he squeezed her breast again. "Right now, I think we should eat," he said. His hand slowly slid away from her breast and she trembled as his fingers brushed across her nipple. He hesitated only a second before letting her go and turning her to face him. Desire burned hot in his eyes, and she looked for signs that he was upset about her hesitancy. She was the one who'd asked him, and kissed him like a maniac before leaving Columbia, so he had every right to be frustrated with her.

He leaned over and brushed his lips briefly across hers before chuckling.

"Why are you laughing?" she asked.

He brought her hand to his lips. "Because, I can't believe I just told you that. Malcolm would have a heart attack if he could see me now."

She nodded. "This friend and lover thing is new to you, but don't worry, it's only for one weekend."

Disappointment flashed in his eyes so briefly she couldn't be sure if it was really there. Regardless of what he may think, this couldn't last more than a weekend. Once her virginity was gone, she could start looking for a husband. Jared was the last man she needed to keep around if she wanted to get married.

Instead of replying to her comment, he tugged on her arm. "Come on. Let's go eat before I say anything else that can be classified as romantic, noble, or decent."

She laughed and followed him out.

CHAPTER 12

Jared cursed himself a thousand times as he and Tasha walked along the pier in Waterfront Park. He couldn't believe he'd told her they didn't have to sleep together until Sunday. He was really acting like a punk. The minute he'd seen her standing in the bedroom he'd wanted her, but her racing heart and stiff body had gotten to him. He knew she wanted him too, but he didn't want to rush her first time. Still, the amount of lust coursing through him was playing havoc with his patience.

He could have easily overcome her anxiety—the way her body melted when he kissed her neck told him that—but he wanted her to come to him, the same way she had at the park and in her house before they left: without hesitancy. But to give her until Sunday to relax and come to him was a bit much.

He walked behind her on purpose. His eyes followed the soft sway of her hips beneath her dress. He would have a serious case of blue balls if she wasn't ready until Sunday. There weren't any panty lines visible beneath her dress. His erection had doubled in size when he'd felt her bare breast earlier. Did she just slip out of the shower and into that dress? All he had to do was slide it up and glide himself right into her wetness.

Jared groaned and she turned to face him with a frown. "Are you okay?"

He nodded. "Yeah, I'm good."

"Then why are you groaning?"

"Just thinking about something I need to do for my product line. We're trying to get my line at the Farmers Market and I forgot to update the superintendent." He lied easily. One good thing about being a player was he could come up with quick excuses. He ignored the twist in his stomach at the thought of playing Tasha. That wasn't what he was trying to do with her.

She smiled and walked over to lean on the rail overlooking the river. "That's one of the things I like about you. You've always pursued your dream with tenacity. Even way back when I first met you and you were just starting out as a personal trainer, you pushed your services and your fitness ideas with such enthusiasm."

Jared rubbed his jaw as he walked to stand beside her at the rail. "You make me sound like some hustler."

"Not like that. I just mean I could tell you really believed in yourself and what you were offering. Plus you care about your clients. You never were just another muscle head leading people from machine to machine. You want them to succeed. I knew you would be successful one day. I just didn't realize how successful."

He turned to look at the harbor. "I'm doing okay."

"Okay?" she said with a laugh. "You have an infomercial."

"Sales ad," he quipped.

She rolled her eyes. "Infomercial, and from what I hear it rivals the top selling workouts in sales and intensity. You recently launched your product in two large retailers, and you own a huge production facility. And let's not forget the gym franchise."

"It's only a few dozen gyms."

She playfully hit his shoulder. "Will you stop being modest, it doesn't suit you, Casanova. On the real, I'm proud of what you've done. It's a testament to you and your skills."

As Jared looked at Tasha's upturned face there was a tightening near his heart. He'd had women praise his workouts, looks, and dick size, but never his skills outside of the gym or bedroom—two of his best rooms if anyone were to ask. Until that moment, he hadn't believed her when she said she'd picked him because she respected what he did. He'd assumed she was like the other women he knew that wanted him in their bed.

The sunlight brought out red highlights in her curly hair and he couldn't resist the urge to play with a tendril that blew softly in the breeze.

He leaned down and softly kissed her. "Thank you," he said.

She blushed but didn't pull away. "You're welcome."

He ran his hand across her cheek and studied her face. He may have given her until Sunday to say "let's get it on" but that didn't mean he couldn't try to speed her along. And right now, the only thing he wanted to do was kiss her until she insisted they forget food and go back to his condo.

"Let's get something to eat," he told her, but didn't remove his hand from her face.

"Then let's go back to your place."

"Are you sure?"

She stood on tiptoe and kissed him again. "Yes."

To hell with food, was Jared's immediate thought. He could always order something afterwards. *Calm down, man. At least now you know you won't have to wait until Sunday.*

"How about we get something quick?" he said.

"What do you want to eat?"

"You." It was an automatic response.

She blinked a few times before lowering her eyes. "That won't fill you up."

He stepped close. "We'll both be satisfied once I'm done."

Tasha turned to lean on the rail. The wind blew the hair away from her face and the humid smell of the river drifted over them. "I doubt it. I don't see what the fuss is about. It's messy for men and uncomfortable for women. The entire act is overrated."

Jared laughed loud enough to draw the attention of a few passersby. "Are you sure you've done it before? Or were you only trying to get to me?"

Tasha looked around before whispering. "I've done it before. I just didn't like it."

"Who was he?"

She shrugged as if it were no big deal. "My high school boyfriend."

Jared waved his hand dismissively. "That's the problem. We don't know what we're doing in high school. He probably went at it like he was eating an apple."

"More like a dog lapping water from a bowl," she said with a shudder.

He chuckled. "Even worse."

She turned and placed a hand on her hip. "What makes you so good? The act is the same no matter who's doing it."

Jared leaned over and lowered his voice. "Because I don't *eat* it. I kiss it. I use my tongue, teeth, and lips to taste, kiss, and savor every drop of goodness coming from you."

The cockiness of male pride filled his chest when her breathing increased. He knew she wanted to know if he could do it better, and he was absolutely certain he could. She licked her lips and his tongue itched to retrace her actions.

She looked at him and he almost lost himself in her honey colored eyes. "You said you only do it with the right people. What makes me right?"

Jared couldn't answer that question. He hadn't kissed a woman's lower lips since a Hollywood writer had decided to give a play-by-play of his technique on her blog six months ago. The blog had caused women to throw themselves at him for over a month, but they were all disappointed. He didn't like his business in the street and wasn't going to give another woman fuel.

But ever since Tasha had come to him with her request, he couldn't stop himself from wanting to taste her. He wanted to see her face when he gave her the ultimate lovers' kiss, and feel her body climax around his tongue. She didn't need to know how much he craved it—he didn't understand it himself.

"I want to introduce you to your sexuality. I can't hold back any of my techniques if I were to do that," he said.

She frowned and he loved the way her nose crinkled up. "Maybe you shouldn't do that. I should save something for my husband."

Jared checked his annoyance at the mention of a non-existent husband. "Number one, you have to know what you like so that you can tell your husband."

"He'll know what to do."

"Men aren't mind readers, Tasha. You have to say what you like, otherwise he's going in blind. Just like your high school sweetheart. Number two, you love my kisses and I know you want me to kiss you everywhere." He ran his hand slowly down her arm. Goose bumps raised on her soft skin, sending his already heated body went into overdrive.

He bit back a smile—her thoughts were back on him.

"I wouldn't say that I love your kisses," she said softly.

"Well, I damn sure like yours." He pulled her close and lowered his lips to hers. He couldn't get enough of kissing her. He didn't care that they were on the harbor surrounded by tourists. He'd ignored Monica's calls offering easy ass ever since Tasha asked him to take her virginity, and he could barely walk straight from the constant arousal. He'd be damned if he got through the weekend without her feeling the same.

His tongue glided back and forth over the fullness of her lower lip until she opened her mouth with a sigh. Wasting no time at all, his tongue slipped past her lips to kiss her fully. He loved every inch of her mouth until she was weak and clinging to him. Thoughts of doing the same to every fold of her lower lips caused his dick to throb and he pressed it against her, letting her feel just how hard she'd made him.

"Get a room," somebody called out.

Tasha stiffened and tried to pull away but he didn't let her. Instead, he leisurely ended the kiss, sucking gently on her lower lip before gradually letting it slide between his lips. Her eyes were like molten pools of caramel as she stared up at him. Damn, if they weren't so exposed he'd hike up her dress and take it right here.

"I think it's time to stop the torture. Let's go back to my condo and let me make love to you." He'd never told a woman he wanted to make love to her. Let's have sex, do it, or fuck were common phrases he'd used, but not make love. Yet, that was what he thought of with Tasha. He'd always been a giving sex partner, with women coming back for more, but he wanted to do more than pleasure Tasha's body. He wanted to worship her body.

"Let's go."

He couldn't stop the cocky grin from spreading his face. He grabbed her hand and nearly sprinted back to his place. There was no need to try and hide his anticipation, she wanted him just as much. He was going to make sure the feel of his body remained with Tasha for the rest of her life.

CHAPTER 13

Tasha didn't have time to think as Jared hurried the few blocks to his condo. It amazed her things could accelerate so quickly between the two of them. Thirty minutes had barely passed since she was hyperventilating as he'd held her. Now, she was just as anxious as he to get back to his place and, as he said, end the torture. Just thinking about him kissing every part of her body the way he'd kissed her mouth on the harbor had her on fire. Saying she should leave something for a future husband was her last attempt to keep herself from getting completely caught up in Jared's spell.

The inside of the lobby was a blur on the way to his condo. On his floor, Jared rushed inside and pulled her into his arms in a flash. In the next instant, his mouth was on hers and Tasha softened against him. He lifted her up and she wrapped her legs around his waist. Instead of carrying her to the bedroom, he placed her back against the wall and kissed her with as much tenacity as he'd done on the harbor. Every sweep of his tongue against hers caused heat to pulse between her legs. She was so wet she wouldn't have been surprised if his shorts were damp where they pressed against her.

Jared broke the kiss and Tasha groaned in disappointment. He laughed softly against her throat. "Don't worry, I'll kiss you some more."

"That's not the only place I want you to kiss me."

His head lifted from her neck and his eyes met hers. A wicked grin spread across his face. "That's what I'm talking about. Tell me what you want."

Tasha carefully took her hands from around his shoulders, afraid that if she let go she might fall. He didn't show a sign that her letting go made it harder for him to hold her. His arms flexed beneath her behind and around her waist and another rush of desire flooded her. His strength was so damn erotic.

She pushed the dress away from her shoulders and pulled her arms from the straps exposing her breasts. She didn't think it was possible but she felt him get harder between her legs and she flexed the muscles of her sex in response.

"Kiss my breasts." It was barely a whisper she was so embarrassed to say it out loud.

"Hold them for me," he said.

She blushed as she took a breast in each hand and lifted them up. Jared hoisted her higher so that her breasts were at eye level and she tensed in anticipation. He buried his head between the two mounds, kissing the valley in between. Tasha moaned as he licked the same spot before kissing and licking his way up the sides. He sucked each of her fingers on his way to her nipple, which became pebble hard and aching for his touch. When his warm mouth finally covered the peak she gasped as pleasure rocked within her. He gently sucked one breast before moving to the other. Tasha gyrated her hips against him, his rigid stiffness creating mounting waves of excitement whenever her aching flesh pressed against it. Her movements became more frantic as the pleasure built. Between his mouth on her breasts and the pressure between her thighs she felt as if she was on the way to an explosion.

When she was on the edge of ecstasy, he pulled away from her breast with one last suck and carried her from the wall.

"No, you don't. You're not coming until I'm ready."

She tried to press her body against his but he kept space between them. "What are you doing? Why did you stop me?" She grabbed his face and kissed him frantically as she tried to press her hot center back on his hardness.

Jared carried her into the bedroom. He dropped her on the bed, then climbed on, his knees between her thighs and a hand on each side of her head. "Dammit, Tasha, I want to take it slow but if you keep this up I can't promise that."

Slow. Not when her body was on fire from within and she was so close. "I didn't ask you to take it slow."

She sat up and pulled his shirt over his head. His muscles seemed to bulge even more than usual and the veins in his arms were prominent beneath his tan skin. She ran her hands up and down his arms, then ran them over his chest to pause at his pecs. "Make them jump."

He smiled. "You like that?"

"Yes."

Jared flexed his right one before doing the left. Then he picked up the pace flexing them both at the same time. Tasha leaned forward to kiss his chest and smiled when she felt his body tremble. Her lips closed around one of his hard nipples and Jared cursed before pushing her away. Tasha pushed his hand away and took the other nipple in her mouth.

He pressed her shoulders back against the mattress and pulled her dress roughly down her hips. She lifted her legs so he could pull it off and he threw the garment across the room. His hands rested at the waistband of her thong as his eyes traveled over the length of her.

"Your body is beautiful."

For the first time since they'd started Tasha felt shy but didn't cover herself. The look in his eyes was a mixture of desire and adoration, as if he'd never seen another woman's body as beautiful as hers. She knew that wasn't true, but she didn't want to think about how many other women he'd said that to.

The throbbing between her legs was insistent. Without thought, she ran her hand down her belly and into the waistband of her thong. Jared's breathing hitched and his eyes grew darker. With one smooth motion, he pulled her underwear off. She jerked her hand away, but he took her wrist in his hand. "Touch yourself."

She didn't know if her face burned from self-consciousness or desire. She'd masturbated before—just because she was a virgin didn't mean she was completely unknowledgeable—but obviously never in front of another person. But the heat in his eyes evaporated any shame she may have felt. There was something erotic about the way he watched her.

She slowly began to massage her outer lips, spreading her wetness around. She used her fingers to open herself and slowly rubbed her clitoris. Jared's dark eyes were focused on her movements. His body was tense and his breathing labored as he rubbed the rock hard staff between his legs. Tasha lifted one leg and closed her eyes as she slipped her middle finger inside of her dripping core.

"That's it. Show me what you like," he whispered.

Turned on by his encouragement Tasha's eyes closed as she continued to glide her finger inside of her, before slipping it out and over her aching nub. She became so engrossed in her own pleasure, her moans and sighs echoing in the room, that she wasn't aware of Jared moving lower until he moved her hand and replaced her fingers with his tongue. Tasha cried out as he slowly licked from one end of her goodness to the other. True to his words, Jared kissed her lower lips just as thoroughly as he kissed her mouth, his tongue doing a wicked dance with every nook and cranny. She thought her heart would stop from the pleasure. When his mouth closed around her swollen clit she yelled as an orgasm unlike any she'd ever felt rocked her body. The spasms clenched in her womb and stars burst behind her eyelids.

She tried to curl up into a fetal position as the aftershocks went through her body, but he didn't let her. He opened her legs and reached into his pocket for a condom. She watched as he pulled down his shorts and underwear and his erection sprang forth. She'd seen penises before—mostly in porn that Shayla sent her—but Jared could give any porn star a run for his money. He tore open the packet with his teeth and quickly slid on the protection.

His movements were effortless, another sign he'd done this often.

"It'll only hurt a second…I think," he said.

She opened her mouth to answer but Jared pushed into her with one quick thrust. When she cried out this time it was in pain. She'd known it would hurt, but this was excruciating. He needed to get off, now!

"Damn, Jared, that hurts. I don't think I can do this," she said between clenched teeth.

"It's done now. Shit, Tasha, you feel so good," he said through clenched teeth of his own.

She tried to move back but he held fast to her waist. "Don't move. Take a second to feel it." He groaned.

Tasha went still. This wasn't nearly as good as what he'd told her it would be. This was painful.

"Relax, Tasha." He leaned back slightly to move one hand from her waist and slowly rubbed her clit. "Give it time." His eyes met hers, concern mixed with his desire. His body was as tense as hers and he was gritting his teeth as if in pain. She slowly let her body relax as he continued to massage where they were joined. The pain began to subside as pleasure ran through her. She clenched her muscles around him and was surprised at how good he felt inside of her. She hesitantly moved her hips and Jared groaned. "I've got to move now."

"Move," she said.

He pulled back slowly, then pushed in to the hilt. Tasha gasped with pleasure when his thickness rubbed against her inner walls. He repeated the move and her eyes rolled to the back of her head. This was more like it.

"That's it. Feel me inside you," he said.

"Move, Jared," she moaned.

He picked up the pace and Tasha's hips tentatively meet his. She wrapped her legs around his waist to get more of him inside. He continued to rub between her legs and Tasha felt the building of another orgasm.

"Move, move, please move!"

"Shit, yeah." He increased his speed, but his movements were deliberate, as if he was still mindful that this was new to her.

Tasha felt her orgasm coming. And she wanted it more than she wanted the first one. "Jared, yes! Move, dammit!"

He squeezed her clit between his thumb and forefinger and Tasha's world exploded. "Jared, Jared, Jared!" she cried out over and over and she climaxed around him.

He grabbed her hips with both hands and pumped into her twice more before coming himself. "Damn, Tasha! Fuck!" He collapsed on top of her and they both tried to calm their breathing.

After a few moments, Jared lifted up and looked at her in awe. "Where did you learn to have sex like that?"

Tasha was still trying to catch her breath as she spoke. "You, I guess. It felt like what I should be doing with you."

All emotion drained from his eyes. He'd shut himself off. He hadn't pulled away from her, he was still inside of her, but emotionally he wasn't there. She tried not to be upset about it. Sure, they'd just had what she thought had to be mind-blowing sex, but it was only for this weekend. She didn't need him to cuddle with her afterwards or tell her romantic words.

She looked away, unable to continue holding his stare. "Now that it's done we don't have to stay all weekend."

"What are you talking about?"

She looked back at his now frowning face. "I don't know what to do next, Jared. You're still inside of me, but you look as if you don't want me here anymore."

He lowered his head. A few seconds later, he looked back at her. "I want you to stay all weekend."

She should go back. Her virginity was gone and she had one round of great sex to get her through the months or years it took to find a husband. But one round wasn't enough. Just this weekend. She'd get through the weekend and not get caught up in him pulling away after sex. They weren't a couple and she didn't love him. So she could do this again.

She moved her hips to take more of him inside her. Desire quickly filled his eyes and she smiled. "I'll stay all weekend."

He grinned and just like that, Jared was back. "Good."

*

Hunger pangs woke Tasha later that night. She looked at the clock; it was half past midnight. She was officially thirty and no longer a virgin. She and Jared hadn't left his condo since having sex earlier. He snored softly beside her and she smiled. He truly knew his way around a bedroom. He also knew his way around a couch, against a wall, and in the bathtub. She couldn't believe how many times they'd had sex. It wasn't all on him. She couldn't get enough of him either. They'd completely forgotten about food and concentrated on feeding their sexual appetites. Now, she was starving.

She turned and studied him in the dim light from the moon shining in through the windows. The light cast a silver glow against his tan skin and created shadows, which highlighted his muscular frame. The bed sheets were tangled in his feet, exposing his body for her to study. He'd pulled them over her before she'd fallen asleep. Her eyes paused between his legs. Even unaroused his size was impressive. She reached out to touch him but stopped herself. No need to start that up again. Despite how much she'd enjoyed the day locked in a room with him, her body ached. Especially between her legs. She did want him again, but didn't think she could handle it.

She'd avoided saying anything about how right things felt between them, and he hadn't shut down on her emotionally again. It was true, though, albeit foolish, that she did feel that way. As soon as he touched her, her shyness evaporated and she forgot he wasn't her type. She only wanted him to touch her again, and that was scary. All afternoon his hands had been on her—both during and after sex. Even now, in sleep, his hand was on her waist. It would be easy to become flattered and think she was special, but he could be this way with all of his lovers.

You're getting caught up and reading too much into this, her mind warned. *Jared is a ladies' man. That's why you asked him to do this. Don't become a statistic.* It was a good thing she'd only agreed to a weekend. If she routinely slept with Jared, she'd forget what she truly wanted in a man and see more to their relationship than there was.

Her stomach growled, reminding her why she'd woken up. She would love a slice of pizza, but quickly dismissed that thought. It was too late to eat anything heavy. She hadn't brought any snacks, but he mentioned packing some of his protein bars in his bag earlier.

Tasha carefully slid out of the bed. There was enough light for her to make her way across the room. Her feet barely made a sound as she softly padded across the hardwood floors. She slowly unzipped his bag only to gasp after opening it. There were over a dozen condoms in the bag. He must have planned nothing but sex all weekend. She was amazed and annoyed by his cockiness.

She pushed the condoms aside and dug around until she found the bars. Her mouth watered as she pulled it out. Finally food.

"What are you doing?" The frigid tone of Jared voice startled her.

She turned to see him sitting on the bed glaring at her. She held up the bar. "I was hungry, so I got a protein bar out of your bag."

He continued to eye her with mistrust until her stomach growled loudly. He finally relaxed and a small smile played on his lips. "I guess I did forget to feed you."

Upset by his anger Tasha sat on the floor and frowned. "Why did you get so upset? You looked ready to kick me out."

He ran his hand over his face before lying down on his back. She thought he wasn't going to answer her but then he turned on his side and faced her. "I don't trust too many women."

Her eyebrows shot up. "Why?" Her stomach growled again and she opened the bar and took a bite.

"Because you can't trust women. They all want something. Money, sex, attention. Even the ones you think might be cool end up trying to take all they can get," he said matter-of-factly.

Tasha swallowed hard before replying. "Damn, who broke your heart?"

Jared chuckled. "No one. I never let anyone close enough to break my heart."

"So you've never been in love?"

"Hell no! And I don't plan to be. My view of women has been pretty accurate. They want my money or they want to have sex. I'm more than happy to sleep with them, though only a few are worth spending money on." His shoulder lifted in a depreciating shrug. "So far it's been a win-win situation."

Tasha finished her bar in silence. His view of women was another reason she couldn't get too caught up in this. She felt stupid for even entertaining the thought that things felt right with him. It was wrong. There wasn't another way to describe it. To Jared all women were sex objects he couldn't trust. No wonder he'd treated her like the rest after she'd asked him to take her virginity. She'd come to him for sex and in his world, that's what women wanted.

He watched her while she ate. He hadn't offered an explanation for his feelings, or tried to back pedal and make his opinion less harsh.

"I guess I'm no different really," she finally said. "I came to you for sex, then asked you to treat me like a friend. I shouldn't have done that. What we're doing isn't different from what you do with other women."

He sighed and shook his head. "I thought that, until you said you admire my work. You're the first woman, outside of my PR agent Cassandra, to truly appreciate all that I've accomplished."

"I meant what I said. After this weekend, I'll still be a fan of your brand and your work. And I promise I won't ask for sex anymore."

He flinched. "Don't promise that, because I refuse to promise not to ask you."

She shook her head. "I told you, after this we're through."

He sat up and Tasha almost forgot to listen to him as his abs flexed with the movement. "You're no longer a virgin, and there's no need to be celibate. No reason not to have a lover until you find your perfect husband."

The absurdity of that took her mind off his body. "That's the dumbest thing I've ever heard. I can't date a man while sleeping with someone else."

He snorted and looked as if he wanted to argue but shook his head and smiled instead. "You're almost refreshing." He leaned back against the headboard, distracting her once again by flexing his pecs. "Since you plan to cut off the good thing we've started here come Monday, let's not waste the weekend. Grab a condom and get over here."

Tasha laughed. "You mean one of the dozens you have in here?"

He shrugged innocently. "What's the problem? I have a big sexual appetite so I grabbed every condom in my drawer. Don't you think it'll be fun to see how many we can use?"

"I don't know if my body can handle it. I'm sore as it is."

He winked. "Don't worry, I'll go slow this time."

She watched as his erection slowly grew to life. Despite her soreness, desire gathered wetly between her legs. "You're going to kill me."

He licked his lips and smiled. "What a beautiful way to die."

With a half groan and a laugh she grabbed a handful of condoms and came to bed. He eyed the stash in her hand and grinned. "That's my girl."

CHAPTER 14

The next morning Jared got up at six and left Tasha sleeping in bed while he worked out in the condominium's gym. He was still exhausted from the day, and night, before but didn't want to miss another workout. When he returned two hours later, she was still where he'd left her. He smiled and admired her smooth caramel skin exposed by the sheet. Desire caused his dick to stiffen, letting him know he was up for another type of workout.

She turned him on more than he'd expected. She wasn't the first woman he'd slept with multiple times in one day, but never four times in less than twenty-four hours. That was a record even for him. He couldn't get enough of her, and he could feel it. His erection was sore, like a muscle he'd overused. It didn't stop him from wanting her again, but if he was feeling the effects of their continuous sexcapades, then so was she. It hadn't escaped his notice when she winced slightly as he slid into her warm body shortly before four. He only wanted her to experience pleasure when they were together, not pain. Pain would make it harder for him to convince her to continue sleeping with him after the weekend. Having Tasha as a routine sexual partner wouldn't be too bad.

He'd let her sleep in before starting their day. Since it was her birthday, he was prepared to do whatever she wanted and had even planned a few surprises for her. Jared walked over to the bed and leaned down to kiss her shoulder. He squeezed her round butt cheek not covered by the sheet. She sighed and whispered his name in her sleep. A satisfied smile curved his lips before he kissed her shoulder again and went into the bathroom to take a shower.

Afterwards, he came back into the room and reached into his bag for clothes. Tasha was still asleep. She would be hungry when she woke up. There wasn't any food in his fridge, so he decided to run to the store for weekend essentials. Sliding on a pair of basketball shorts and a t-shirt, Jared looked through the nightstand for a pad to leave a note when the piercing sound of his cell phone ringing broke the silence. Tasha frowned in her sleep and turned over. He dropped the pad and looked around for his phone. Another ring came from under the bed, causing Tasha to stir again. He fell to his knees and reached under the bed. When he felt the cool plastic exterior of the phone he quickly pulled it out and answered the call.

"Hello?" he said quietly.

"Hi, Jared, it's your mother."

He froze. His mother hadn't called him directly in years. They always spoke through Malcolm, at his request.

"Were you looking for Malcolm?"

"No, I wanted to talk to you."

Jared took a deep breath and looked at Tasha. Her breathing was deep and steady as she slept. He quietly backed out of the bedroom and shut the door.

"Why do you want to talk to me? There isn't anything we have to say," he said.

"There's a lot to say, but you refuse to talk to me. It's been fifteen years since your father died. Why are you still holding this against me?"

His mother's voice was pleading, but Jared didn't care. He'd stopped caring the day his dad died. "You're the reason he died and we both know that."

"No, you think that. You jumped to conclusions and haven't talked to me since. You're thirty-three now, Jared, not eighteen. It's time to act like an adult and face this."

Jared clenched his jaw to keep from lashing out. "You know what? I don't have time for this. If you need something just tell Malcolm. I'll help him get it."

"The only thing I need is for my son to talk to me."

"Yeah, well, you and Mr. Carter killed that when you killed my dad."

"Stop saying that," she snapped. "Your dad had a heart attack."

"After finding you in the arms of another man."

"That's not what happened. At the time, I didn't think I could tell you what really happened. If I'd have known you would have refused to come around me for the next fifteen years I would have explained."

"I don't need the sleazy details. Now, unless you have a point, I'm ending this call. Call Malcolm, he still thinks you're a good mother."

Jared didn't care if his words were harsh. He'd stopped caring after he'd watched his father fall to the floor in agony after seeing his mother in Mr. Carter's arms.

"Jared, I'm calling you because I'm getting married. I wanted you to hear it from me." Her voice sounded tired.

Jared laughed bitterly. "Who did you trick?"

"I'm marrying Mr. Carter."

He froze. The only sound was his heart beating loudly in his chest. He couldn't breathe and fell heavily on the couch. He tried to take in air as his stomach rolled in disgust. "How could you do that?"

"We need to talk, Jared. You have to understand what happened that day." Concern laced her voice but Jared barely noticed as rage filled him.

"I…I can't talk to you anymore," he said and ended the call.

He squeezed the phone in his hands and covered his face. But the pain was too great; he couldn't sit still. He jumped from the couch and threw the phone with a curse. It hit the wall and fell to the floor in two pieces. He paced back and forth, rubbing his hands over his face frantically. The vision of Mr. Carter holding his mother and his father falling to the floor gripping his chest played over and over in his head. He stopped pacing and reached back to slam his fist into the wall.

"Jared!"

His arm stopped mid swing. He turned to Tasha standing in the door to the bedroom with the sheet around her. Damn, she was beautiful, her hair tousled and her lips swollen from the night before. He wanted to hate her for looking so beautiful, so innocent, when he knew she wasn't. She was just another deceitful woman. One who would be useful and take his mind off of the conversation with his mother.

Three quick strides had him across the room. He wrapped his arms around her waist, sweeping her up against his chest. He didn't want to think about his mother's betrayal. It was typical of a woman, and right now, he needed to forget his pain between Tasha's legs.

He dropped her on the bed and reached for one of the condoms on the nightstand. In a flash, Tasha scrambled to the other side of the bed and held up her hand. Anger and desire coursed through him as he watched her try to cover her naked body. Her eyes were hard as she looked at him.

"You're not going to screw me in order to forget your problems. That isn't how this works. I heard enough of your conversation to know that you're hurting, but you're not going to take it out on me."

"I don't hurt," he said through clenched teeth.

"Bullshit, Jared. You think your mom and some Carter guy killed your dad, and whatever she said on the other end of the phone set you off."

"Eavesdropping?"

"It's not eavesdropping when you're yelling in the next room." The anger left her and concern filled her eyes. "Jared, why don't you go to the police if you think she had something to do with it? Why are you walking around with this?"

"Why do you give a damn?" he bit out.

"Because." She paused. Her eyebrows furled before she held up her hand. "Because I just do, all right?"

He gazed at her and the tension slowly left his body. Tasha was always trying to help someone. At the center, she was viewed as a surrogate mother, sister, or friend who was always willing to help. Another reason why he'd stayed away from her. She was too nice for him to run game on.

"She didn't kill my dad." He sat on the edge of the bed with his back to her. "I was eighteen. My dad and I went fishing that morning. When we got back, he went in the house while I put up the gear. When I came in my dad was peeping through the door to our home office. I walked up and he looked at me, looked back at the door, and clutched his chest. He fell to the floor and I saw my mom kissing my dad's friend, Randall Carter. They broke apart when I cried out and my mom came running up to help, but it was too late. He died of a heart attack on the way to the hospital." His voice was flat as he finished the story. Pain filled his chest.

He heard the rustle of the sheet as she walked around the bed to sit beside him. She reached over and put her hand on his leg and squeezed gently. Her hand was warm and smooth against his skin. It was funny that he could actually enjoy her touch in a non-sexual way. It was nice, and comforting. He almost reached over to place his hand on hers, but stopped himself.

"I've never told anyone what happened that day. Not even my brother Malcolm. He was so worried about our mother after dad died, I couldn't tell him. He'd always been closer to her than I was."

She brought one leg onto the bed and faced him. "Why are you telling me?"

He sighed and rubbed his face. "Shit if I know."

She smiled slightly. "What did she say that upset you?"

Jared closed his eyes as the anger came back. "She's marrying Mr. Carter. Ain't that a bitch? She called to tell me that." Tasha gasped and he laughed humorlessly. "Your reaction is more fitting than mine, I guess."

"Why would she call with that?"

He shrugged. "She says we need to talk. That there's more to the story than what I saw."

Tasha rubbed his leg. "Maybe there is."

He pushed her hand away. "I don't want to hear a damn thing she has to say about that day. If my dad hadn't seen them together, he wouldn't have had the heart attack and died. As far as I'm concerned there's nothing more to say."

Tasha slapped his arm. "Stop it, Jared. Don't push me away like I'm nothing. I know that we aren't together, but what I gave you... what we did...was special. I'm just trying to be a friend. Don't mistrust what I'm offering."

He turned to look at her. Instead of feeling his usual annoyance when a woman said what they had was special, he felt something click inside of him. Like a switch shining a light on the truth of what she said. What they'd done was pretty damn incredible. The best he'd ever had. And for her it was life changing. It couldn't be described as anything but special.

Warning bells rang in his head. He couldn't be falling for her, that was impossible, but maybe he did trust her a little. Or maybe the great sex was turning his brain into mush. But she was right. What was between them wasn't like anything he'd had with the other women he'd slept with. She wasn't out to trap him or his money. If anything, Tasha was the most honest female he knew. Even Cassandra was shady when it came to getting hers. But not Tasha. He'd never seen her lie to anyone; she was always up front even if it wasn't what you wanted to hear. But she was also compassionate, loving, and trusting. Why in the hell had she chosen him to take her virginity?

He reached over and brushed the hair from her face. He ran his fingers through the silky curls before cupping the back of her head and pulling her forward to kiss her softly. "Thank you for listening."

Her eyes softened. "It's the least I could do."

His gaze traveled to the swell of her breasts above the sheet. "Is it?" Now that he'd poured the equivalent of his heart out to her, his mind easily transitioned to other things. He still wanted the distraction her body promised.

She slid away. "Hold up, cowboy. I don't think my body can handle any more."

"Are you hurting?"

Dark lashes lowered over her eyes as she looked away. "A little sore."

He stood and brushed his hand across her cheek. "Fill up the tub and take a bath."

She grabbed her stomach. "I'm starving. A shower makes more sense."

"Take a bath and I'll run out for something to eat. You soak and when you're done, I'll have food ready. After we eat, we'll go out and do some sightseeing. It's your birthday, so I'm willing to do whatever you want to do."

She smiled at him, her light brown eyes shining. "Thanks for making my birthday special even when you're hurting."

An unfamiliar tightening in his chest made him back up. He had to get out of here before he had a warm and fuzzy moment. Snatching his keys off the nightstand he turned to the door before tossing them back on the bed. "I'll run to one of the bakeries around the corner. When I get back you'd better be in the tub." He said over his shoulder as he walked out the door.

CHAPTER 15

"Why were you a twenty-nine-year-old virgin?"

Tasha froze mid-step. They'd spent what was left of the morning exploring the sites in downtown Charleston and were walking back to his car after ending the day on the Isle of Palms. He'd still been upset about his mother's call, so she'd made an effort to keep his mind off of things. True to his promise, he didn't complain as she'd dragged him through the old slave market, into the various shops and around the College of Charleston campus.

Surprisingly, he'd opened up about his childhood memories of hunting and fishing with his brother and father. Though he'd tried to appear relaxed, his tense shoulders and compressed lips proved he was in pain. She'd quickly changed the subject to the joys and pains of growing up under her father's strict rule.

A breeze blew her hair into her face and she pushed it away. She would have preferred to put it in a ponytail, but he'd asked her to keep it loose. "What did you say?"

"I didn't stutter. Why were you still a virgin?"

She laughed and started walking again. "Religious beliefs."

He snorted. "Come on, Tasha. Give me more than that."

She sighed. "I'm serious. I grew up with my parents telling me it was a sin to sleep with someone before you were married. My dad preaches about it as much at home as he does in church. As I got older and realized there were a lot of people sinning, my parents scared us on the consequences of sex, like disease and pregnancy."

"You can prevent both," he said.

"Says the man with a lifetime supply of condoms," she said gently bumping him with her shoulder. "Yes, I know that. For a while it was fun to be the virgin." He looked at her skeptically and she giggled. "I know it sounds silly, but it was. I was different from the other girls. Guys treated me differently. They respected me more. Plus, I was into the same things they were, working out and sports. It was fun. But as I got older, guys' attitudes changed. They either looked at me as a challenge or undateable. The last guy I dated actually told me I was nice, but if we weren't having sex then we should just end it."

He took her hand and steered her out of the way of another couple going toward the beach on the path. He didn't release her hand after. "I still don't understand why you asked your favor."

She shrugged. "I could have met my husband ten men ago, but maybe he was scared away because I was a virgin looking for marriage. I'm tired of the pressure to save myself for a man who might not be willing to wait."

"That makes absolutely no sense."

"Really, so you're telling me you would marry someone without sleeping with them?"

He cringed. "No, but I don't plan to ever get married. You caved in to the pressure."

"No, *I'm* tired of waiting. I'm thirty years old. My best friend has amazing sex apparently with every guy she meets and I have to hear about it. My sister is married and I have to walk in on her and my brother-in-law feeling each other up in every room at their home. I'm the only single person I know and I want a husband, but I'm tired of scaring guys away with my 'wait until marriage' speech. Especially when I don't believe waiting will make a man love me any more or less. I want to meet a guy, go out, feel attracted to him, and if it's right, *finally* sleep with him."

His brows furled, the afternoon sunlight reflected in his eyes making them appear light brown instead of their usual chocolate. "And if it doesn't work out, then what? You've slept with someone no good and you're still single. Except now you're heartbroken."

"Are you going to break my heart?"

He shook his head and laughed quietly. "Tasha…"

"What we're doing isn't much different. I know you. I'm attracted to you, so we slept together. When it's done my heart won't be broken."

"That's because we aren't dating. What if you fall in love and the guy doesn't feel the same?"

She looked away. "Why do you act like you care? What happens after we're finished doesn't matter. I'm not going to sleep with every guy I meet. I can't do the things I've done with you with just anyone. He has to be special."

She dropped his hand and rushed ahead to the parking lot. He plan wasn't fool proof. There was a likelihood that she'd still meet a guy just as sorry as Charles. But it was none of Jared's business. Him acting as if he cared about her possibly getting hurt in the future caused her emotions, already wrapped into him more than they should be, to swell into dangerous territory.

They reached his car and she stopped her before getting in. "I didn't mean to upset you. I was just curious, ya know?"

"Let's just forget about it." She said with a wave of the hand.

They rode back to his condo in companionable silence. Her heart rate picked up once they parked in the garage. Her body still ached wonderfully from the night before, but after spending the day with him just the idea of sleeping with him again made her wet.

"Hey, let's walk down to the harbor." He said once they got out of the car.

She groaned. "Really? We've walked all day. I'm tired."

He took her hand and pulled her along. "Come on. I indulged you all day, you can give me this one thing."

"Yeah, but it's *my* birthday."

The breezed carried the sound of his chuckle back to her. With a sigh, she stopped dragging her feet and followed him around the block to the front of the condominium. A guy dressed in jeans and a plaid shirt with long red hair pulled into a ponytail leaned against the building. He held a guitar in his hands and jumped up when they rounded the corner. Jared stopped and pulled her against his side.

"Why are we…" her voice trailed off as the guy started singing happy birthday. His smooth alto voice glided over the words into the night air. Tasha gasped and looked to Jared, who grinned at her.

"Malcolm got the singing voice in our family. So I found someone to sing for me. Happy birthday, Tasha."

She was in trouble. Deep trouble. Jared was more than the playboy she'd taken him form. His softer side was playing a number on her romantic's heart and she was perilously close to wishing there was more to this situation.

"You didn't have to." She said after the guy finished singing.

Jared shrugged as if it were no big deal. "Hey, you only turn thirty once." He turned to the guy and gave him pound. "Thanks, man."

"No problem, Jared." He smiled at Tasha. "Happy birthday, beautiful." He saluted then turned and ambled down the street.

She tried to hide how much she appreciated the effort as she met Jared's eye. "I can't believe—" He cut her off with a kiss. His warm tongue gently probed her mouth open. With a sigh, she wrapped he arms around his neck.

His dark eyes burned with desire when he broke the kiss. "Instead of telling me what I shouldn't do, let's go upstairs and end your birthday right."

Without a word, she took his hand and rushed back to the entrance.

*

Tasha stood at one of the windows in Jared's condo and stared at the boats gliding along the water in the Cooper River. It was Sunday.

Time to go home and the end the best birthday weekend she'd ever had. It wasn't just losing her virginity—although the sex had been amazing—it was spending time with Jared. The effort he'd put into making her birthday special was a gift she'd cherish forever. Despite his playboy persona, the man knew how to make a woman feel wonderful. It may be old hat for him, but she decided to accept it for what it was and celebrate in the fact that her thirtieth birthday and loss of virginity was a memory worth cherishing. Memories of the way he'd slowly made love to her the night before hijacked her mind causing her nipples to pebble beneath her shirt.

She shook her head and pressed her temples. They did not make love. It was sex. Sweet, wonderful, perfect sex, but that was all. Love had no place in this.

He came out of the bedroom carrying their overnight bags. His biceps, revealed by the red cutoff shirt he wore, flexed as he dropped them by the door. He was in basketball shorts and her gaze dropped to the crotch. Her face burned; just looking at the man summoned memories of what they'd done. When he walked over to stand beside her at the window, it took everything in her not to lean into him.

What do you say at the end of an affair? She looked to him for guidance, but he was scowling.

She touched her face. "What?"

He reached over and pulled the clip out of her hair. "Wear your hair down when we're together."

His long fingers caressed the base of her scalp. Her eyes fluttered, heat infused her, but she straightened her shoulders and stepped away. "I think we should stop before it gets out of hand."

His scowl deepened. "Out of hand?"

She tucked her hair behind her ears. "Jared, I did this so that it would take the pressure off of dating. I still hope to find a husband. I can't do that if I'm sleeping with you."

He smiled devilishly and took her elbow to pull her close. "No one will be hurt if we sleep together until you meet someone else."

She laughed softly, but pulled away. "Says the man with a trail of broken hearts behind him. No, this weekend was it. Thank you, for everything."

He rolled his eyes and looked out the window. "You can stop thanking me for sex. The pleasure was all mine."

"It's not just the sex. Yesterday was…the best birthday I've ever had. Despite your mom's call, you helped me celebrate in a beautiful city and now we can go home as friends. Nothing more." She stared at him, hoping he wouldn't see how hard it was for her to say those words.

Jared cocked a brow. Crossing his arms, he leaned against the window and watched her. "You've gotten a taste, Tasha. It won't be so easy to forget."

"You're pretty confident."

He shrugged and grinned. "I have a reason to be." He motioned with his head for her to come closer.

A smart woman would refuse, but the smoldering of his dark eyes and curve of his lips was a temptation hard to deny. Her feet slid across the hardwoods as she approached. He wrapped an arm around her waist and pulled her closer. She melted against the heat of his body. Something flared in his eyes as they stared into hers. "You'll call me when you want me, and I'll be ready."

She shivered. "I'm not calling."

His head lowered until their lips barely touched. Gently he rubbed his nose across hers. Her face lifted, her breathing hitched, and he pressed her body against his.

Jared's lips curved in a knowing grin. "I'll be waiting."

Straightening, he let her go and damned if she didn't sway slightly with the loss of contact. Shaking the fog out of her head, she glared at him. His smile didn't waiver. "I'll take the bags down and we can go."

She didn't respond to his goading. God help her. She'd have to pray constantly to resist calling him.

CHAPTER 16

"Tasha, did you hear a word I said?"

Tasha blinked several times and turned to her dad. "What?"

He shook his head and smiled, his white teeth gleaming in his tan face. Seeing the thin man with dark-framed glasses and a receding hairline sitting at the head of the table, you would never expect he could preach a sermon loud enough to shake the rafters in the church. Luckily, Angie's daughters hadn't done anything this Sunday to warrant a sermon. "You haven't paid attention to anything going on at the table," he said. "You've spent the entire dinner staring off. Have you met a man?"

She shook her head frantically. "No! It's work, that's all. I've got a lot on my plate."

"You work too hard, Tasha," her mom said from across the table. "You didn't even get to celebrate your birthday two weeks ago. Are you sure you don't need to take a vacation?"

Tasha avoided her mom's gaze by looking at the meatloaf on her plate. "No, the conference wasn't so bad. It was almost like a vacation."

Angie snorted. "I bet."

Tasha glared at her sister before turning to her dad. "What were you asking?"

Her dad leaned back in his chair. "I asked what you thought of my sermon today. Some people think it's old fashioned when I preach about saving yourself until marriage, but you've been able to keep yourself pure for thirty years. I almost used you for an example." He laughed.

Tasha's eyes widened. "Please don't do that. I really don't want that type of attention."

"Why not, Tasha? It's something to be proud of," Angie said with a twisted smile and raised eyebrow.

She hadn't told her sister about her weekend with Jared, although Angie had probably figured it out. She hadn't talked to anyone about it, including Shayla. It was hard enough to not think about Jared, no need to purposefully talk about him.

"I don't want to talk about my personal life any more than you do. It's not the congregation's business," she said to her sister.

Angie shook her head and took a bite of the meatloaf.

Her dad waved his hand to get their attention. "I wouldn't do you like that, but I am proud of you. So many women out there get caught up in temptation. That's why we have so many diseases and babies out of wedlock. Whenever people tell me I'm being old-fashioned, I want to say, 'Hold up. Look at my two girls.' One gave herself only to her husband and the other is still waiting. You girls are a true blessing."

"Amen," her mom agreed with a smile.

Angie caught Tasha's gaze and both of them nodded frozenly. What would her dad say if he knew that at this moment she wanted to leave their house and run straight to Jared's? He promised to be ready when she called, and God help her she wanted to call him every day. Pride stopped her. Pride, and the fact he hadn't called her.

Memories of the way he'd kissed her from head to toe were her constant companion. She squirmed in her seat and her breathing became shallow. Every time he'd slid inside of her, it had felt so right, so wonderful.

"Tasha, are you okay? You look flushed." Her mom's voice broke into her thoughts.

She looked up with a start, her cheeks flaming. Here her dad was talking about how proud he was of his virgin daughter and she was fantasizing about her only sexual partner.

"I'm not feeling too good. I think I'm going to go home early," she said as she slid her chair from the table.

"You can always stay here if you're feeling bad," her dad offered, concern in his eyes.

"No, I just think I'm tired." She grabbed her plate from the table and hurried into the kitchen. She dropped her plate in the sink and rested her forehead in her hand. She would not call him.

She hurried from the kitchen before her sister could follow and question her mood, quickly kissed her parents goodbye, and left, avoiding Angie's gaze the entire time.

When she got home she cleaned the house from top to bottom, but it didn't distract her. All it did was make it easier for memories of her weekend in Charleston to hijack her exhausted brain when she finally lay down to go to sleep. Her breasts and the wet spot between her legs ached for more. With a groan, she hit the pillow and rolled over, willing herself to go to sleep.

The next day work was a typical Monday. Although summer camp at the center wouldn't start for another two months, they had to arrange the schedules and confirm locations for traveling field trips. The water park they always took the kids to was under new management and wanted to raise the price for the field trip. After a frustrating call where she negotiated the new price, she then had to get with the various counselors about the after school schedule. Standardized testing was starting and they tried to supplement the student's studies with information that would help them on the tests. After lunch, she got with the head of the local League of Women's voters to arrange the group's rental of the facility for a fundraiser later that month. By the time three o'clock hit, Tasha had a screaming headache.

Latiffa came when she got out of school at three to work the front desk. The teenager poked her head in after knocking. "Ms. Tasha, you have a call on line one. You want me to send it over?"

She didn't want to talk with anyone, but was expecting a call from one of the councilmen about funding for the center. The city was in the middle of budget talks and now was the time to press the case for continued funding.

"Sure, Latiffa."

The girl nodded and went back to the desk. A few seconds later, her phone rang. "Central Midlands Rec Commission, Tasha speaking."

"It's been two weeks." Jared's voice came through the phone. A deep tremor ran through her body. Her heart vibrated and her thighs clenched.

She took a deep breath before answering. "Jared. It's nice to hear from you."

He chuckled. "Nice to hear from me? Okay, so you want to keep up the fight."

"There is no fight. I told you it was only for that weekend."

"I've thought about kissing you every night since we got back. And I'm not talking about just your mouth."

Tasha swallowed hard. "Jared, I need to find a husband."

"Is there anyone in the running right now?"

"No."

"Have you met someone in the past two weeks that you're even thinking about dating?"

"No, but—"

"But nothing. Why deny both of us what we want when there's no need to. You're an adult and so am I. We can do this for a while. When you meet someone else, I'll walk away, no problem."

It was tempting, but she couldn't do it. She got too wrapped up in Jared and that was scary. "No. I can't open myself to another man if I'm fooling around with you."

"Just tell me one thing. Do you think about that weekend?"

She wanted to deny it, but what was the point? He knew how good it had been. "Every day. That's why I can't do it anymore."

She heard him sigh. "I'll be ready when you come around." He ended the call.

She wanted to scream. Now she had a headache and she was horny. Damn him and his good sex. She snatched up her phone to call Shayla, but didn't make the call. She didn't need Shayla to push her into something she already wanted to do. She'd wished for his call since they'd returned. Truthfully, she'd waited on him to call and prove he wanted her just as much as she wanted him.

What he'd said was true. She wasn't seeing anyone right now. Would it really hurt to sleep with him one or two more times? Just to get it out of her system. And if she felt herself getting tied up in knots, she would stop. She could stop anytime she wanted. *You sound like a junkie!*

She jumped up from her desk and grabbed her purse from the coat rack. There was no time to think about this. The longer she thought, the longer she'd say no.

"Oh, Ms. Tasha, can you help me?" Latiffa called as soon as she exited her office. "This man wants to sign up for the men's basketball league, and I can't find the paperwork." She pointed to a guy across the counter.

Not paying attention to the man, Shayla walked over to Latiffa. "Craig had copies made this morning. He probably has them in his office." She pointed to the office of the director of intramural sports.

Latiffa nodded and jumped up from the desk to go to Craig's office. Not wanting to leave the man standing there, Tasha finally looked up and smiled. She paused when she met warm black eyes set in a handsome brown face. His wide shoulders strained the seams of the hospital scrubs he wore. His hair was styled in a small afro that was tapered at the sides. When he smiled back at her, his full lips revealed even white teeth.

"You're Tasha Smith," he said in a smooth baritone voice.

"I am. Do I know you?"

He shook his head. "No, a friend of mine works out in your gym and mentioned you. He was right, you are a very attractive woman."

Tasha blushed and fought the urge to straighten her hair. "What's your friend's name? I'll have to thank him for such a wonderful compliment."

"Charles Worthington."

The smile left Tasha's face. Charles Worthington, the asshole her sister had hooked her up with.

The man's eyes widened when she frowned. "Did I say something wrong?"

"No, it's just that Charles and I aren't friends."

He held up a hand, regret in his eyes. "I didn't mean to upset you. I guess I goofed up my introduction with a beautiful woman." He reached out his hand. "I'm Dr. Kevis Flynn. No relation to Charles Worthington, and I only play ball with him occasionally. Please don't hold it against me."

Tasha accepted the handshake. His large warm hand squeezed hers firmly, but not tightly. She quickly removed her hand from his and smoothed her hair back. "Doctor?"

"Yes, I'm an ER doctor at Palmetto Health Baptist. Just started a few weeks ago."

As handsome as Dr. Flynn was, his friendship with Charles's dampened her attraction. Too bad, he might have been worth getting to know better.

"Well, Dr. Flynn, I really need to go."

He smiled. "Please, call me Kevis. I hope you'll come watch me play ball sometime. I'll score twenty points just for you."

Tasha laughed. "Are you always such a flirt?"

He shrugged. "Only when I see someone worth flirting with."

Latiffa came back with the paperwork and passed it to Kevis. Tasha smiled at him. "Have a nice day, Kevis."

"You too, Tasha."

His voice could give Barry White a run for his money. She felt his eyes on her as she walked out, but didn't turn around. His relationship with Charles was enough to rule him out, and her mind quickly turned back to Jared.

*

Tasha didn't give herself time to think about what she was doing on her way to Jared's. Showing up unannounced was a bold move, but she had to be bold or else she'd chicken out. A part of her hoped he wasn't at home or was in the middle of a training session. It would give her the out she knew she didn't have the guts to make.

She pulled into his driveway and was thankful there were no other cars there. It was a good sign that he was either alone, or not at home. She took a deep breath and smoothed her hair back into the ponytail before getting out of the car and ringing his doorbell.

Just two or three more times to get him out of your system, she said to herself.

The door swung open and Tasha froze. Her sister's best friend, and Jared's soon to be sister-in-law, stood on the other side.

Surprise was obvious in Kenyatta's face, but she smiled openly. "Hey, Tasha, what are you doing here?"

Tasha gaped for a second before catching herself. "Um, Jared forgot to…um…turn in the mentor forms." She coughed. "I came over to…get them. Because, you know, we've got to make sure we report that with budget hearings coming up." Good Lord, she was rambling. She cleared her throat. "What are you doing here?"

Kenyatta smiled and her brown eyes sparkled. It was not surprising Kenyatta had attracted the attention of one of the Patterson brothers. She was smart, beautiful, and curvaceous. "I'm helping Malcolm and Jared plan their mother's birthday party. I got off work early and Malcolm is meeting me over here." She winked at Tasha. "Plus, I want to get Jared's help on a picking a location for our honeymoon. Malcolm mentioned this fishing trip he took to Canada with Jared a few years ago. So I'm picking his brain before Malcolm gets here."

Relief and disappointment warred within Tasha. She had her way out, but now she wasn't sure she wanted it. "I can come back later."

Kenyatta waved a hand and ushered her in. "Don't be silly. Knowing Jared, your forms are on the seat of his car or something. If you want, stick around. I haven't seen you in a while. We can catch up."

"I wouldn't want to intrude. I'll grab them and go."

Kenyatta closed the door behind Tasha at the same time as Jared rounded the corner into the entryway. He froze when he saw her. Desire filled his eyes as he looked her over from head to toe. His gaze was like a caress. Her heartbeat speed up, and her breathing became shallow.

"Tasha," he said.

"Jared," she answered.

Kenyatta looked between them. She raised an eyebrow then smiled. "Jared, I'm going to use your office computer to look up that place in Canada."

He nodded. Kenyatta shook her head before walking away.

The heat in Jared's gaze set Tasha's body on fire. Blood rushed in her ears. How quickly could he get out of those clothes? It shouldn't take long; he was in his standard attire: basketball shorts and a sleeveless t-shirt. But it was still too many clothes.

She closed her eyes to regain composure. *Two or three times, Tasha. That's it.*

She opened her eyes and met his gaze. "I thought…"

He didn't let her finish. He quickly eliminated the distance between them and picked her up. Her legs wrapped around his waist as their mouths met in a passionate kiss. He pressed her against the door as his tongue danced with hers. She moaned and brought her hands up to his face as she met his kiss head on.

Jared moved one arm to run his hand up her thigh. She loved it when he held her as if she weighed nothing. When his hand went up her khaki skirt, he didn't pause before sliding a finger in the side of her underwear.

He groaned when his finger slid through her slick heat. "Damn, you're wet already."

His mouth moved to kiss her throat and Tasha gasped when he slid a finger inside her. He moved in and out slowly, making her whimper in pleasure.

"Jared, you're going to make me come," she panted.

"Not yet. I want to be inside you." He reached for the waistband of his shorts and pushed them down. His erection bounced against her. She bit her lip to keep from crying out. He rubbed himself against her underwear and cursed. "No condom."

"In my purse. I stopped to buy some."

He looked up, and she pulled the purse off her shoulder. Jared continued to press against her as she dug out the protection.

"We can't do it here. Kenyatta," she said.

"Is downstairs in my office." He took the condom from her and ripped open the package with his teeth. He shifted her weight as he slipped it on while still holding her.

"You've done this before," she teased.

"Not with you." He reached between them to push aside her underwear and slid inside of her with one smooth stoke.

"Oh God!"

"Damn!"

They gasped in union. Tasha tightened her legs around him and buried her face in his neck. He pumped his hips and she smiled decadently as he rubbed within her.

"Hold your head up," he told her.

She lifted her head and put it against the door.

"Grab my shoulders." When she did, he took a step back and grabbed her waist. He tilted her pelvis forward and increased his speed.

Tasha's shoulders pressed into the door, but she didn't care. She looked down at where they were joined and her arousal grew with every slide of his body within hers. Her climax came suddenly and strongly. Still mindful someone was in the house she bit her lip to keep from yelling out.

Jared came a second after she did. Keeping her legs wrapped tight, he moved forward until they were pressed against each other. Their gazes locked as their breathing slowly came back to normal.

CHAPTER 17

Jared handed Tasha a glass of wine before leaning on the bar and eyeing her over his own glass. Thankfully, Kenyatta left a few minutes after he and Tasha had finished in the entryway. She'd said Malcolm couldn't get off work, and he hoped that was the truth. He didn't need her running to tell Malcolm which virgin he'd deflowered.

It was unlike him to jump Tasha when she was only two feet in his home. But no other woman ever drove him crazy with just a look. He did have the common sense to take her to bed after Kenyatta left. The door had barely closed behind Kenyatta before he picked Tasha up and sprinted to his bedroom. But once there, he'd taken his time reacquainting himself with every inch of her body. He'd been rewarded with soft sighs and cries of pleasure that he couldn't get enough of.

She'd snuggled against him afterwards. As if she was supposed to be there. Even scarier, he liked it. Needless to say he'd panicked. Jared Patterson didn't snuggle. He'd jumped out of bed and offered her a glass of wine.

The disappointment in her eyes was quickly replaced with gratitude. He knew his withdrawal was callous, but surprisingly she didn't ask what was wrong or pout like other women tended to do. She'd agreed to the wine and ignored the awkward moment. He could've kissed her for that while also wondering why she didn't seem to care.

He looked at her now. She'd put on his bathrobe and he lost his train of thought ever time the soft swell of her breasts was revealed by the gaping fabric. And savored the smell of her clean scent mingled with the smell of their lovemaking. Why did this former virgin turn him on more than any other woman he knew?

"You're looking at me like I'm a puzzle you can't figure out," she said with a smile.

He lowered his glass. "Because I can't figure you out. It wasn't an hour ago you said you wouldn't sleep with me again, yet you show up and sex me at my front door."

She laughed. "Don't blame that on me. I was about to tell you I came over for the mentor reports and you cut me off mid-sentence."

He grinned and leaned forward. "I don't mentor on Mondays. So what gives? Why did you show up and let me cut you off mid-sentence?"

Tasha's eyes lowered, but the smile remained on her face. "You made a good point. I'm not seeing anyone right now. It won't hurt to sleep with you once or twice. Just to get it out of my system."

He cocked an eyebrow. "Once or twice? If that's the case, then it should be out of your system."

She looked back at him. Her honey eyes and flushed cheeks were adorable. Adorable? Where had that come from?

"I want to do this. Just for a few weeks."

He crossed his arms on the bar. "Do what?"

Her blush deepened, but she kept eye contact. "Let's sleep together."

Hell yeah, was his first thought. But when he looked into her eyes he could still see the good girl who'd asked him to treat her like a friend. Not the usual woman he dated who understood the boundaries of a sex only relationship.

He straightened and shook his head. "I'm not that type of guy."

She cocked her head to the side. "Yes you are. You sleep with women all the time."

"Yeah, with women like me. Only in it for sex. I'm not a relationship guy. I'm not going to fall in love with you, and I'm not going to marry you. If you ever ask me where this is going I'm gonna tell you nowhere."

She pushed her wine away with a frown. "You were the one who insisted we do this. I know who you are, and I don't expect anything from you. You're the last man on earth I want to end up with."

He came around the bar to stand before her. "I know you've said that, but let's face it, Tasha, I'm your first." He reached out to brush the hair from her face. "You're going to get caught up if we do this."

She tensed before slapping his hand away. She jumped from the chair and pushed his chest. He stepped back, not from the force but to give her space.

"I'm not going to get caught up. This is only for a few weeks until I start dating someone else. Maybe shorter than that. I met a very handsome doctor this afternoon and he called me beautiful."

Jared clenched his jaw and took a step toward her. "What did I say about mentioning other men when you're with me?"

She smirked. "It looks like you're more caught up than I am."

She had him on that one. He lectured against getting feelings involved, but was jealous at the mention of another guy. It had to be sexual frustration. He'd gone to bed frustrated and hard every night since they'd come back from Charleston, despite the continued calls from the ever persistent Monica. He was used to women coming back, but Monica was on another level. He would've changed his number if he hadn't been waiting on Tasha to call.

He'd picked up the phone to call Tasha a dozen times, but never had the balls to do it until today. He was the one behaving like a novice.

He relaxed and stepped back. "You've got me on that one," he said. "You don't belong to me any more than I belong to you."

She smiled softly. "And we never will. So we'll do this for a few weeks, okay?"

Jared considered what she said. In the past other women had enticed him enough to want more than a one night stand—true, none had affected him as much as Tasha—but he'd be over this in a few weeks.

He bit his lip and looked at her from the corner of his eye before answering. "Okay."

She sighed and reached for her wine. "Let's change the subject." She bounced back into her chair as if they'd just agreed on ordering take out. "What's up with you planning a birthday party for your mom?" She took a sip from the glass.

Jared flinched and walked back around to the other side of the bar. "Nothing's up. I promised Malcolm I'd help before we went to Charleston. I can't back out without telling him why."

Fortunately, his mom hadn't called again. It was hard enough to stomach listening to Malcolm talk about it. Malcolm said he was fine with their mom remarrying, but he'd seen the sadness in his brother's eyes when he first brought it up. Their dad was long gone, but their mom remarrying didn't erase how much they missed him. Especially since Jared wanted to strangle Mr. Carter every time he thought about *how* his dad died.

"Why don't you tell Malcolm?" Tasha asked.

He shrugged. "He lost one parent. No need for him to lose both of them like I have." He downed the rest of his wine and poured another.

Tasha's hand paused as she lifted her glass to her mouth. Sympathy filled her eyes before she looked away. "That's fair, I guess," she said. "Are you okay…with helping I mean?"

"I'm fine. It's no different from any other time she's needed something. She asks Malcolm, he arranges, and I throw money at the problem."

Her brows furled. "Your mom asks for money often?"

"No." He scoffed. "Never, actually. She lets Malcolm know when something is wrong with the house and we fix it."

Her eyebrows lifted. "I'm surprised you do that."

He sighed and gulped his wine. "She's still my mom, even if she's a bad one. Plus, it's my dad's house."

She tilted her head to one side and studied him. "I think you still care. Maybe you should talk to her."

Jared pushed away from the bar and downed the rest of the wine. "I think…I'm tired of this conversation. Are you spending the night?"

If she was surprised by his change of subject she didn't show it. Instead she shook her head and stood. "No, that's too much. I'm going to get dressed and go home."

His shoulders slumped. He never kicked women out afterwards, but he also never stopped them from assuming he wanted them to leave. It surprised him how much he wanted her to stay.

"Come back tomorrow," he said.

"Why come here?"

"Because my home is more secluded. Everyone would know what was going on if I come to you."

"We'll make up something. Say I'm helping you edit the manuscript for your fitness book or something. That's what would be going on," she said with a laugh. "Besides, you'd never stay the night."

She was right. If he said she was helping with work, people would believe it because that's the type of person Tasha was. But he wanted her here, in his home and bed. "Doesn't matter. Come here tomorrow."

She frowned. "You aren't ruling this."

Jared walked around the bar and slid his hands beneath the bathrobe to cup her bottom and pull her close. He leaned down and softly kissed her lips. "Come here, please."

She looked into his eyes and he kissed her again. When he pulled away she was smiling. "Fine, I'll come here tomorrow."

CHAPTER 18

Tasha dropped her purse in her hall and slumped against the front door. She pinched her nose and willed the stuffiness go to away. Usually she was long gone from the Rec Commission before the monthly pet adoption drive, but today she'd had to stick around and complete the budget. She'd been so wrapped up she'd forgotten today was the day the center would be overrun with shelter animals from the two county area. Even though the animals had been outside, she'd had to walk through the various penned dogs and cats, while being stopped by employees who wanted her to "ooh" and "ahh" over the cute puppies and kittens. The itching and sneezing had started in less than five minutes.

She slowly rolled her head toward the mirror in her entryway and shook her head at the reflection. Red rimmed eyes, swollen nose, and flushed skin. She stood closer to the mirror and groaned. The rash was starting. Sneezing, she turned away and dragged her feet across the floor to her bathroom. She frantically searched the medicine cabinet until she found the Benadryl. Cupping water from the sink, she swallowed two of the pills and prayed they worked fast.

Of course, everyone had understood when she'd sneezed and ran off, but the damage was done. She'd be good for nothing for the rest of the night as she waited for the reaction to pass. Hopefully she'd make it to work the next morning.

She dragged herself from the bathroom to her kitchen where she made a pot of green tea. It usually helped when she broke out. She took the pot and a warmer into the living room, poured a cup, wrapped up in a blanket, and turned the TV to ESPN. She was watching *Pardon the Interruption* when her phone rang.

Jared's picture popped up on her touch screen and she smiled before answering. "Hello?" She flinched when she heard the scratchy sound of her voice.

"Are you okay?"

"Yeah, today was pet adoption day at the center and I'm allergic to dogs. I try to get out of there before they arrive, but got caught up in work."

"Do you need anything?"

She smiled at his concern. "No. I've taken Benadryl, now I'm drinking green tea and watching ESPN. I should be fine."

"So I guess you won't be coming over tonight." Disappointment clouded his voice.

"Not tonight." Her voice mirrored his disappointment. In the two weeks since they'd agreed to whatever it was they were doing, she'd gone to his house every night. Except Wednesdays when he mentored and Sundays. She couldn't go to church and eat dinner with her family, then go sleep with Jared. She knew she was sinning the rest of the week, but she wouldn't include the day she pretended to be her father's perfect virgin daughter.

It was risky to see him so much, but she couldn't help it. She enjoyed sleeping with him, and since she knew the rules, she chose to take it for what it was. But she'd have to end it soon. She was becoming too attached.

The always flirty Dr. Kevis Flynn had shown up at the Rec Commission a few times for open court games of basketball. She was still wary, because of his connection to Charles, but it wouldn't hurt to get to know him better.

Jared sighed into the phone. "Well, I guess I'll talk with you later."

"So you only called to see if I was coming over?" As soon as she asked, she realized she sounded like an irritated girlfriend.

"You know the rules, Tasha."

She sneezed. "Forget I even asked, all right? I've got to go." She hung up the phone and reached for a tissue on the coffee table to wipe her nose.

Stupid, stupid, stupid. Why else would he call? They were not together. Over the past two weeks he'd only called or texted to see if she was coming over. She'd insisted they not do anything to cause the other one to get more involved than necessary. So why was she upset that he only wanted to know if she was available for another booty call?

Throwing the tissue on the floor in disgust, Tasha took a gulp of her tea and gasped as it burned her tongue. With a curse, she put the cup back down and lay on the couch. She focused on every word spoken on the television so she wouldn't think about Jared, or if her unavailability meant he was going to find someone else tonight.

After an hour of television, a slight calming of her sneezing but an increase in itching, Tasha was prepared to take two more Benadryl and will sleep to overtake her. No matter how hard she tried, she still imagined Jared wrapped up in some other woman's arms. And each time the picture filled her mind she got mad at herself for even caring. She knew who Jared was and he wasn't monogamous. Especially after she'd insisted she couldn't possibly care about him.

She got up from the couch with the blanket still wrapped around her and was heading for the kitchen when her doorbell rang. She pulled the blanket tighter as she shuffled to the door and jerked it open.

Her heart thumped double time. Jared stood there with a plastic grocery bag in his hand. Relief swept through her like the winds of a hurricane. He wasn't sleeping with someone else.

He held up the bag while she continued to stare at him dumfounded. "I know nothing about allergies, but thought since soup worked for a cold it had to be good for allergies."

Tasha chuckled and shook her head. "Yes, soup is useful for a lot of things."

He looked over his shoulder then back at her. "So can I come in, or are you going to just take my soup and shut the door?"

She stepped back and he walked in. Her entryway seemed ten times smaller as his large frame filled the space. He didn't wear cologne, but the now familiar scent of his body wash invaded her senses, reminding her of what it was like to have his body pressed against hers. Swallowing hard she closed the door and took a few calming breaths. When she turned around, he was still standing behind her and examined her face.

"You look awful," he said.

She hit his shoulder. "That's a messed up thing to say."

He laughed. "I'm sorry, Tasha, but you don't look good. Are you sure you'll be okay?"

She nodded while checking her reflection in the mirror. There was a definite rash along her skin now. Damn dogs. "I was going to take two more Benadryl. I'll be fine."

He cocked his head to the side. "Are you sure that's smart? You don't need to overdose on over-the-counter meds."

It was her turn to laugh. "I'm not going to overdose. I've done it before."

He frowned. "I'm serious, Tasha, don't take anything else. If you're still feeling bad tomorrow, I'll take you to the doctor."

"You can't be serious."

He gave her a hard stare. "Do I look like I'm playing?"

Unnerved by his show of concern, Tasha cleared her throat and scratched her chin. "What are you doing here anyway? Did you come to boss me around?"

Jared took her arm and led her into the living room. "No, you didn't sound good on the phone so I came to check on you."

"Oh."

What else was there to say? She should say he didn't have to because it was beyond the boundaries of their arrangement. But she welcomed the warming around her heart because he wanted check on her.

He sat her on the couch and touched her forehead. Tasha laughed and pushed his hand away. "It's an allergic reaction, not a fever."

He smiled. "Look, it's my first time playing nursemaid, all right? So just sit down and let me figure this out."

She shook her head but agreed. "Okay, boss."

Jared winked at her and went into the kitchen. Tasha curled back up on the couch and flipped the TV to the basketball game. She watched the game while Jared heated the soup in the kitchen. She'd eaten a few crackers with her tea earlier, but that was all. Whenever she had an allergic reaction, she wasn't very hungry, but as the smell of chicken noodle soup filled her house her stomach grumbled.

A few minutes later, Jared came out of the kitchen carrying two bowls of soup. He handed one to Tasha and sat beside her with the other.

Tasha breathed in the smell of the soup and sighed. "This smells great. Did it come from a can?"

He scowled. "I don't eat out of a can. It's a soup that I made and froze. Try it and you'll stop eating canned soup."

Tasha took a spoonful and blew it off before tasting. "Oh my, this is good."

He smiled at her. "I know. Now eat."

They watched the game while they ate. Miami was playing Boston. They both cheered for Miami, although Tasha wasn't too upset whenever Boston scored. She'd always had a crush on Kevin Garnett.

She put her bowl down and scratched her arm. Jared watched her with a frown. He'd frowned every time she scratched or sneezed. She must look like a freak, scratching and sneezing every five seconds, but she'd been through this before.

Jared reached over and took her hand. He stretched her arm out and ran his hand over her irritated skin. Tasha sighed as his gentle touch relieved the itch, if only temporarily.

"Do you have something to put on this?" he asked.

"There's hydrocortisone in my medicine cabinet, but it's not that bad."

He jumped up from the sofa. "I'll get it." He went into her bathroom and came back a few seconds later with the cream. He took her arm and smoothed the medicine on the rough patches.

When he finished with her arms, he slid closer and put some on her face. It was impossible to ignore the lighting flashes of desire running through her with each rub of his fingers against her face. The muscles in his arms, exposed by the sleeveless t-shirt he wore, flexed with each movement and Tasha watched as the eagle tattoo on his arm stirred with each play of muscle.

Her breathing hitched and she prayed she didn't sneeze in his face. When he finished he looked in her eyes and cupped her face with his hand. "You don't look awful."

"No, I don't."

He smiled. "I like you, Tasha."

There her heart went, doing a silly flip flop. But Jared was not the guy for her. "Jared…"

"Don't tell me not to say that. I've always liked you, even when we were just starting out at the Rec Commission. You say what you feel, but you're also compassionate. I respect you for that. I'm not trying to blur the lines of what we're doing, we both know this will end soon, but don't ever forget that I like you."

Tasha nodded. "I like you too, Jared."

"Good." He leaned over and kissed her quickly before sitting back. "Feel better?"

"Yes, the itching is getting better."

He pulled her against his side and they watched the game. Although he pretended to be relaxed, tension radiated off him. He wanted to talk. It was one of the things she'd picked up on in Charleston and in the weeks they'd been together. He often worked harder to appear calm when something bothered him, but his body would be hard with tension. Eventually he'd blurt out whatever bothered him: a new client, his deal with the Farmers Market, or something at the production facility. He hadn't talked about his mother since the last time she'd brought it up.

Tasha leaned into him and rubbed his chest. She told herself it was to relax him, but really, it gave her an excuse to touch him. She loved feeling his abs and chest almost as much as she loved seeing him without his shirt on.

"I can't go to my mom's party," he said after a few minutes.

Tasha's hand froze for a second before she continued rubbing him. "Don't go."

He sighed. "Malcolm got pissed when I mentioned I might not make it."

"Why was he mad?"

"He said it's because he doesn't want to embarrass or upset my mom on her birthday. I think he just wants me there when she announces she's getting remarried. Malcolm doesn't have a problem with Mr. Carter, but he's not eager to see mom get married."

"Why not?"

"He's too much of a good guy to admit he would rather our mom mourn for our dad for the rest of her life. Dad died the day before Malcolm got back to Georgia. He never said goodbye, and that's always bothered him. That's why he always tries to visit our mom, or calls and checks on her. Now that she's getting married, he's going to have to truly say goodbye to our dad."

"If you're there it's easier for him to wish her well."

"Yeah. But I can't go down there and smile and act happy. I hate her for what she did to my dad. To know she's marrying Mr. Carter makes me sick. I'll end up saying something and making a bad night worse."

Tasha looked up at his profile. He stared unseeing at the television, his jaw clenched. "Jared, you need to talk to her and settle this. You can't go through the rest of your life pretending as if everything is okay."

He shook his head. "I don't want to hear her lies."

She reached over to lay her hand on his hand, which was clenched in a fist on his lap. "You still care about your mom, or you would have told Malcolm a long time ago what she did. You can't love and hate someone at the same time."

He scoffed. "Why not? I hate the fact that I still care when I know what she did."

"Maybe it's because you know what you saw, and yes it was messed up, but you also know your mother didn't literally kill your father. You don't have to be as close to your mom as Malcolm, but you need to clear the air."

He was quiet as he continued to stare at the television. Tasha laid her head back on his shoulder and watched the game. He finally opened his hand and clasped hers. "Come to the party."

She sat up slowly. She didn't face him but could feel his gaze on her. She wanted to go. She wanted to be there for him during something she knew would be difficult. She wanted to hold his hand as he tried to be nonchalant but tension clenched his body. She wanted him to squeeze her hand like he did now when things were tough. She wanted to end the night wrapped in his arms while they talked about what happened. She wanted it so much it scared her.

This was going horribly wrong. She should have known. How many books and movies were made about people who thought they could sleep together and not fall in love, but did in the end. Only this wasn't a love story. She'd fall in love, and Jared would move on to the next woman.

"I'm going to get something to drink."

When she tried to get up, he held onto her hand. "Are you going to ignore me?"

She looked in his eyes. "Jared, we both know I don't need to go. Do you want your family to think we're together? If Malcolm's there, then Kenyatta will be and she'll tell my sister. Then before you know it, my dad is asking me to bring you to the next Sunday dinner. I can't tell him it's not proper to bring my lover to dinner."

He studied her for a second before a small smile twisted his full lips. "It's this whole friend, lover thing. The lines get blurry." He pulled her back against him. "Forget I asked."

"You can call me after the party," she said.

He kissed the top of her head. "No need to worry about it until I'm sure I'm going."

"You need to go."

"Then go with me." When she stiffened he laughed. "I'm joking, Tasha. Let's change the subject, okay?"

"Yes, lets."

"In Charleston, you said a guy had to be special for you to sleep with him. Now that your virginity's gone, am I special to you?"

She sat up and groaned. "Why do you ask questions like that?"

"The hell if I know."

"Maybe it's time to stop this."

"I think you're right."

They sat on the couch and stared at the television, ignoring the game. Just that quick, he was ready to end things. His agreement hurt more than it should have. She didn't want to stop sleeping with him, but she needed to. What was supposed to be one night had lasted long past its expiration date. It was better to cut things off now, before she became too accustomed to being with him every night.

She opened her mouth to tell him but sneezed instead. Luckily, she was quick enough to sneeze into the crook of her elbow instead of on him. He jumped up and reached for a tissue. She took it and wiped her nose and he smiled.

"I never do the right thing," he said. "We'll stop next week."

She lay back on the couch and he pulled her feet onto his lap. "That sounds good."

He began to rub her feet and she snuggled into the cushions. Yes, they were blurring the lines of their relationship. Yes, she was beginning to care about him. But right now she was achy and tired and didn't want to think about how minutes before she'd been lost at the thought of ending their arrangement. Right now, she just wanted to enjoy the fact he was there and was content to rub her feet and watch the game.

CHAPTER 19

Jared was satisfied Tasha was getting over her allergic reaction when he left her at seven the next morning. The rash was fading and she'd stopped sneezing shortly before ten. He didn't like the way she casually popped Benadryl that morning, but couldn't blame her too much since she hadn't taken any more the night before.

He didn't know why he cared so much; it must be because of what he'd said the night before. He did like her. He usually didn't know a woman long enough to like her before they slept together. It put him in an odd position. He didn't want to care, but couldn't help it.

He'd lied through his teeth when he said they would end things next week. He wasn't close to being tired of sleeping with her, and he planned to continue this arrangement for as long as possible. He just hoped he didn't hurt her too much when it ended, because it would end one day.

Jared had three training sessions set for the morning that he eagerly went through. Afterwards he met with Sam at the production facility and went over the operations for the week. Things were running smoothly as usual and he once again complemented Sam on his hard work before going to meet Malcolm. He wasn't in the mood to discuss his mother's engagement party, but Malcolm insisted since he was leaving town for a conference tomorrow.

With a groan, Jared parked his car on Main Street before getting out and entering Malcolm's office building.

When he stepped off onto Malcolm's floor, he was immediately grateful he didn't work in "corporate America." The sight of the men in button up shirts and slacks and the women in pantyhose made him shudder. He didn't feel the least bit out of place in his t-shirt and workout shorts.

He smiled at the front desk receptionist, who nodded and said it was okay for him to go down the hall. He greeted some of his brother's co-workers before entering Malcolm's office.

Malcolm sat at his desk reading something, dressed in a shirt, tie, and slacks. Malcolm's straight-laced appearance was one of the things Kenyatta loved about him. He thought it made his brother look even more like the choirboy he always accused him of being.

"What's up, bruh," Jared said as he came into the office and sat in the chair across from Malcolm's desk.

Malcolm looked up and frowned. "What happened to you last night? Devin and I thought you were meeting us for drinks."

Jared flinched. He'd completely forgotten about meeting them. "My bad, man. Something came up."

"Something or someone?" Malcolm asked with a raised brow.

Jared hated when he looked like that. It was the same look their dad had used when he'd been scolding them. "Someone, if you must know. You know how I do," he said with a grin.

"Is that someone Tasha Smith?"

The grin dropped from his face. "How did you find out?"

"Kenyatta figured it out the other day." He lowered his voice. "That's the virgin you took out of town."

Jared shrugged. "And so what?"

Malcolm rolled his eyes. "So what? She's the sister of my fiancée's best friend. If you fuck around with her then *I'm* going to suffer."

"Please. You're overreacting," Jared said.

"Kenyatta and Angie spent two hours on the phone the other night talking about how my no good brother is going to break this poor girl's heart. Believe me, I will suffer."

Jared frowned and sat up in the chair. "I'm not going to break Tasha's heart. We have an understanding."

"Virgins don't know the meaning of *understanding*," Malcolm said sarcastically.

Jared held up a finger and smiled. "Number one, she's no longer a virgin." He lifted another finger. "Number two, she gets me. She knows who I am and I know who she is. What we got is working."

Malcolm studied him. "How long will it work?"

Jared shrugged. "Until one of us gets caught up."

"Meaning until Tasha falls in love with you."

"I'll stop it before it gets there," Jared said, but he didn't meet Malcolm's eyes. What would it be like for Tasha to say she loved him? He'd probably freak out before the words were out of her mouth, but it would be different to be loved by a nice woman. Tasha wouldn't say it for clothes, money, or connections. If she said it she would mean it.

"You don't look convinced," Malcolm said.

He met Malcolm's gaze head on. "Look, you tell Kenyatta and Angie to mind their own damn business. Tasha is thirty years old and can make her own decisions."

"And I'd usually agree with you, but I know Tasha. She's a nice girl. Jared, you're used to playing around with women who are used to the game. You shouldn't be messing around with a good girl."

He scowled. "What, just because I've been around I don't deserve to have her care about me?"

Comprehension flashed Malcolm's eyes. "You want her to care about you."

Jared scoffed. "Whatever."

"Whatever, hell. You do. I can see it in your eyes. You want this girl to fall for you. Jared, that's wrong."

Jared jumped up from the chair and paced back and forth. "Look, I didn't come here for a lecture on my sex life. Tasha is happy, I'm happy, and what we're doing is working." He walked toward the door. "Pick out whatever you want for Ma and *Mr. Carter*, I don't give a damn anyway." He stormed out of the office.

His brother wouldn't chase him down the hall. It would make a scene at his job, and Malcolm hated being the object of rumors. Jared didn't care what Malcolm, Kenyatta, or Angie thought. It would be nice to have Tasha care about him. He hated when she acted as if he wasn't good enough for her to marry. It may be true, but that didn't make it any less annoying every time she said he wasn't what she wanted. But he wasn't deliberately trying to make her fall in love with him.

Sure, he treated her better than any other woman he'd slept with. And yeah, he continued to blur the lines of their relationship in an effort to shake her up a bit. She was always so damn calm about their situation. Always insisting she leave after they had sex, making him wish she would stay. She didn't want people to know about them, and acted as if he were another co-worker when he showed up for mentoring at the Center. Even when he was deliberately abrasive, she never complained or cried. He was used to women crying and acting as if he'd broken their hearts, when in reality he'd only broken their dreams of uniting with his money. She didn't want anything from him and dammit, he wanted her to want something from him.

Outside, he stopped at his car. What did he want her to ask for? Not marriage. He didn't trust women enough to marry one. But it wouldn't hurt for her to want to be with him.

He smiled. He'd never considered having a long-term lover. It would be hard to convince her to put off marriage. But it would only be for a few months, until they grew tired of the arrangement. If he applied a little pressure, showed her what it would be like, then it should be easier to convince her. She liked what they had going just as much as he, and the sex was amazing.

Whistling, Jared got in his car and headed for the Rec Commission. It was time to turn up the heat and convince Tasha there was no need to rush and find a husband when she had a perfectly good lover at her service.

CHAPTER 20

The buzzing of Tasha's cell phone interrupted her count of the basketball equipment. She sighed in frustration, not because of the phone's interruption, but because she'd have to count the equipment for the tenth time. Thoughts of Jared had distracted her the previous nine times. She pulled her phone from her pocket and saw a text from Shayla.

Big party in ATL this weekend. Come, you need the break.

Tasha put the phone back in her pocket. She did need the distraction. Her agreement with Jared to continue their arrangement for one week had easily turned into two. He'd turned up the heat so much, by the end of the first week she hadn't even brought up ending things. She'd gotten caught up. The realization wasn't surprising. All it took was a phone call or text from Jared and she was ready.

She'd been with him almost every night for the past four weeks. Now she was hooked and it was getting harder to get out of his bed and go home. He always said she didn't have to leave, but he never asked her to stay. Refusing to spend the night was the last front she could put up to pretend she didn't crave him, but it was useless. She wanted to stay, and he wanted her there.

If it were just sex then maybe she wouldn't have gotten attached. But she'd learned more about Jared over the past weeks than she'd known in the years of working with him. They talked about his business, a new offer to reissue his DVD, their childhood memories, and happenings at the Rec Commission. Since the night he'd tended to her allergies, there'd been other nights they hadn't had sex and just hung out and watched the NBA playoffs. The lines were so blurry Tasha didn't even know what label to put on what they were doing.

But she could label what was happening to her: she was falling for Jared, and she was falling hard.

Her phone buzzed again. Cursing, she put down her clipboard and checked the message.

I'm hungry.

It was Jared. *Damn, damn, damn.* She knew what he was hungry for and it wasn't food. Her face flushed as she remembered the last time he'd texted those words. He'd shown up at the Center twenty minutes later and feasted on her inside one of the storage rooms. Her panties became damp as her mind's eye visualized what they must have looked like: her back against the wall, legs open, and Jared kneeling, dining to his heart's content.

Tasha kicked the wall and grabbed her foot as pain sliced through her big toe. She never should have asked him for the favor. That's why Shayla invited her to Atlanta. The birthday party for Jared's mother was this weekend. Once Tasha had updated Shayla on her current situation with Jared and how he continued to ask her to go, Shayla had quickly pointed out it was time to stop sleeping with Jared and move on.

Her phone buzzed again and she seriously considered throwing it against the wall. Instead, she pulled it from her hip again and checked the message.

Hey girl. I hope we can catch up for lunch soon. I really need to talk to another Christian woman.

She should have thrown the phone into the wall. Monica Javers was the newest attendee at her father's church and for some reason the woman had designated herself as Tasha's newest friend. She was usually happy to welcome any new members to her father's church, but Monica's immediate connection to her was unnerving. Tasha cringed because as the preacher's daughter, eventually she'd have to accept Monica's lunch invitation.

She pulled out her phone one more time to check the time; it was almost six. It was the first night of the intramural basketball league so she'd stayed late to make sure things kicked off okay. Giving up on her count of equipment, she grabbed a bag of balls and left the storage room. Two teenage boys she recognized from the mentoring program nearly knocked her over as they ran down the hall.

"My bad, Ms. Smith," said Jevaras Jones, a seventeen-year-old who had on a t-shirt that swallowed his thin frame and shorts that looked more like oversized pants.

"Yeah, we didn't see you," Tony Wilson, the sixteen-year-old Jared mentored, spoke up. He was a miniature version of his mentor in a sleeveless t-shirt that showed off his developing biceps and basketball shorts.

"You would have seen me if you weren't running in the hall," Tasha said with a scowl. She shoved the bag into Tony's hands. "Take these to the gym. I know that's where you're headed."

"You know it," said Tony, laughing. "We got to see what these old dudes can do."

Javaras crossed his arms and pursed his lips. "Why you don't let us play in the league, Ms. Smith?"

"Because you boys only want to pretend you're LeBron, or fight each other, instead of playing the game. Now take the balls and stop running in the halls," she said, tapping her toe.

"Dang, no need to be all nasty," said Javarus. He tapped Tony on the shoulder. "She must be PMSing."

"What did you just say?" Tasha snapped. Tony took off down the hall with a mumbled apology and Javarus quickly followed.

Shaking her head Tasha followed. She wasn't PMSing. She froze. In fact, she hadn't experienced PMS or her cycle since before Charleston. She mentally counted the weeks and groaned. Six weeks had passed.

Her vision blurred and she gasped for breath. *No, no, no, no, no. This can't be happening*, she thought. *I'm just stressed. I've been late before due to stress.* She placed her hand against the wall to brace herself.

"Are you okay? You look as if you're going to faint." A warm hand grasped her shoulder. She looked up and met the concerned eyes of Dr. Kevis Flynn.

Tasha nodded and gave him a shaky smile. "I'm fine. I just… had a bad thought."

He still frowned as he turned her to face him. He lifted her chin and looked into her eyes. "It must have been some thought. You're shaking."

Tasha grasped his hand to remove it from her chin. Instead, he turned his to clasp hers. "Something one of the mentoring kids said. It was silly. I shouldn't take them serious."

He frowned. "Are they that bad?"

She shook her head. "No, they just don't know when to stop playing." She squeezed his hand and tried for a brighter smile. "See? I'm fine. No more shaking."

He finally smiled back at her. His thumb caressed the back of her hand and, surprisingly, she was comforted by the small gesture. "Good. I thought I would have to rush you to the hospital."

"No need for all that. Are you playing tonight?" she asked to change the subject.

"Yes, the six-thirty game. I was hoping you'd be around to watch me play."

This time her smile came easily. "I only like to watch men who know how to play the game. I'm not into watching showoffs."

"Oh, I know how to play." His baritone voice lowered an octave.

Someone cleared their throat loudly. They both turned as Jared walked up. Although he didn't appear upset, it didn't stop her from feeling guilty. She pulled her hand out of Kevis's and smiled at Jared.

His eyes flicked over her before turning to Kevis. "My bad, man, I didn't mean to break up your flow, but I need to speak to Tasha about something."

Kevis pointed at Jared. "I know you. I work out at your gym and tried your exercise program. It's a great workout, man."

Jared smiled and gave Kevis pound. "Glad to hear you liked it." He looked at Tasha, jealousy clear in his dark eyes before he hid it behind a sly grin. "Do you mind if pull her away?"

Kevis shook his head. "Nah, man, but give me a second." He turned to Tasha. "I was just about to ask the lady if she'd go out with me on Saturday."

Tasha kept her eyes on Kevis, but saw Jared stiffen in her periphery. "You move pretty quickly," she said.

Kevis smiled. "When I like what I see there's no need to beat around the bush."

"Tasha, weren't you and your sister coming to my mom's party this weekend?" Jared asked. When she cut her eyes at him, he looked at Kevis. "It's in Atlanta. Tasha's family is pretty close to mine."

Kevis frowned before turning back to Tasha. "If you have plans for this weekend we can make it another night."

She planned to refuse Kevis, until Jared spoke up. Pushing aside her anger with Jared for stepping in she smiled at Kevis. "The party isn't until Saturday. How about we go out Friday?"

A huge grin replaced Kevis's frown. "Sounds good." He walked backwards away from her. "Don't forget to come watch me play. Remember, I'll score double digits just for you."

Tasha laughed. "I knew you were a showoff."

Kevis laughed, turned, and hurried down the hall. When he rounded the corner, Tasha whipped around to face Jared. "What was that about? I never said I was going to your mom's party."

He stepped back and held up his hands. "Tasha, quit playing. You know you're coming."

"Why are you insisting I go? I know it's going to be hard, but you need to go and air things out with your mom. You don't need me there to hold your hand."

He crossed his arms. "I could call Cassandra and have her fly in to hold my hand?"

Jealously churned in her gut. He'd told her about his previous relationship with Cassandra. At first, she couldn't understand how he could work so well with someone he used to sleep with, but now she empathized with the woman. One day that would be her, forced to work with Jared, while remembering what it felt like to be with him.

She bit her lip and inwardly counted to five. "If that's what you need to do, fine." She spun to walk down the hall but Jared reached for her hand. When she turned around he gently pulled her back.

"Stop. I don't want to fight you." His voice was soft. "I'm not calling anyone else." He leaned down to look her in the eye. "For anything. You got that? I'm only calling you."

Her heart rate to speed up and her stomach fluttered. That's all it took from him, a few soft words and those soft eyes and she was pudding in his hands. "Jared, I'm not asking you to do that. I think it's time—"

"It's not time," he interrupted. "You don't want this to be over."

"I don't, and that's exactly why it's time."

"Because of him?" He motioned down the hall in the direction Kevis had taken.

"Not just because of him. Because I'm starting..." Her voice trailed off.

Excitement filled his dark eyes. "Starting to what?"

"I'm starting to ca—"

"Jared, what are you doing here?"

Tasha blinked rapidly. She'd almost told him she was starting to care. With a sigh of relief, she turned to see who'd saved her from herself. A tall, handsome guy with tan skin, high cheekbones any woman would die for, and a slim but sculpted build walked up to them. He looked familiar but she couldn't place where they might have met.

"Devin, what's up man?" Jared said without sincerity. He and Devin gave each other a one-arm hug.

"A few of us doctors put together a basketball team. We're playing tonight." His eyes left Jared and turned to Tasha.

Jared cleared his throat. "Devin, this is Tasha. She's the assistant director at the Rec Commission."

Tasha smiled and shook Devin's hand. "Nice to meet you. Although, you do look familiar."

Devin smiled warmly. "I get that a lot. Where are you from?"

"I grew up in West Columbia."

He frowned as if he were trying to place her. "West Columbia. I had a friend in high school who used to hang out over there."

"Kenyatta's best friend Angie is my sister. We may have met in passing through her and Malcolm," Tasha said.

He nodded. "Yeah, that may be where."

Tasha took the opportunity to escape. "Well, I'll let you two talk. I'm going to watch the first game." She looked at Jared. "I like the guy playing," she said before walking away.

CHAPTER 21

Jared started to follow Tasha down the hall but Devin placed a hand on his arm. "Hey man, don't even go there."

Jared turned to his friend. "Why not?"

Devin let him go. "You had your fun, but it's time to move on to the next one."

"I don't have time for this," Jared said going after Tasha.

Devin followed. "I talked to Malcolm."

"Aw hell."

"He said you're messing around with a good woman."

He cut his eyes at Devin. "So what, I can't be with a good woman?"

"Not if you're only trying to sleep around. Look, Jared, we all know the type of guy you are."

Jared stopped at the entrance of the gym and frowned at Devin. "What type of guy am I?"

"Don't get pissed at me, man. You've never tried to hide you only want a woman for one thing. You clown me whenever I date a woman for an extended period of time and you questioned Malcolm about marrying Kenyatta. I don't have a problem with your viewpoint, because usually you're dealing with women who ain't about nothing. But, when you start messing with *virgins*, you've got to admit that's pretty messed up."

Jared turned and pointed at Devin. "Let's get a few things straight. I'm not messing with virgins; I did one virgin a favor by being her first, at her request. Sleeping with her wasn't even on my radar before she came to me with that. Second, she chose to keep this thing going. I can't help it if honey got hooked on a brotha. I've been upfront with her from the start, so both you and

Malcolm can quit acting like I'm hanging around the playground picking up young girls."

Devin pushed Jared's hand away. "I'm not trying to start nothing with you. I'm just letting you know that when you mess with a woman like that, their feelings get involved. She's gonna end up hurt."

"How do you know that? For your information, I was thinking about keeping her around for a while," Jared said and turned to scan the gym for Tasha.

"What's a while?"

Jared shrugged. "I don't know, man, a while." His eyes landed on Tasha seated in the bleachers. The guy from earlier, he hadn't gotten his name, was stretching out his legs on the bleacher in front of her. "She's cool, all right. We've always been cool; I just never hooked up with someone I respected before. I like it." He frowned when Tasha laughed at something the guy said.

"You like *it*, or you like *her*?"

Jared shrugged again. "Her, I guess. Who the hell is that dude?"

Devin turned to follow Jared's gaze and grinned. "That is Dr. Kevis Flynn. He's an ER doctor, moved here from Charlotte. That dude has every female doctor, nurse, and orderly at the hospital panting after him."

"So he's a player?"

"Nah, he's straight and narrow. Nice to all the ladies, but not running through them. I hear he's on the lookout for a wife."

Jared's frown deepened. "Where'd you hear that?"

"Some of the nurses were gushing about how he mentioned being ready to settle down and have kids."

"Damn, that's just what I need." Jared wanted to spit fire when Tasha laughed again. Was the dude a comedian or something?

"What you mean?"

Jared sighed. "Me and Tasha agreed to do our thing until she met someone else. The good doctor over there just asked her out.

I tried to block, but she just went around. He's exactly the kind of man she's looking for." *And I'm exactly the type of man she doesn't want,* he thought.

"Are you looking to marry and have kids?" Devin asked.

"Hell nah!"

"Then it's time to move on. Kevis is a good dude. Let the chips fall."

Jared shook his head. "No, I'm not ready."

"Then you better lay something on the line that'll make her stay." Jared opened his mouth to interrupt but Devin kept going. "And I'm not talking about sex. If you like her, tell her."

"I already did."

Devin did a double take. "Hell must have frozen over. I never thought I'd see the day when you told a woman you liked her."

Jared pushed Devin's shoulder. "I ain't said I love her or anything like that."

Devin smiled. "Sorry, man, but love is probably the only thing that'll keep a girl like that."

Jared frowned and turned back to Tasha and the good doctor. She would expect something like that. He liked her—a lot—but love? He didn't even know what love was.

"I'm not telling you to say it just to get what you want either," Devin said.

Jared nodded. "I don't play dirty like that. I'll find another way to keep this going."

Devin shook his head. "What you want may not equate to what's good for her."

"Damn, y'all act like I'm Lucifer or something. I'm not going to kill the woman."

Devin laughed. "I know. But you will crush her heart. Think about what I said, man. I gotta warm up."

Jared watched Devin as he walked over to Tasha and Kevis. They said a few words and then Kevis joined Devin on the court to warm up. *Good looking out,* he thought. Devin would have his back, even if he didn't agree with him.

Tasha glared at Jared before turning her body away from him. He guessed she figured out what Devin was doing. Jared walked to the other side of the gym. He passed his mentee, Tony, who was flirting with Tasha's front desk helper, Latiffa.

"What's going on, Tony?" Jared reached out to give Tony a one-arm hug.

"Nothing much, Jared. Just came to watch these old dudes ball," Tony said with a laugh.

"Yeah, well, remember this old dude can still whip your ass on the court," Jared replied.

"I been lifting, man. Don't underestimate." Tony flexed his biceps and Latiffa's eyes lit up.

Jared shook his head and kept walking. He sat in the bleachers directly across from Tasha. The fact that she kept her eyes trained on everyone in the gym except him told him she knew where he was.

The game started after a few minutes. The team of doctors quickly took the lead against their opponents. Jared would have been happy for Devin, if the good doctor wasn't on the team. Jared scowled after Kevis scored a three point shot, kissed his fingertips, and pointed at Tasha, who smiled back. Did he look that stupid when he'd done the same motion to women in the stands? The good doctor was laying it on thick.

Jared pulled out his cell phone. Time to remind Tasha of what they had.

I'm still hungry, he texted.

Tasha pulled her phone from her hip and read his text. He smiled when her lips parted as she took a deep breath.

Burger King is open. Go get a whopper.

I'm not hungry for a whopper. I'm hungry for you.

I'm not going to be your booty call whenever you get horny.

You're more than a booty call, Tasha.

Really? You could have surprised me.

Don't trip. We have fun even when we aren't having sex. Remember the game the other day?

He watched her smile and shake her head. *Yeah I remember.*

Come on girl. Don't break up what we got going.

What do we have going?

Why we got to label it? All I know is I've never done this before but I like it. I like you.

*I like you too *sigh**

So are you going to feed me?

We can't do this forever.

But we can do it now. Let me taste you.

Jared looked across the gym. Tasha looked up from her phone at him. She smiled briefly before turning back to the game. He kept his eyes trained on her, willing her to say yes. His heart speed up when she finally got up and walked out of the gym. A few seconds later, his phone buzzed.

Meet me in my office.

Hell yeah! Jared caught Devin's eye and lifted his chin with a smile. Devin shook his head. Jared didn't care what his friend thought. He was going to handle his business.

CHAPTER 22

Tasha groaned with a mixture of desire and self-loathing when Jared leaned down to kiss the side of her neck. The satin sheets were strewn across his bed from where he'd thoroughly explored every inch of her body. For the second time in two days, she regretted her actions. The night before he'd tasted her so meticulously she'd practically begged him to fuck her on the wall of her office. There was no other word to describe what she'd wanted him to do. Instead, he'd left her panting, soaking wet, and horny as a teenager, while he walked out with a cocky look in his eye. She was too embarrassed to go back to the game, so she'd briskly given the maintenance crew instructions for closing up.

It wasn't hard to figure out why he'd left. Even though he'd been just as turned on as she, he'd wanted to leave her wanting more. More from him and no one else. And dammit, like a junkie she'd run over after work today so he could finish what he started. It was crazy, reckless, stupid, and every other adjective out there used for bad judgment.

She tried to push him off. Instead, he slowly slid out of her and she gasped at the pleasure and loss.

He rubbed his cheek against hers. "I could do this every day."

Her heart thumped repeatedly. She pulled his head up so she could look into his eyes. "Do you mean that?"

He froze. His mouth opened and closed regret clear in his eyes. He hadn't meant those words the way she'd taken them.

She tried to smile, but it was more of a grimace. "Of course you do. What man wouldn't want to have great sex every day?"

He didn't stop her when she slid away from him and sat on the edge of his bed. She pushed her thick hair out of her face and stared at the wall. If he didn't want to commit to her now, why would he if her fears were confirmed? Even after he'd left her wanting him, her last thought and prayer the night before was for her period to come in the morning. It hadn't. Jared's expression confirmed what she'd already known. He was content to sleep with her every day, but that was all. What would he say if she was pregnant? What would she say? She couldn't imagine facing her parents, her father's church members, or even herself in the mirror. Jared was always clear he didn't want marriage or kids. She had only herself to call a fool if she was pregnant.

Jared's hand brushed her back and she jumped. "What's wrong, Tasha?"

As if he didn't know. She wanted to yell at him for being so callous. For not caring about her the way she cared about him. Instead, she shook her head. "Nothing." She hopped off the bed. She pulled the sheet with her and wrapped it around body. "I've got to go."

"You don't have to go."

She whipped around to face him. "I can't stay here."

"Why not? You can't possibly tell me you feel like driving after what we just did." He smiled.

"No, you don't understand. I *can't* stay here."

He frowned and reached for her but she took a step back and held up her hand. "Stop, Jared. Just stop it. Stop acting like you want me here. Stop telling me you *like* me, and calling and texting me when you want me. I know you think nothing is wrong with doing those things, but it is."

His thick arms flexed as he crossed them and leaned against the headboard. "Why don't you tell me why letting you know that I want you is wrong?"

She glared in response to his calm voice. "You're acting like we're together, when we're not."

"I'm giving you what you want. You asked me to treat you differently from my usual women. That's what I'm doing."

"That's the problem."

He rolled his eyes. "You're making no sense."

"I know." She paused and took a deep breath. "Look, I'm not cut out to do this. I ignored the consequences."

His eyes narrowed. "What consequences?"

She looked away. "I have to think about the future and what I want." Her gaze returned to his. "Right now all I want is you."

He jumped off the bed so quickly she jumped. He reached for her hands and pulled her close. "You've got me. We can do this for as long as you want."

"Will you marry me?"

He dropped her hands and stepped back. "I'm not talking about marriage, Tasha."

"Well, I am. I want a husband and kids. I don't want to be someone's jump off or baby momma."

He screwed up his face. "You're not my jump off, and you're damn sure not going to be a baby momma. We protect ourselves from that."

"It's not one hundred percent," she whispered.

He shook his head. "It's been foolproof for me so far. Besides, if we ever had an accident I'd take care of it." She flinched and he cursed. "Tasha…"

She held up her hand. "No, I needed to hear that. I've never asked you to hide who you are. Just like I can't hide who I am. I *can't* do this anymore. I'm caught up, Jared. I'm falling so damn hard for you and I can't afford to stay."

He rubbed the back of his head and looked away. That simple movement broke her heart. He didn't feel the same. She was even more naïve than she'd thought.

"I'm gonna get my stuff and go," she said.

"Look, why don't I call you tomorrow and we'll talk?"

"There's nothing to talk about." She turned and snatched her clothes from the floor. When she had everything, she headed for his bathroom. She dressed slowly. Her eyes trailing to the door as she waited for the knock, for him to tell her he still wanted her to stay. If he said he felt a smidgeon of what she felt for him then she'd keep this up. She would even tell him about her fears. If he cared, he couldn't possibly hurt her by "taking care of an accident."

The knock never came. Her feet were like lead as she left the bathroom. He looked at her before getting off the bed and sliding into a pair of basketball shorts. He walked over and kissed her cheek. "I'll call you tomorrow. We'll talk."

Tasha stiffened. He expected her to come running back to his bed. And she'd been the stupid fool who gave him that impression. She'd been running to his bed for weeks. Every time she said she was through she came back. There was no reason for him to believe she was done.

She looked into his eyes. "Don't bother calling. Tomorrow's Friday. I have a date." His eyes turned cold and she walked out.

CHAPTER 23

Instead of going to Atlanta on Friday, Jared waited until that night to pull out his cell and call Malcolm. He'd used work as an excuse to get out of helping with last minute preparations and arrive later, but as the day wore on and he thought about smiling in the faces of his mom and Mr. Carter, he couldn't bring himself to go.

If Tasha were coming, it would be different. In the six weeks since Charleston she'd become a fixture in his life. After a day of training, putting out fires for his business, and working deals with Cassandra, it was nice to come home and have someone there to talk to. She'd push him to talk whenever he tried to change the subject. No one else did that. She'd listen and offer advice without being pushy or opinionated. He'd never had that before.

Her consistent refusal to come to his mother's party impressed and irritated him. When other women would jump at the chance to meet his family, she'd insisted it would give the wrong impression. He didn't care what his family thought. He wanted her in his life. At what capacity he wasn't sure. Every time he thought about the dreaded L word, he broke out in a sweat. He'd choked the night before when he should have admitted that he cared too. How could he possibly admit to something stronger?

Malcolm's voice mail picked up. "Hey, Malcolm, it looks like I need to leave town and…" His message was cut off by the beep from call waiting. Malcolm was calling him back. He switched calls. "I was just leaving you a message."

"My bad, man, I was getting settled here with Mr. Carter and didn't pick up in time. Are you in Atlanta yet?"

Jared frowned. "Mr. Carter. What are you doing with him?"

"Kenyatta went to see a movie with Mom, so Mr. Carter and I decided to get a drink. I was hoping you were calling to let me know you were here and could join us."

"Even if I were in town I wouldn't join you for drinks," Jared said.

"Excuse me for a second, Mr. Carter," Malcolm said. There was shuffling in the background before the murmurs of bar conversations disappeared. When Malcolm spoke again he didn't try to hide his hostility. "Jared, it's time for you to stop acting like a kid and accept the fact that Mom's moving on. I'm not thrilled about it, but I want her to be happy. Why can't you do the same?"

"Because I don't care if she's happy, especially if it's with someone like Mr. Carter. That man's no good and I don't want anything to do with him."

"What's wrong with you, man? Why are you being so hateful? It's our mom."

"You don't want to know."

"How about you stop telling me what I do and don't want to know. I'm a grown man, and I don't need my *little* brother trying to think for me. So you either start talking or your ass better be here tomorrow for the party."

Jared looked up and shook his head. "Look, Malcolm, I had some stuff come up and I need to go—"

"I don't care what came up. Your ass better be here tomorrow or I'm gonna personally kick the shit out of it when I get back in town." Malcolm paused and Jared could picture his brother trying to calm himself down. "If you don't want to do it for Mom, then do it for me. I need my brother beside me."

"Look, man, I'll see what I can do, all right?" Jared said before ending the call. It wasn't the answer Malcolm would want, and sure enough, his phone rang almost instantly. Jared turned off his phone. He rubbed his eyes and pushed aside the guilt for letting Malcolm down. He didn't doubt his brother would come straight to his house after leaving Atlanta just to kick his ass.

A fight with Malcolm was preferable to going to the party. Sure the party would be tough for Malcolm, but he'd have Kenyatta by his side. Tasha wouldn't be there to make it easier for him.

He'd texted and called all day, but her phone went straight to voice mail. He'd even called her office and was somewhat mollified when they told him she was in meetings all day. But she would have had some breaks to check her phone and call him. He looked at his watch: ten on the dot. Her date with the doctor should be coming to an end.

He wasn't worried about one date with the good doctor. She'd said herself she was falling for him. What concerned him more was thinking she'd keep up this silent treatment as a way to end what they had.

What should be a simple confession would get her to Atlanta with him. It would keep her from looking at another man ever again. But it would require putting his feelings out there. How could he—self declared playboy and denouncer of long-term commitment—tell her he was just as caught up in what they had as she? How could he explain how much he wanted her in his life, but ask her to leave out the marriage and kids part?

Jared snapped his fingers. He didn't have to tell her. He could leave the long drawn out discussion about their future for another day. Right now, all she needed was to know he wasn't interested in anyone except her. It should be enough to calm her fears, kill any thoughts she had about the good doctor, and get her to Atlanta. *Yeah, but that's messed up when you know what she wants,* his conscience intervened. He shook the thought out of his head. He pushed away from his desk and grabbed his keys. Right now he had to get to Tasha's before he chickened out.

CHAPTER 24

When Tasha turned her cell phone on briefly at lunch, she ignored the texts from Jared and called Kevis to confirm their date. Kevis's message telling her to dress casually piqued her curiosity. But she wouldn't complain after spending a day in heels and a suit. He'd agreed to meet her at city hall then follow her home so she could change. The air was balmy when she walked out of city hall at six, but Kevis looked fresh and comfortable as he waited for her in a graphic t-shirt that hugged his muscular chest, jeans, and sneakers.

Tasha smiled at him in greeting. "You really meant casual."

"You're going to have to change," he said. He openly admired her legs below the hem of her grey pinstripe suit skirt.

Her smile widened. "Sounds good to me."

He drove her to her car, which was parked in a nearby garage and followed her home. She quickly changed into a red and orange tank top, flowing white linen skirt, and gold sandals. She pulled her hair out of the ponytail she'd worn all day and let her natural curls frame her face. Jared liked her with her hair down, so Kevis probably would too. He sat on her couch and waited for her to change exactly where she'd left him. Unlike another man who'd roamed around looking at everything during his first visit.

"I'm ready," she said.

He stood up and paused. "Wow, if this is casual I'd hate to see dressed up."

She blushed and reached for her purse. "Thank you."

She led the way out and he opened the door to his car so she could slide in. As he drove back downtown she talked about sitting through various meetings with Richland County and

City of Columbia staff to gain continued support for the Rec Commission. From there the conversation flowed to his night before in the emergency room. He didn't go into detail about any of the patients, but the compassion in his voice proved that he cared about what he did.

Downtown he parked in front of Macs on Main and had her wait while he ran inside. He came out with bags of takeout. From there they went to Finlay Park.

"How does a picnic dinner and movie at the park sound?" he asked.

Tasha grinned. "Sounds like a lot of fun." It was her first real date in over a month. Getting together with Jared every night at his house didn't count. She couldn't resist the familiar excitement of a first date.

They found a spot in the grass before the stage where Kevis spread out the blanket he'd brought. Tasha tried to help but he insisted she relax. She sat back and sipped on a soda as he laid out their food as carefully as if he were laying out a meal for the queen. Their conversation flowed around first date topics: where are you from, where's your family from, what are your hobbies.

Kevis pushed his finished plate aside and met her eye. "What are you looking for in a relationship?"

Tasha froze mid-chew, before slowly swallowing the peach cobbler. That question would have been so much easier six weeks ago.

He softened his features and smiled. "I'm not trying to scare you off or anything, but I'm at a point in my life when I don't want to play games. I'm ready to settle down and have a family, and if that isn't in your long term plans, I'd like to know. I'm not saying we'll get married, but I would like to know I'm dating someone who isn't playing the field."

Tasha took a long drag from her soda can. Kevis was exactly what she'd been looking for—before she'd stupidly asked Jared to sleep with her. She meant what she'd said the night before, she couldn't keep sleeping with Jared, but until she knew for sure that she wasn't pregnant—and she prayed every night she wasn't—she couldn't say he was completely out of her life.

"I don't play games," she said. "I do want to get married one day, but it's too early to say who I'll do that with."

Kevis smiled. "Fair enough. Just as long as we're straight with each other."

It was dusk and the park staff announced the start of the movie. Tasha leaned back on her elbows on one end of the blanket to watch. Her eyes widened, but she didn't move when Kevis scooted close enough for their hips to touch. Her heart didn't flutter as it did when Jared touched her, but she enjoyed the pleasant scent of his cologne, the warmth of his body, and the solidness of his frame. By the end of the movie, she was leaning into his side and he'd wrapped his arm lightly around her waist. It was a nice date. Not earth shattering or mind blowing, but nice. So nice, she let him hold her hand on the way to the car, and later when he walked her to her front door.

Tasha turned to smile at him. "I really enjoyed myself, Kevis."

He returned her smile. "So did I. Maybe we can do this again sometime?"

She nodded. "I'd like that."

His gaze left hers to settle on her lips. "I'd really like a goodnight kiss."

Her heart sped up. She'd forgotten the good night kiss. Would she'd enjoy anyone's kiss after Jared? Only one way to find out.

"I'd like that too," she whispered.

Kevis took a step closer to her, his wide shoulders blocking the glow from her porch light. She breathed in the scent of his cologne and although it didn't increase her arousal, it was nice. When his lips settled on hers, she was disappointed there wasn't an immediate rush of desire. But she didn't pull away when his tongue grazed along her bottom lip. She opened her mouth to let him deepen the kiss and slowly slight warmth started in her belly. His hand came up to the side of her breast, but instead of cupping it, he pulled back.

"I'd better go before I get ahead of myself." His deep voice was heavy with desire and Tasha could feel the evidence pressing against her.

She cleared her throat and took a step back. "That was nice."

He smirked. "Nice? I'd hoped for something a bit more."

Her eyes widened. "No, I didn't mean it in a bad way. I definitely enjoyed it."

He smiled crookedly. "That's better."

She laughed and he joined in. "Give me a call when you get back in town."

She frowned, then remembered Jared had given the impression she was going to his mother's party. She wasn't going, but hadn't dismissed the idea of going to the party Shayla invited her to. Not because it would put her in the same town as Jared—or so she told herself.

She nodded. "I will."

He leaned in and kissed her cheek. "I'll call you tomorrow."

Her smile froze on her face as Jared's voice went through her head. It was stupid to think of him and the fact that he'd said the same every night before she left, but she couldn't help it. Thankfully, Kevis didn't notice. She had to force the smile to remain on her face as he walked off the porch to his car. He watched as she unlocked her door and went inside. Once inside, her face fell. Why did he have to say that? Now her mind raced with memories of Jared kissing her before she left him when it should be racing with thoughts of her first kiss with Kevis.

There was a knock on her door and she released a shuddering breath. He'd come back. Maybe she could kiss him again and get thoughts of Jared out of her mind.

Grinning, she opened the door. "I'm glad you came back."

Jared stood on her porch. "Well, when the person you want ignores your calls all day you have to pop up."

Tasha's smile crumbled. She mentally shook her head and stood on her toes to look over his shoulder. "What are you doing, did Kevis see you?"

He smirked. "I waved at him as I drove up."

Tasha rolled her eyes. "Are you crazy? Now he's going to think…"

"That there's something between us." He stopped smiling and stared at her solemnly. "Isn't there?"

Tasha felt herself melting as she looked into his eyes and she cursed herself a thousand times. "No." She tried to slam the door but he pushed it open. "Get out of my house."

"Why did you kiss him?"

Her jaw dropped. "You were watching."

"I was parked across the street. Did you kiss him because I was there?"

"I didn't see your car, stalker. And for your information I kissed him because I wanted to." She turned and went further into the house. "If I would have known you were watching I would have let him come in."

He followed her. "He asked to come in?"

She whipped around to face him. "Did he see you parked across the street, watching my house?"

He shrugged. "I don't know and I don't care. He doesn't matter."

She stomped her foot. "Yes, he does. Look, Jared, I wasn't joking last night when I said this was over. I had fun tonight with Kevis. It was a real date, something we've never had."

"That's because you didn't want anyone to know about us."

"Because we were only supposed to be a one-time thing. What happened later was…a mistake, okay? Kevis wants what I want."

"How do you know that?"

She sighed and sat on the couch. "Because he told me. He's looking to settle down, Jared. I can't date a guy like that while sleeping with you."

He sat beside her. "What if you date me instead?"

She closed her eyes and sat back on the couch. "Do you want the long or the short answer?"

"I'm serious, Tasha."

She looked at him out of one eye, he was smiling. "Jared, I don't have time for these games. You don't want to date me. You just want to keep sleeping with me. Dating is just a nice name to put on it, but we both know it'll go nowhere. Let's just chalk up our losses and move on."

"You know we can't move on. There're consequences to what we've been doing."

Tasha stiffened. Had he realized they'd had uninterrupted sex for over a month? "What consequences?"

He leaned closer to her. "Last night you said you were falling hard for me."

She turned away with a groan. "Please don't go there."

He held onto her arm and turned her back toward him. "I didn't want to say it, but I…" He stopped.

She opened her eyes and gave him a wary glace. "You what?"

"I'm falling for you too, Tasha."

Instead of falling into the gooey puddle of happiness his words invoked, she jerked her hand away, stood, and pointed a finger in his face. "Don't give me that load of crap, Jared. You think you can just come over here, say you're falling for me, and I'll jump right back into bed with you? That's weak, especially for you. Go run that game on some other chick, because I'm not that stupid."

She turned away and he jumped up from the couch and took her arm. "I'm not running game on you."

"Really? I'm supposed to believe you suddenly realized you're falling for me? And what next, Jared? We keep on sleeping together, maybe we even let our families know we're lovers, just to break things off immediately afterward because you can't handle a relationship. I'm not letting myself get wrapped up in you only to find myself broken hearted and alone."

She tried to jerk away but he held fast. "Dammit, Tasha, it's not like that." He paused and glared at her before the tension slowly left his body and he let her arm go. "Okay, maybe it was like that..." When she sucked her teeth, he hurried on. "At first. I did come over here to tell you I was caught up, hoping you'd stay with me. But when I saw you with him, when I saw you kiss him, I realized I wouldn't be saying it just because. I've never been in love with a woman before—I don't know how to say it, or even if what I'm feeling is love. All I know is that the bad things in my life don't seem so bad when you're around. I *like* coming home and seeing your car in my driveway. I *like* watching basketball with you, talking to you, and, yes, making love to you. I'm not usually a jealous man, but when I saw the good doctor kiss you, I wanted to rip his arms out of the sockets. The only explanation I have for that is because I love you."

Tasha couldn't breathe. It was as if each word out of Jared's mouth sucked some of the air out of the room. She was afraid to speak, because if she spoke maybe she would wake up and realize this was just a wonderful dream.

Jared reached out and cupped the side of her face. "I just poured my heart out and you're gaping at me like a fish. Say something."

She finally took a shaky breath before smiling. "You mean it?"

He nodded. "Yes." He laughed. "I just surprised my damn self."

She laughed with him before reaching up to pull his face down. His mouth glided over hers and intense heat erupted below her skin. There was no slow build up when Jared kissed her, it always crashed over her like a tidal wave: forceful, uncontrollable, and sweeping her under.

He lifted her and carried her into the bedroom. For once, she didn't feel hurried as he kissed her. She had a lifetime to enjoy him and wanted to savor every moment starting now. He slid her body down his and she marveled at the softness of his skin contrasting with the rock hardness of muscle underneath. They undressed each other slowly, both taking the time to kiss every bit of skin revealed. When Tasha pulled down Jared's pants and underwear, she gasped at the sight of his erection, large and proud before her. She took it into her hands and kissed the top before slowly taking him into her mouth. He'd loved her like this so many times, but she'd only returned the favor once. She took her time learning every inch of it and became more aroused by his quickened breathing and groans as he dug his hands in her hair. She tasted the salty sweetness of his pre-cum and moaned with satisfaction.

Jared lifted her up and slammed his mouth down on hers. "I'm coming inside of you, Tasha."

She grinned. "That would have been inside of me."

"Damn, you know exactly what to say," he groaned before laying her down on the bed.

Jared kissed her with unbridled passion before making his way down her body. He paid homage to her neck, breasts, and stomach before reaching his ultimate destination. He kissed the folds of her sweetness before using every part of his mouth: tongue, teeth, and lips to worship her goodness. When she felt the coming waves of a climax, he pulled up and she groaned in frustration.

"Not until you tell me what I want to hear," he whispered.

Tasha groaned. "What…don't stop."

He grinned before reaching over and getting a condom out of her bedside table. He opened it and easily slid it on before teasing the edge of her wet walls with his blunt head. "Tell me," he slid one delicious inch inside of her, "you love me." He slid out and she whimpered.

"Jared, please," she begged.

"Tell me," he slid two inches inside of her before pulling out, "you love me."

Mindless with passion Tasha, lifted her hips. "You know how I feel."

"Tasha," he slid three inches inside of her, "Look at me." She opened her eyes and met his, which were filled with uncertainty. "Tell me you love me."

Any last strains of doubt about his feelings fell away as she met his eyes. "I love you, Jared. God help me, but I do."

He slid into her completely and she cried out in pleasure. "Oh, God, I love you," she panted. He kissed her neck as he thrust slowly in and out of her.

"Say it again," he demanded.

"I love you."

He quickened his pace. "Again."

"I love you."

His speed increased and when his lips met hers she climaxed. He swallowed her screams with a kiss, but broke away to cry out with his own orgasm. He buried his head in her neck as their breathing slowed down. When he slowly slid out of her, she moaned.

He didn't roll away—instead, he lifted his head and stared in her eyes. "I do love you, Tasha."

Tasha's heart soared. It didn't matter what happened tomorrow because he loved her. If her scare turned out to be legitimate, they would work it out together. If her family thought she was crazy they'd have to get over it. She'd known deep down the first time he kissed her she would fall under his spell. Now she knew it was because it was leading them to this.

She reached up and touched his cheek. "I love you too, Jared."

He smiled his cocky smile, her heart skipped a beat, and he kissed her again.

CHAPTER 25

Tasha squeezed Jared's hands as they entered the doors of the banquet facility where his mom's party was being held. It was a standalone building with a lobby decorated in shades of gold and cream. Small sitting areas were in each corner and double doors led to the main banquet hall. At the last minute, the party had been changed to a birthday and engagement celebration. Luckily, Malcolm and Kenyatta had rented the entire facility for the party.

Tasha had finally agreed to come around noon. They'd barely gotten out of bed, dressed, and arrived in Atlanta before the start of the party. But remembering Jared whisper in her ear he loved her as they made love during the night was worth every hurried second to get there.

On the way, Jared said they'd invited all of his mom's friends from college, church, her job, and the old neighborhood. Based on the full parking lot and the large number of people mingling, everyone invited must have shown up.

Jared winked at her between smiling and nodding to various people. To anyone else he would appear to be at ease, but his nervousness and tension was as plain to her as the nose on his face. His smile was tight, his movements jerky, and laughter forced. After watching Jared agonize over this event for the past few weeks, she was nervous.

Jared was right—what he'd seen was hard to justify, but for his sake, she prayed there was more to the story. Despite her anxiety, she had to stifle a yawn as they entered the main room.

Jared caught her yawning and concern filled his eyes. "Are you tired?"

She smiled. "After last night, you're surprised?"

He grinned. "You're right."

166

She rolled her eyes and looked away. She was exhausted, and that pissed her off. Angie had been exhausted during her pregnancies. Her recent fatigue combined with a still absent period probably meant the worst. Her breathing picked up. What Jared would say? When he'd said he loved her the night before she'd thought things would be okay, but today she wasn't so sure. He didn't trust women. His newfound feelings for her might dissipate as soon as she voiced her suspicion. She wouldn't say anything to him until she worked up the nerve to take a pregnancy test.

His grip on her hand tightened and she looked up. He wasn't looking at her and her gaze followed his to Malcolm and Kenyatta talking to an older couple. The woman's features were so similar to Jared's, she could only be his mother. A tall, well-built man had his hand around her waist and she assumed it was Mr. Carter.

"Are you ready?" she asked.

He clenched his jaw before taking a deep breath and visibly relaxing. "Let the games begin."

Tasha felt Jared's hands become sweaty as they approached his family. She reached over to place her other hand over his.

"I'm here," Jared said to his brother. "Where's the bar?"

Surprise was the first emotion on Malcolm's face before annoyance replaced it. "Jared," he said through clenched teeth.

"It's okay, Malcolm," Mrs. Patterson said. She smiled warmly at Malcolm before turning to Jared and Tasha. The warmth in her eyes and was replaced with cool indifference as she looked at Jared. It was an expression so similar to his, the exact same mask he put on to hide his hurt. "Hello, Jared." Her eyes flicked coldly and dismissively over Tasha. "I see you brought a friend."

Jared pulled Tasha closer to his side. "Tasha, this is my mother, Gladys Patterson. Mother, this is Tasha."

"It's nice to meet you, Tasha." Although the words were cordial, the warmth behind them was as welcoming as the Antarctic. "This is Mr. Carter, my fiancé." She raised a slim hand to Mr. Carter.

Jared squeezed her hand again and she pasted a smile on her face. "It's nice to meet you, Mr. Carter."

"Please, call me Randall," he said sincerely. There was warmth in his gaze, and after the cold reception of Jared's mother, she couldn't help but respond with an open smile. She hadn't expected hugs and kisses, but a little pleasantness would've been nice.

"Don't call him anything," Jared said before she could respond.

Randall's smile was replaced with a somber expression. "Look, Jared, I don't care how you feel about me, but for your mom's sake, don't make tonight harder than it has to be."

Jared sneered. "And why should I do that?"

"Jared, please," Tasha said.

Gladys held up a hand. "Don't, my son stopped caring about me a long time ago."

All pretense of calm left Jared, his body visibly stiffening. "Since the day my dad died."

Malcolm stepped up. "I think we need to talk. Tonight."

Jared laughed bitterly. "No need. Tonight's all about celebrating love...and life." He looked at Tasha. "Come help me find the bar."

"There isn't a bar," Malcolm said.

Jared cringed. "I'm supposed to do this sober?"

"I've had enough of your attitude," Randall said, taking his hand from around Gladys's waist.

Jared glared back. "I really don't give a f—"

"Gladys, I'm so excited."

Tasha sighed with relief as a middle-aged woman rushed over to hug Jared's mom. "Celebrating a birthday and an engagement at the same time. It's about time you found some joy in life. I thank the good Lord it was with Randall." The lady turned to look at Malcolm then Jared. "And both of your boys are here. You boys must be so happy for your mom."

"We are, Mrs. Jeffries, thank you," Malcolm said.

"Ecstatic," Jared said.

If Mrs. Jeffries noticed Jared's lack of enthusiasm, it wasn't apparent. "Well, we all knew in college Randall loved Gladys, but she had a soft spot for your father. Good thing too, because she saved his life. God bless him. I think even he would approve of this match." Jared snorted but Mrs. Jeffries continued on. "Now, Malcolm, I've met your girlfriend."

"Fiancée," he said, smiling and holding up Kenyatta's hand to show of the ring.

"Oh, Lord, another reason to celebrate. Congratulations!" She turned to Jared. "Are you next?"

"No, excuse us." Jared turned and walked away, pulling Tasha along with him.

"That was rude," Tasha said when they were out of earshot.

"Mrs. Jeffries will talk to a wall. Believe me, I did you a favor," he said. "Can you believe that nonsense? So he's wanted my mom since college? I wonder if their affair lasted that long. And what did she mean, *saving his life*? How did my mom save my dad's life?"

Tasha hurried to keep up with his pace. "You were too busy hightailing it out of there to find out. It's obvious you have more questions than answers. You need to talk to her, tonight."

"I thought I could, but seeing them together…" He sighed. She squeezed his hand and he nodded. "Tomorrow, I'll try tomorrow."

She stopped. When he turned to face her she stared pointedly. "Tonight."

He looked as if he would argue, but didn't. Instead, he lifted her hand and kissed it. "I'll try."

They walked over to the buffet table where Jared's friend Devin was piling food on his plate.

"Man, you and my brother love filling your body with junk," Jared said, slapping Devin on the back.

Devin turned and grinned. "Hey, man, I'm just trying to let Kenyatta feel good about the food she ordered."

169

"Whatever. You remember Tasha?" He pulled Tasha to his side.

Surprise flashed across Devin's face before he covered it with a smile. "I do. Nice to see you again."

"Same here."

Devin turned back to Jared. "So have you pissed Malcolm off yet?"

"I think so. I'll steer clear of him tonight."

Devin shook his head. "I'm staying out of this family drama."

Before Jared could answer, Kenyatta came up to their group and pinched Jared on the arm. Tasha admired her beaded lavender jumpsuit and wished she'd taken more time to pick out something for the evening. Jared had complemented her yellow maxi dress, but Kenyatta looked more polished than she felt.

"You know Malcolm's gonna kill you," Kenyatta said to Jared.

"He'll be all right. I'll keep my distance for the rest of the night."

Devin laughed and shook his head. "You must have really pissed him off."

Kenyatta nodded. "I didn't order them, but I think they'll be fireworks."

Jared grinned at her. "Why don't you take him to some dark corner and distract him? That'll get him off my case."

"At your mom's party? You must be crazy."

It was the first time Tasha had been with Jared around other people. She'd thought his openness with her was something special. But he teased Kenyatta with an open friendliness she'd never seen him give other women. Maybe she was deluding herself into thinking she was more special to Jared than she was.

"Tasha, girl, I am so glad to see you," Kenyatta said.

Tasha blinked several times. As much as Angie complained about her spending time with Jared, she'd figured Kenyatta would feel the same. Angie had even told her previously Kenyatta thought Jared was a dog.

"Really? What's up?"

Kenyatta smiled and clasped her hands to her chest. "Can you help me with something in the kitchen? I tried to make the pasta salad recipe I got from Angie. You know the one your mom makes that everyone loves? Well, it needs some work."

"I thought you catered the party?" Jared asked.

"I did, but some of your mom's friends asked if they could bring food, and since I didn't want them to think Malcolm was marrying a woman who can't cook, I figured I'd make something too."

Tasha laughed. "Kenyatta, you can cook."

"Only when necessary. Malcolm and I eat out most days of the week because of our schedules. I know you can, Tasha. You're almost better than your mom, but don't ever tell her I said that. Will you help?"

Tasha laughed at the obvious compliment. "For that, I'd make a red velvet cake. Sure, I'll help."

Kenyatta's eyes lit up. "Great. Come on."

Tasha looked and Jared who raised an eyebrow. She shrugged helplessly before Kenyatta pulled her away. They didn't talk much as Kenyatta wove her way through the thickening crowd. Before they got to the kitchen, Gladys stopped Kenyatta.

"I can't believe he did that. He'll never listen to me."

Pain laced Jared's mother's voice. She stepped around Kenyatta to offer sympathy, but when Gladys saw her, the hurt in her eyes was quickly replaced with disappointment.

"Never mind, Kenyatta, we'll talk later," she said before turning and walking away.

Tasha frowned and followed Kenyatta into the kitchen. "What was that look for?"

Kenyatta sighed and pulled Tasha out of the way of a caterer with a tray of sandwiches on his shoulder. "That's why I pulled you in here. Jared's mom is upset he brought you."

Tasha scowled. "You must be joking." How dare his mom be upset about her presence when she was the one in the wrong? As soon as the thought came she felt bad. She was no better than Jared. But that didn't ease the pain of knowing Jared's mom didn't like her.

"Come on, Tasha, we all know the type of woman Jared usually dates. She thinks he brought some dumb broad he can paw on in front of her friends all night to embarrass her."

"Did you tell her you know me?"

"Yes, but it didn't change much. Just because we're friends doesn't mean you're not a slut."

Tasha cringed. "Kenyatta."

Kenyatta bit her bottom lip. "Sorry, her words, not mine."

Tasha took a deep breath and pinched the bridge of her nose. "It's not like that with me and Jared."

Kenyatta looked skeptical. "Maybe you think that…"

"I don't *think* anything. I *know*." She crossed her arms.

"Tasha, you're my best friend's little sister, and I care about you and your happiness. But, Jared is no good. I mean, he's a decent person and all, but when it comes to women, he's a dog. Angie's really worried you're in over your head."

Tasha uncrossed her arms to put her hands on her hips. "Angie's being overprotective. I know you guys are trying to do what you think is right, but I know what I'm doing. You don't have to protect me from the same type of mistakes you all made."

Kenyatta reached out to take her hand. "This isn't about that, it's about us caring about you. Jared uses women. We're worried he's using you."

She snatched her hand back. "Jared isn't using me, he loves me." The words were out before she could think about it. She hadn't meant to go professing their love for each other so soon, but now that she had she was ready to fight anyone who doubted it. What she wasn't ready for was the pity in Kenyatta's eyes.

"You really believe that?"

She clenched her fists to keep from shaking her sister's best friend. "I believe it because he said it. Jared loves me."

Movement at the door caught her eye and she turned to see Malcolm standing there, a stricken look on his face.

He took a small step toward her. "Do you love my brother?"

His tone begged her to say no. The anger in his eyes made her more uneasy than anything her sister or Kenyatta could say. Why was everyone so against her and Jared being together? She wanted to cry, instead she clenched her fists. It had to be hormones.

"Yes," she answered. He cursed and she flinched. "Is it really so terrible?"

He held up his hands. "I didn't mean it like that."

"It doesn't matter how you meant it. If you'll both excuse me, I'm going to look for the one person in your family who's actually happy I'm here." She rushed past him back into the main room.

Jared was the first person she saw. She couldn't shake the unease from the scene in the kitchen, but when he looked at her and smiled, it was almost forgotten as warmth spread within her. She'd fallen in love with him, and hoped she wasn't stupid for believing he loved her too. He wasn't despicable enough to tell her such a hurtful lie. Was he?

As handsome as he was in the silk peach shirt and tan slacks he'd worn, she wished he was wearing his customary basketball shorts and sleeveless t-shirt, and that they were sitting on his couch watching television instead of here. Surrounded by people who didn't believe what they had was real.

When his eyes met hers his smile faded, and he rushed over. "Are you okay?" He took her hand.

She smiled and squeezed. "Yes. Perfect."

He didn't look convinced. "Are you sure? Was Kenyatta's pasta salad that bad?"

She laughed. She'd completely forgotten about the excuse

Kenyatta had used to get her in the kitchen. "Let's just say stay away from the pasta salad."

He continued to study her face and she looked toward the dance floor. "Let's dance. I feel like dancing."

He hesitated for a second before smiling. "All right, let's see what you got."

CHAPTER 26

Jared spent the half hour since Tasha had disappeared with Kenyatta avoiding his brother and mother, while keeping an eye on Tasha. He'd known Kenyatta's pasta salad excuse was just a way for her to get Tasha alone. When Malcolm followed them into the kitchen, and Tasha came out looking like a kid who'd just been told Santa wasn't real, his suspicion was confirmed. She'd tried to act as if everything was okay, but the worry line in the middle of her forehead told a different story.

He was tempted to grab his soon to be sister-in-law and find out what was up, but Malcolm would only follow. His brother followed Kenyatta around like a trained puppy. He would usually tease Malcolm about it, but he was doing the same thing with Tasha. His gaze followed her around the party and whenever she left his side, he was quick to follow. He'd deny it if anyone knew how attached he'd become. It wasn't anyone's business what was between him and Tasha.

They were limited in the people they spoke with. He only wanted to talk to his father's friends, but after a few conversations, he began to wonder if he'd entered the Twilight Zone. Most of his dad's friends were happy about the match. Some even commented it wasn't surprising his mom and Mr. Carter ended up together. With each well wish his stomach knotted up. His mom's affair with Mr. Carter must have been well known.

After they walked away from another of his dad's friends, Tasha frowned at him. "Jared, I think there's more to the story about your mom and Mr. Carter."

"Yeah, it sounds like they were together throughout my parents' marriage."

Her frown deepened. "No, I don't think everyone would be so happy if that were true. It seems like they're happy she's happy. I don't know. Did your parents ever have problems?"

"Not that I know of." He pulled her to his side. "Obviously I was wrong."

She shrugged. "You'll find out tomorrow when you talk to your family."

He didn't say anything. He didn't want to talk to his family and confirm his mother had been unhappy during her entire marriage. It would undermine everything he'd ever thought growing up. Knowing all of the smiles his mom had given to his father, the hugs and kisses they'd openly shared were all fake on her end would shatter the little bit of faith he was starting to have in relationships. He looked at Tasha who was watching the couples on the dance floor. Could she be that fake too?

The music changed to the "Cha Cha Slide." Tasha beamed up at him. "Come on, Jared. Let's dance."

He began shaking his head before the last word was out of her mouth. "No, ma'am. I gave you one dance earlier and that's it."

She pouted and immediately he wanted to take her lower lip into his mouth. Damn, she could turn him on with the simplest gestures. It had to be love.

"Are you really gonna have me stand around all night?"

He leaned over to kiss her cheek. "No, you can dance all you want."

"Fine. I've gotta have some fun tonight."

"You'll have plenty of fun later."

She licked her lips and leaned toward him. His body tingled and he lowered his head for her kiss. Her eyes shifted to his left and she leaned back. "Later."

His shoulders slumped when she turned away and hurried to join the line of people dancing. He looked to his left and saw his mom. She shook her head and walked away. Jared cursed and turned back to the dance floor. Kenyatta joined Tasha in line. Tasha slid back until she was in line behind Kenyatta. What was that about?

He looked back to where his mom had been standing. Malcolm marched toward him. Not in the mood to talk to his brother, he went in the opposite direction toward the door. His steps slowed when a large bald man dressed in all black entered. With a fierce scowl on his face, the man could easily pass for a club bouncer. Jared's face broke out into a grin and he quickened his steps. "Uncle Bruce. What are you doing here?"

The frown on his uncle's face immediately dissolved into a huge grin that showed off the one gold tooth in a line of otherwise perfect white teeth. "What's up, nephew? It's good to see you, young blood."

They clasped hands and embraced before stepping back and sizing each other up. His uncle's massive build was one of the reasons Jared had begun lifting weights in high school. But after watching his dad die of a heart attack, health and fitness had become more important that just being buff. His uncle was still a big man, but he was starting to get soft in the middle.

"Looks like you're staying out of the gym, Unc," Jared teased.

Bruce rubbed his rounding stomach. "Yeah, well, I still got the ladies all over me."

Jared laughed. "That's because you own a strip club."

Bruce grinned. "Doesn't matter why they're on me, as long as they're on me."

"So what are you doing here?"

"Why do you think? To wish my sister well."

Jared scowled. "You must be losing your mind and your muscle. She *was* your sister-in-law."

Bruce shrugged. "Family is family. I'll always be there for your mom. She knows that."

"Why, don't you know she's—"

Bruce held up his hand. "Look, I know you and your mom haven't been close since Mike died, but she deserves some happiness. Hell, I'm even happy it's with Randall. He fought hard for your mom before Mike got her."

Jared snorted. "Dad knew about Mom and Mr. Carter?"

Bruce laughed. "Knew about him, hell it was full on warfare to win your mom back in the day. Most of the guys on campus were trying to impress her, but only Randall and Mike had any real chance. I would say the old Patterson charm got her, but that wasn't what did it."

Jared shook his head. "Then what did, because as far as I can tell, Dad wasn't as lucky as he thought. Mom was cheating with Mr. Carter during their whole marriage."

Bruce's frown returned with full force. "Hold up, young blood. I don't know who's been telling you lies, but your mom only had eyes for your dad."

"Then why is everyone saying this was meant to be? Why aren't people surprised they're together?" Uncle Bruce was the only family member he trusted to tell him the truth.

"Jared, don't you know how Gladys and Mike got together?"

"They met in college."

"True, but why your mom chose him over Randall?"

"She didn't choose one over the other. She had her cake and ate it too."

Bruce's scowl was so fierce Jared understood why lesser men cowered when faced with it. "You're not going to talk about your mom like that to me. Your mom is the reason your dad survived college. Didn't you know your daddy was a junkie?"

The music became a dim thumping in the background, the only sound his blood rushing through his veins as he tried to absorb his uncle's words. He shook his head to clear it before responding. "What?"

Bruce put his hand on Jared's shoulder and pulled him to

the side of the door. He lowered his voice and Jared had to lean close to hear. "Mike was hooked on heroin. He said it made him smarter. We all tried to get him off that stuff, but Gladys was the only one who could. She locked herself with him in his apartment for weeks. Threw out all his shit and fought him like a man when he tried to leave. We tried to convince her to let us in to help, but she refused. When the smoke cleared your dad went to rehab, got cleaned up, and they were joined at the hip forever. Randall knew he was out of the picture then, but they did remain friends. Hell, everyone cemented around them to keep Mike clean."

Jared shook his head. "What?"

"You didn't know?"

"That my dad was a fucking junkie? Hell no." He rubbed his jaw. "It doesn't change what I saw."

"You mean when Robert kissed your mom before his heart attack?"

Jared froze. "You know about that?"

"I spoke to both of them after it happened. Mike had started using again. Randall came to tell her and, like a fool, kissed her. Mike saw it, but the only thing he did was ask Randall why he'd ratted on him before clutching his chest and falling. I know you saw it, your mom told me, but I thought you knew the whole story."

Jared looked away. There were too many emotions running through him to deal with before an audience. He patted Bruce on the shoulder. "Now I know. Excuse me."

He went around his uncle into the entryway and around the corner of the lobby where the lights were dimmer and it was quieter. He braced his hands on the wall and closed his eyes. His dad had been a junkie? His mind raced back to that last day. They'd gone fishing. His dad had been fidgety and distracted. Stress at work was what he'd said when Jared mentioned it. That was the only weird thing about that day. They'd caught fish, laughed, talked. Had his dad been craving a hit the entire time?

He hit the wall and cursed. Why hadn't anyone told him? His dad had been a deacon in the church, always telling him and Malcolm to do right and keep their noses clean. He'd spent the past fifteen years thinking his dad was perfect when he'd been a drug addict!

"Jared, Uncle Bruce said I needed to check on you."

Malcolm's footsteps were hesitant and he approached. Jared shook his head. "Why didn't you tell me about dad?"

Malcolm sighed. "You thought he was perfect, I didn't want to take that from you."

He kept his head down. "You don't keep something like that from me."

"We both know you were dad's favorite. I'm not upset about it, he loved me too, but let's face, it you were more like him than I was. You idolized him, I lost that when I found out he struggled with his addiction."

He looked up. "When did you find out?"

Malcolm leaned his back against the wall next to Jared. "High school. He caught me smoking a joint and told me his story. You should have seen him, man. It was difficult for him to even throw away the joint. It was hard on him, and it hurt to see him so weak. You wouldn't have wanted to see that."

"So you've been lying to me since high school?"

"I didn't lie."

"We can argue that later. When did he start using again?"

Malcolm rubbed his face and sighed. "I don't know. Mom called me in college to say Dad was having a hard time, but I didn't ask with what. I didn't want to know, but I suspected. There was heroin in his system when they did the autopsy."

"Hell no!" Jared pushed away from the wall. "I was with him all day. He didn't do anything when we were out."

"Were you with him every minute of that day?"

He opened his mouth to say yes but stopped. He remembered his dad rushing into the house when they'd gotten back. He'd stayed out and put up the fishing equipment. Could he have gone in to get a hit?

"Just as I thought," Malcolm said.

Frustrated, Jared rubbed his eyes. "This is some bullshit. I'm gonna grab Tasha and we're out of here."

Malcolm pushed away from the wall. "You can't keep running from difficult situations. That's why I didn't tell you in the first place."

"I don't run from situations."

"Yes, you do. Anytime a conversation is too tough or too serious you bail. You shake your head, say you don't have time for it, and haul ass out the door. Randall's right, it's time for you to grow the fuck up."

"You and Randall can kiss my ass."

Malcolm shook his head. "That's real mature. Face it, Jared, you're still a kid. You ran after Dad died instead of facing Mom. You ran from California when Cassandra started wanting more than a business relationship. And you lied to Tasha to get her here so you wouldn't have to face your family. The first two only hurt you, but this shit with Tasha is messed up."

"What the hell is that supposed to mean?"

Malcolm got in Jared's face. "You told her you loved her? Come on, Jared, I could see it in your face that day in my office—you wanted to make her fall for you. You were supposed to end it before that."

"No, you assumed I would," Jared said, pointing a finger in Malcolm's chest.

Malcolm scowled. "Tasha's a nice girl. I know you like running game on women, but this is low even for you."

Jared wasn't about to tell Malcolm he was in love with Tasha. It wasn't any of his damn business anyway. What they had was working, and until he was used to the idea of loving, and trusting her, no one needed to know what was going on. "You think I care what you think? She's here, isn't she? Tasha's happy and that's all you need to worry about."

"Is that why you told me you loved me? Because you wanted me here?" Tasha's voice hit him like a ton of bricks.

He closed his eyes and took a deep breath. He turned away from Malcolm to face her. "Tasha, don't listen to Malcolm."

She waved her hand as she approached him. Her face a mask of pain and confusion. "No, I think I should listen to him. I should have listened to him, my sister, Kenyatta, and everyone else who told me I was in over my head."

"It's not what you think."

"Isn't it? I break it off with you, told you why, and you still..." She broke off and held up her hand. "You know what, it doesn't matter."

"Tasha..."

Devin strolled up beside Tasha. "Malcolm, Jared, Kenyatta's looking for you. It's time to cut the cake." He looked from one face to the other and frowned. "What's going on?"

"Nothing," Tasha said, turning to Devin. "Can you give me a ride somewhere?"

"Where?" Jared asked.

She whipped around to glare at him. Her usually warm honey eyes were cold. "That's none of your damn business." She turned back to Devin. "Please. It'll only take a minute."

Devin looked from Tasha to Jared, who shook his head, then to Malcolm, who nodded. When he looked back at Tasha, he nodded. "I will."

She sighed. "Thank you."

Jared stepped up. "Wait a minute."

She pointed at him. "No, you wait a minute. I'm tired of this. I thought I knew what I was doing, but it was wrong. From the start, it was wrong. I shouldn't even be mad at you for doing what you do. That's why I picked you in the first place. But right now, I am mad and if I have to look at you any longer I'll say something I'll regret."

Tell her you love her, screamed his brain. He opened his mouth then closed it. Devin watched expectantly. Malcolm glowered as if he would choke him if he didn't say it. He couldn't say it with everyone standing there. He wouldn't beg in front of Devin and Malcolm. He would talk to Tasha when she wasn't so angry and they didn't have an audience.

He swallowed before forcing out the words, "Maybe you should go."

The pain that flashed in her eyes was like a knife in his chest. He would have expected hysterics or crying from any other woman. Her ability to be strong when things hit her hard was one of the things he loved about her. His hands flexed with the need to grab her and kiss her, but instead he stepped back.

Devin shook his head and glared at Jared. "Let's go, Tasha."

She nodded and turned. Jared bit the inside of his jaw to keep from calling her back. Devin gave him a scathing look before turning and following Tasha. It was a bad scene, but he would get her back. When they were alone, and he wasn't pressed by Malcolm and Devin to pour his heart out, he'd talk to her and get her back.

CHAPTER 27

"So where are we going?" Devin asked as they buckled their seatbelts in his black Ford F-150.

Tasha blinked back the tears that threatened to spill the moment Jared admitted he'd lied about loving her. She'd suspected it, even accused him of it, but stupidly let him convince her otherwise.

"My friend is at a party at the St. Regis hotel in Buckhead, can you take me there?"

He nodded. "Sure."

Tasha thanked him and pulled out her cell phone to call Shayla. She hadn't told her friend she was coming to Atlanta with Jared. It had been such a whirlwind decision she hadn't told anybody. It would be a miracle if Kenyatta didn't tell Angie as soon as she left the party.

Shayla answered after a few rings, the sounds of laughter and talking were in the background. "I can't believe you have the nerve to call me after avoiding my calls all day. You better not be wrapped up with Jared somewhere and coming up for air just to tell me you're not coming to my party. I could have figured that out myself."

Despite her crushed spirits, Tasha mustered a small laugh. "You're a fool. No, I'm calling to tell you I'll be there in about thirty minutes."

"Are you serious? It's after…ten. And *you* don't leave the house that late."

"Unusual circumstances."

"You came with him, didn't you? Is he coming too?"

"No."

"Oh." A slight pause. "Fine, come on, girl. You can tell me the story when you get here."

"Thanks, girl. I'll see you soon."

She hung up and looked out the window. "I can't believe he lied to me," she whispered.

"Neither can I."

She turned toward Devin who glanced at her out of the corner of his eye. "Why would he say…what he said?"

Devin shrugged. "That's a new low, even for Jared. But sometimes I don't think he understands himself."

Tasha rolled her eyes and turned away. "Spare me. I know he doesn't trust women, doesn't believe in love, and doesn't believe in marriage. This is my fault."

Devin didn't say anything and Tasha leaned her head against the seat rest. She closed her eyes and images of her time with Jared flashed in her mind. The way he looked at her, touched her, made love to her. It had all felt so right. They'd clicked, or at least she'd thought they had. But with the good images came the bad. He'd manipulated her to stay every time she'd tried to end it, starting in Charleston when she'd known he was too much for her to handle. She should have trusted her instincts then and walked away. Now she was broken hearted and…pregnant. She bit her lip to keep from sobbing. If Devin noticed, thankfully he didn't say anything.

Thirty minutes later the car stopped. She opened her eyes and stared at the front of the St. Regis hotel. She blinked several times as the valet attendant came over to open her door.

"Thank you, Devin," she said.

"I'll walk you in."

"There's no need for that."

"I know, but it's against my nature to drop you off at the door."

Tasha smiled. "Thanks."

He got out and told the attendant he'd be right back. They walked into the hotel and Shayla immediately ran up to Tasha. She looked flawless as usual in a sleeveless red dress that hugged her perfect figure and complemented her smooth brown skin.

"Girl, you look like someone stole your dog." She embraced her friend. "I told you it was time to break it off. I told you not to come here with him. But I also agreed you should sleep with him in the first place. Don't listen to me when it comes to men."

Tasha sighed and pulled away. "Amen to that."

Shayla sucked her teeth before looking over Tasha's shoulder and freezing. Her mouth fell open and she pulled at the top of her dress. Tasha turned to see what had stunned her friend. Devin wore a similar expression. His gaze ran over Shayla's figure from the top of her perfectly flat-ironed shoulder-length brown hair to her pedicured feet in black peep toe heels.

"Devin," Shayla gasped, her almond-shaped eyes wide.

Devin swallowed before answering. "Hello, Shayla."

Confused, Tasha looked between the two. She could light a match with the electricity firing between them. Shayla always had an effect on men, but she'd never seen Shayla reduced to staring.

Tasha pointed from one to the other. "You two know each other?"

Shayla cleared her throat and looked away from Devin. "Devin Jones," she said. Tasha raised her eyebrows and shrugged. Shayla shook her head and said, "Devin Jones from high school."

Tasha's eyes bulged and she looked back at Devin. "You're Shayla's Devin?"

"I'm not Shayla's Devin," he answered.

Shayla pointed at Devin. "You didn't recognize him?"

"I never met him. You two were at Helena High, I went to Airport, remember? He only dropped you off at my house once. You always kept *Your Devin* to yourself."

"I'm not her Devin. She was my teammate's girlfriend."

Shayla stiffened. "That's right. Remember, Tasha? Devin and I weren't cool after I started dating Tony."

Tasha frowned. "You didn't start dating Tony. That ass took advantage—"

Shayla cut her off with a wave of the hand. "It doesn't matter, that was years ago."

"Years ago," Devin agreed.

She didn't like how Shayla had breezed over what she was about to say. Tony was a jerk who'd taken advantage of Shayla, but she respected her friend's wish and left it alone.

Tasha turned to Devin. "Thanks for the ride."

He opened his mouth to respond when a man approached. He walked with a swagger and an air of arrogance in his blue eyes. He presented Tasha and Devin with a large fake smile, before turning to Shayla. "I was able to get away for a minute. We can have that talk now."

The look in his eye gave Tasha the impression he was interested in more than talking.

Shayla glanced briefly at Devin before pulling the man to the side. "Mark, my friend just got here and she's upset. I'll call you tomorrow."

Mark rubbed his chin, the light gleaming off the gold band on his left hand. He looked at Tasha quickly before turning back to Shayla. "I'm free tonight."

Shayla crossed her arms and stepped back. "Then we'll talk another time."

Mark smirked. "Fine." He ran a finger down her arm. "Tomorrow." Without so much as a word to Tasha or Devin, he turned and walked away.

Tasha didn't like him. "Shayla?"

Shayla held up her hand. "Don't even start. We'll talk about this after we talk about you." She looked at Devin. "I guess I still disappoint you, huh?"

Devin's eyes were sad as he shook his head. "It's not about disappointing me. You know what you're worth." Shayla stiffened and he sighed. "You look beautiful, Shayla," he said before turning away.

"Devin," Tasha called. He turned to look at her. "Please don't tell Jared where you brought me. I don't want to talk to him."

He nodded and walked out. After he left, Tasha turned narrowed eyes on Shayla. "What was that all about? And who was that man?"

Shayla crossed her arms. "Forget the man. I can't believe you brought Devin Jones here. Ever since Tony he's only found fault with me."

"Don't yell at me. I didn't know he was *Your Devin*. Maybe he wouldn't find fault if you'd tell him the truth about Tony."

Shayla scoffed. "Doesn't matter. That was years ago, and since I have no plans to move back to Helena, hopefully I'll never see him again." Tasha started to interrupt but Shayla shook her head. "No more talk about Devin Jones. I'll get my stuff and you can tell me about Jared Patterson." She turned to walk away.

"I think I'm pregnant," Tasha blurted out.

Shayla spun around so fast Tasha was surprised she didn't trip over her five inch heels. "No."

Tears burned the backs of her eyes but she wasn't going to cry. This was her mess and she had to deal with it. "Yes."

"No, no, no, Tasha. This shit isn't supposed to happen to you. This is the type of mess that happens to me," Shayla said walking back to her.

"Tell me about it," Tasha said.

Shayla laughed and Tasha joined in before they turned into sobs. Shayla pulled her into her arms. "Stop it. You don't cry over a man, remember?"

Tasha nodded and tried to stop the tears.

Shayla put her hands on her shoulders and held her away. "Now you said you think you're pregnant. Have you taken a test?"

"No," Tasha answered, wiping the tears from her face.

Shayla nodded. "Okay, I have one at my house."

"Why?"

Shayla shrugged. "You never know when you need one."

Tasha shook her head. "You're a mess."

"Tell me about it."

They laughed again and Shayla squeezed her shoulders. "It'll be okay."

"How am I going to tell my father?"

"Daddy, I'm pregnant."

Tasha rolled her eyes. "It's not that simple."

"I know. Preacher isn't going to be too happy about this, but what can he do? If you are, you are. Unless you don't want to be."

Tasha knew what Shayla implied and she shook her head. She knew of at least one abortion Shayla had had years ago, but had never asked her friend if she'd done it again. Tasha couldn't do it, no matter how hard it would be to have this child.

Shayla's lips rose in a small smile. "I didn't think you would. Come on. No need to stand in this lobby looking like two lost souls. Let's go to my house, take the test, and go from there, okay?"

Tasha closed her eyes and took a reassuring breath. "Okay."

"Good. Now let me get my stuff."

Tasha nodded as Shayla walked off. She closed her eyes and sent up a silent prayer that everything would work out. She didn't know how she'd face her father, but telling Jared scared her more. How could she face the man who lied about loving her that she was having his baby?

CHAPTER 28

Jared stood by the door of the banquet hall and checked his watch. An hour had passed since Devin and Tasha left.

He looked across the room at his mom and Uncle Bruce dancing. Pain and anger sliced through him. Why didn't they tell him about his dad? He'd replayed every encounter he'd had with his dad, trying to find signs of addiction. After Malcolm left for college his dad had been busier, working later, and was easily frustrated and distracted. He'd blamed it on his job, but it must have been more. Around that same time, his parents started spending less and less time together. It wasn't anything drastic; his mom started going to church and family functions by herself a lot more because of his dad's schedule. Had his dad been out getting a fix instead of working? Had his mom known the entire time what was going on?

He tapped his toe, checked his watch, and rubbed his jaw before looking out the door toward the entrance. Where in the hell was Devin? He wasn't concerned about getting Tasha back once he explained, but he needed to talk to her. He needed her soothing voice and soft touch to ease his anxiety. He needed to explain to her how his family's lies were tearing him apart.

He stopped his fidgeting and froze. She had to come back to their hotel room. Her clothes were there, and she needed a ride back to South Carolina. His shoulders relaxed and he breathed easier for the first time since she'd walked out the door.

Mildly comforted by these thoughts, he still jumped and hurried toward the entrance when he saw Devin approach.

Devin was shaking his head before Jared even spoke. "Don't ask me where I took her, she doesn't want you to know."

Jared scowled. "You can't be serious. Just tell me where she's at so I can go get her."

"Why? Do you love her?"

Jared tapped his foot and looked away. "Just tell me where she is."

Devin scoffed. "You can't admit it to me, can you? You'd rather keep up the appearance that you're some kind of player than admit you fell for her."

Jared waved dismissively. "You know what? Keep your secret. She has to come back to our room. I'll wait for her there."

He turned to walk out, but Devin stopped him. "She's with a friend and she doesn't have to come back to your room. Do you really think she's going to face seeing you again when you lied to her like that?"

The truth of Devin's statement twisted his gut. Tasha wouldn't leave a friend to come back and face him. He clenched his jaw; she would probably go back to South Carolina without talking to him first.

He gave Devin a hard stare. "She'll be back."

Devin shook his head. "I don't know. She seemed pretty hurt."

"She knows me."

Devin grinned. "So she knows you're an asshole?"

Jared glared at him. "Whatever." He looked around the room, but he didn't see Malcolm or his mom. "Tell Malcolm I'm leaving. I'll call him tomorrow."

He brushed past Devin and headed for the lobby. Anxiety fueled his urgency as he absently waved goodbye to people. His mind went over everything she'd said over the past few weeks. She must have mentioned a friend in Atlanta before.

He stopped abruptly. His mother stood at the glass doors leading out of the building. She stared at him, her eyes calm and assessing. "I knew you would sneak out without talking to me. Bruce told me he filled you in on what happened."

He opened his mouth, but no words came out. What was there too say? They hadn't talked in years, now a jumble of emotions bounced around within him fighting for release. The dominant one was hurt. Hurt no one trusted him enough to tell him the truth about his dad. He'd royally screwed up by not telling Tasha how he felt and letting her walk out of the door. He could use her hand in his, and her soft voice telling him things would be okay.

"Can we talk about this tomorrow?" He moved toward the door.

She didn't move out of his way. "We'll talk now."

"I need to go."

She scowled. "Where, to find that girl you brought here tonight?"

Jared stepped back. "That girl has a name. Tasha."

His mom waved her hand. "What does it matter, Jared? You only brought her here to bother me. I know the type of women you date, so I know she isn't worth you walking out on this discussion."

"You don't know what type of woman I date."

She pushed away from the door and reached for him. "That's because you haven't spoken to me in years."

He stepped back, avoiding her touch. "You should have told me about Dad."

She dropped her hand. "You didn't give me a chance. After it happened, you were so upset."

"I had a right to be upset." His voice was loud, and a few people in the lobby turned to face them. He lowered his voice. "My dad dropped dead from a heart attack after seeing my mom kissing another man. You should have told me."

His mom closed her eyes and crossed her arms. When she looked at Jared again her eyes glistened with tears. "Jared, you wouldn't even look at me in the hospital. You were so angry, if I would have tried to explain, you wouldn't have listened. Then you started college and ran to South Carolina, then Los Angeles."

"That's no excuse. You could have called…"

"For what? I've had to talk to you through Malcolm ever since."

"Then why didn't you tell Malcolm?"

"I'd always assumed you told him, and that he was too principled to say anything to me," she said. "Why didn't you say anything? You hated me so much. I would have expected you to want your brother to hate me as well."

Jared sighed and looked away. "I never hated you. I hated myself because I couldn't. Do you know how hard it is to still care for your mother, even when you think she's the reason your father died? I didn't want Malcolm to feel the same."

His mom gasped and reached out to touch him. Again he stepped back. Pain flashed in her eyes. Eyes the same color as his. She balled her outstretched hand into a fist and put it over her chest. "I'm glad to know you never hated me. Because I've always loved you, Jared."

He hadn't heard his mom say she loved him in years. A rush of emotion hit him, and he didn't know how to take it. He didn't deserve his mother's love. Not after the way he'd treated her. He didn't deserve Tasha's love, either. But he wanted both.

Jared rubbed his hand over his jaw and looked away from him mom. "Look, I've gotta go find Tasha. She's not like the others, she's…she's my rock."

He glanced at his mom who nodded. Saying no more, he brushed past her and left the building.

*

Jared arrived at his hotel in record time. He burst through the door of his room and called out Tasha's name. There was no answer, but still he checked the bedroom and bathroom. He pulled out his cell and called her number. It went straight to voice mail.

"Think, Jared, think," he murmured to himself. Where would she be? Who would she run to? He thought about the friends she'd mentioned over the past few weeks. He snapped his fingers—there was a friend in Atlanta. A female friend, but he couldn't remember her name. That had to be who she'd gone to.

He went into the bedroom and rummaged through her bag. He knew it was useless. No one carried address books anymore. Any contacts she had would be in her cell phone. She might have a card or contact information in her wallet, but that would be with her. He froze in the middle of pulling out her clothes and turned to look at his bag. Her wallet was with him.

He folded his hands in front of him and looked up. "Thank you." When they'd stopped for gas, she'd gotten out her wallet to buy some chips and he told her not to worry about it. She'd thrown her wallet in his bag on the backseat of the car instead of putting it back in her purse. Smiling, he pulled clothes out of his bag. He had to remove everything before finding it. He reached for it and stopped with he saw the silver tip of a condom wrapper sticking out of the panel in the bottom of his duffle bag.

His smile softened as he pulled it out. It had to be left over from the Charleston trip; he'd brought gold condoms to Atlanta. He'd thought they'd used all of them in Charleston. He sat on the edge of the bed and stared at the wall. Charleston seemed like it happened yesterday, but so much had changed. He never would have imagined he'd fall in love with Tasha. Or that he'd be racking his brain trying to find her when she left.

He rubbed the wrapper with his thumb. He'd have to use this one when they made up. Kind of a tribute to their beginning. He frowned. The wrapper wasn't smooth. Instead it was rough, irregular. He lifted it and took a better look. Tiny pin marks broke the surface. He flipped it over; the same thing was on the other side.

A vision of Tasha going through his bag in the middle of the night when they were in Charleston flashed through his mind. He'd believed her when she said she was looking for something to eat, and instead she'd been poking holes in his condoms!

Betrayal pierced his heart like an arrow. She'd played him. She'd been trying to trap him from the start. All of her talk about losing her virginity to find a good man had never sat right with him. He should have known she was up to something more. She was trying to get pregnant, trying to catch him. He stood and balled the spoiled condom in his fist.

Tasha, his Tasha, was no different from the rest of the women he'd dated. They always wanted something. He'd thought she really cared. He'd trusted her more than he'd trusted another woman in his life. And she'd betrayed him—hurt him—more than any woman ever had.

Dear God, please don't let her be pregnant, he prayed. Because if she was, she was in for a big surprise. He didn't want kids, and he'd be damned if he was going to pay for one conceived in deceit. He'd fight her in court for the rest of his life before paying for a child she tricked him into having.

CHAPTER 29

Sunlight cast a cheerful glow in the hotel lobby. Even though the rays were warm on her face, Tasha felt ice cold. Three pregnancy tests were in her purse, all positive. She'd brought them in case Jared didn't believe her. She'd prayed for strength all night. The strength to cope with telling a man who'd deceived her she was carrying his baby. The strength not to cry if he asked her to get rid of it. She'd thrown in a selfish prayer too. She'd prayed he'd take her in his arms, say he loved her, and ask her to marry him. It was a long shot, but that was the point of praying. Too ask God for the impossible.

"Do you want me to come with you?" Shayla reached over and wrapped her warm hand around Tasha's icy one.

Tasha shook her head stiffly. "I'll go alone."

Shayla's glossed lips twisted into a tight smile. "It won't be so bad. Just say, I'm pregnant, it's yours, and I'm keeping it."

"And if he says get rid of it?"

"Then tell him you'll see him in court. It takes two to make a baby."

Tasha closed her eyes and groaned. "I don't even want to go through that. This isn't supposed to happen to me. I'm not supposed to be a baby momma. I'm supposed to be a wife, then a mother."

Shayla shrugged. "Stuff happens. Life happens. You're not a bad person because of a mistake."

Tasha laughed bitterly. "Tell my dad that."

"First you have to tell the father."

Tasha nodded. "You're right." She took a deep breath and squeezed Shayla's hand. "Don't leave yet. Jared isn't as tough as he appears, so I think things will go well but…just in case."

Shayla pulled her in for a hug. "I'm here as long as you need me."

Tasha smiled and left her friend. The elevator ride had to be the fastest in history. Before she could even think of what to say, she was standing in front of their door. Taking another deep breath, she reached into her back pocket and pulled out the room key. Jared was sitting on the couch when she entered. He stared at her with cold and impassive eyes. Her bags were packed and sitting beside the door. Dread washed over her.

"Jared…last night…" She stopped speaking. He hadn't moved. He just continued to stare at her, hurt and anger in his eyes. She frowned. Why was he angry? *He* was the one who'd lied about loving her. He was the one who'd used her for his own gain. "Are you mad at me?"

He narrowed his eyes. "Why did you come back?"

There was a sharp pain in her chest, as if her heart were fracturing. "You didn't want me to come back?"

"Do you have something to tell me? Is that why you came back?"

She nodded. "I do, but first I want to know why you're so angry."

"Let me guess. You're pregnant." He spat out the words.

Another pain pierced her. "How did you know?"

He finally stood and marched over to her. He threw a condom that hit her chest and fell to the floor. Stunned, she looked from the condom to him. "Have you lost your mind?"

"I found your secret. I know you've been punching holes in my condoms. I know you've been trying to trick me into having a baby. I've told you over and over I don't want kids. I swear to God, Tasha, I don't want this kid. You did this, and I'll be damned if you're gonna make me pay for it."

She stood there, her mouth gaping as she tried to comprehend what he was saying. "You think I planned this? You think I want to have your baby? You don't care about anyone but yourself. I'd rather it be anyone's baby than yours."

His eyebrows formed an angry line as he scowled at her. "Are you sure it's even mine? Were you sleeping with the good doctor too?"

She staggered back. "You know I've only slept with you."

"I don't know anything, Tasha. I didn't know you were punching holes in my condoms!"

"I didn't punch holes in your condoms."

He scoffed and turned away. "Then who did? Tell me? What other woman has been in my stash?"

"How the hell am I supposed to know? If anyone was promiscuous in this relationship it was you."

He whipped around and pointed at her. "Don't call what we did a relationship. You were a booty call, that's it. Someone to keep me company at night. Nothing more."

The pain from the shattering of her heart was so great she gasped and clutched her hand to her chest. "So you did lie to me. You never did love me."

"Oh, I was fool enough to believe I was falling in love with you. I should have known better—you can't turn your side piece into your girl. I'm glad I found out what you were before…before I really got caught up."

"Jared, I'm having your baby. Doesn't that count for something?" she whispered.

His face hardened. "It doesn't count for anything when you tricked me. You know how I felt, how I still feel. This is your problem, not mine."

"I didn't trick you."

He picked up the condom and held it in front of her face. "Don't lie to me. Don't stand there looking as if I'm breaking your heart, when you've tap danced all over mine. But that's what you're good at, isn't it? You play the innocent role, you look wounded, you tell me you're getting caught up and I need to commit or you're leaving. Oh, you played me well. So damn well I actually believed you were different. I thought you cared. But you wanted something from me, just like all the rest. And you're not getting a damn thing from me. I don't want this baby, and I don't want you. Get out."

"Jared."

He pointed to the door. "Get out."

Tasha stared at Jared. She was too stunned to cry. She couldn't believe he would think she'd be capable of something so horrible. He couldn't have ever loved her, or truly known her. Not if he could believe she would trick him into having a baby. Her pain was so intense it numbed her. There was nothing left to say, nothing that would heal this hurt. Without a word, she picked up her bags and left the room.

CHAPTER 30

Tasha studied her reflection in the mirror. Her hair was pulled back into a sleek ponytail. Her makeup was simple, but flawless. There wasn't a spot on her white A-line dress. She'd opted for color with red shoes, hopefully, her dad wouldn't be too upset about that. She smiled, shook her head, frowned, and tried again. Wider this time. She laughed out loud. Shaking her head again, she laughed once more, louder and more forcefully. That was better. She turned to the side and smoothed her dress. Her hands hesitated over her midsection before she dropped them and turned back toward the mirror. She took a deep breath, pasted on the smile she liked and left her house.

She didn't feel the warmth of the summer sun. In the two weeks since Jared accused her of deliberately getting pregnant, she hadn't felt warm. She shivered slightly when a humid breeze brushed over her. Her smile faltered, until she saw her neighbor. She fixed her smile and waved, but hurried to the car to avoid being drawn into a conversation. When she got in the car, she turned the radio to an AM station and listened to a gardening segment on her way to her father's church. Music, of any kind, only made her colder.

She checked her smile in the rearview mirror before getting out. Various parishioners waved and called hello as she walked inside, but she didn't stop to talk. Her sister, also in white, was standing just inside the entrance with another usher. Tasha walked over and ignored the frown on Angie's face.

"Good morning," she said with forced cheer.

"You're late. You know Daddy wanted you here for Sunday school," Angie said. She handed a bulletin to the people who'd come in behind Tasha.

"Sorry, I overslept." She took the bulletins from Angie. "You go inside for the start of the service. I'll stand by the door today."

Angie turned to the other usher. "Sister Jones, go on in, I want to talk to Tasha."

Sister Jones nodded and entered the main fellowship hall. Angie narrowed her eyes at Tasha. "Tasha, what's going on with you? Ever since you went to Atlanta…"

"Angie, church is about to start. You'd better get inside, I'll watch the door." She turned away from Angie and greeted the rest of the stragglers. When her sister finally walked into the fellowship hall, she let her smile fall.

A few minutes later, the first strains of music began as service started. She didn't enter; instead, she stood outside of the double doors and took a few deep breaths. Angie wanted to know what had happened in Atlanta, but she was too ashamed to say. She didn't want to face the I-told-you-so look on Angie's face when she heard what Jared accused her of.

She turned to look through the windows of the doors leading into the sanctuary. The choir was singing. She spotted her brother-in-law signing in the back. Her parents, sitting in the pulpit, were scanning the crowd, probably looking for her. She stepped to the side so they wouldn't see her. They were all worried about her. Eventually she'd have to tell them what was going on. But for now she liked to pretend as if it had never happened. As if she weren't pregnant.

But she was, and it wasn't the child's fault. So she'd finally called her doctor and made an appointment for the following week.

The doors of the church opened again and Tasha pasted on her practiced smile before turning to greet the latest arrivals. Her smile was short lived. Jared stood there looking better than she'd ever seen him in a tan silk suit, white shirt, and pink striped tie. Warmth filled her chest as she drank in the sight of him. Pain accompanied the warmth when she remembered he'd rejected her and their baby. The tiniest glimmer of hope formed in her chest that he'd come to apologize. That he'd realized she would never do something so horrible.

He hadn't noticed her yet; he was looking down at the woman he'd come in with. The warmth in her chest immediately went icy. Numbness had been Tasha companion since he'd accused her of deceiving him, but white-hot fury bubbled inside of her as she watched him smile at another woman after treating her so callously. It took a second for it to register that he was with Monica, the same newcomer to the church who'd been trying to get together with Tasha for weeks.

"Monica," Tasha blurted out.

Monica flipped her long black hair over her shoulder—probably a weave—as she turned from Jared and grinned. "Good morning, Tasha."

Tasha didn't return her greeting. She looked at Jared who glared back at her. "What are you doing here?"

"I invited him," Monica said, still smiling. She looked between the two. "Don't tell me you know each other."

"I mentor at the Rec Commission. That's how we know each other," Jared said.

She gasped. "That's how we know each other? You mentor at the Rec Commission?"

Jared didn't answer. They stared at each other and Monica looked between the two. She finally moved forward and reached out her hand. "May I have a bulletin, please?"

Tasha looked from Jared back to Monica. Monica had a small frown on her face and glanced back at Jared before reaching out to touch Tasha's arm. "Are you okay? You look sick," she said in a stage whisper.

Tasha nodded. "Fine. I'm fine."

Monica smiled brightly. "Good." She turned back to Jared and held out her hand. "Come on, baby, the service has already started."

Jared's mouth lifted in the barest of smiles and he took her hand. The sight made Tasha sick. She dropped the remaining bulletins and ran down the hall to the ladies' room. She burst into the first stall and gagged up the toast she'd forced down for breakfast. Even though her stomach was empty, she continued to gag until a sob tore through her. She squeezed her eyes shut and pressed her hands over them. He wasn't worth crying over. He wasn't worth being sick over.

She slowly stood on shaky legs and exited the stall. She wet a paper towel and pressed it against her mouth and the rest of her face. *Get it together*, she thought. She'd made her bed, now she had to lie in it. She was going to get through this with her head held high. No matter what Jared thought, or her family said, she'd never show them or her child how much Jared's rejection hurt.

She took a deep breath and looked in the mirror. Her hair was still smooth, her makeup still in place. She practiced her smile over and over until it was perfect. No one would know she was dead inside.

CHAPTER 31

Jared hated himself for being concerned after Tasha ran down the hall. He shouldn't care if she was sick. Her welfare, or that of the baby, wasn't his problem. Yet he still dropped Monica's hand and followed Tasha.

"Go on in. I'll be back in a minute," he said to Monica over his shoulder and jogged down the hall.

He didn't look back to see if Monica heard him. He wasn't there because she'd invited him. He'd run into her in the parking lot and walked in with her. He was there to catch a glimpse of Tasha. Anxiety and self-loathing had filled him as he'd gotten out of the car in front of Tasha's church. He'd felt like a fool for coming to see her. He'd been overwhelmed with relief when he'd seen Monica in the parking lot. Going in with her hid what a broken-hearted fool he was for pining after a woman who wasn't worth it.

His anger over what Tasha had done hadn't diminished since Atlanta. Now he wanted answers. He wanted to know why she tricked him. Was it for money? Had she known her claims of him not being what she wanted would make him want to be a good man for her? He was used to women using him for their own selfish reasons, but no one had gone so far as to hurt him so completely. And he wouldn't be satisfied until he knew why she'd done it.

He paced outside of the bathroom. He begrudgingly admitted he was worried about the baby. He'd tried not to think about the baby, but knowing she was having his child pressed on him like a heavy weight. He wasn't father material and wouldn't fathom trying to take the baby from her, but he knew he wouldn't be able to keep himself from ensuring she took care of it. It was a part of him, and his family.

His pacing stopped when she came out of the bathroom. The anger, hurt, and disbelief that had been so clear on her face earlier was gone. She looked calm, with a smile on her face that would look genuine to anyone but him. He knew her well enough to tell it was fake. Or at least, he'd thought he knew her well enough.

She froze when she saw him, and to his amazement, her frozen smile widened. "Do you need help finding something in the church?" She sounded like a flight attendant.

"I wanted to..." He couldn't say he wanted to check on her. He wouldn't give her the satisfaction of knowing that despite how much he hated what she'd done, he still wanted her. "I wanted to tell you I'm leaving for L.A. next week. It's Cassandra's birthday."

"You made it abundantly clear that I mean nothing to you. Why are you telling me this?" Her voice was still pleasant and it irked the hell out of him.

"I'm telling you because you're carrying my baby."

"Which you don't want, so your whereabouts mean nothing to me."

He rolled his eyes and turned away from her. Instead of yelling in frustration, he took a calming breath and ran his hands over his face. When he turned back, he said, "So that's your game? Reverse psychology? Tell me all the reasons why I'm wrong so I'll try to do right?"

"I don't know what you're talking about."

She turned to walk away, but he blocked her path. Their eyes met and he almost lost himself in their honey colored depths. He took a deep breath and her clean scent assailed him. Damn, why did she have to smell so good? She broke eye contact first and stepped back; he mirrored her actions.

"Why did you do it, Tasha? Why did you trick me?"

Her smile left her face and she scowled at him. "I didn't trick you. I didn't plan on getting pregnant."

"Just admit it, and I'll move on. I'll give you what you need for the baby if you'll just admit you did this on purpose."

"I won't admit to anything. Why don't you ask Monica? Was she the one you were sleeping with when we were together?"

He scoffed. "I slept with Monica before I slept with you." She turned away and put her face in her hands. "Don't lay blame somewhere else. I saw you going through my bag in Charleston."

She spun to face him. "I didn't go through your bag to punch holes in the damn condoms, I was looking for something to eat."

He clenched his fists. "Dammit, Tasha, stop lying to me. Just tell me why you did it. Did you think I'd marry you?"

She held up one hand and put the other on her forehead. "Let's stop. This is pointless. You are determined to believe the worst about me, and I can't…deal…with knowing how easily I fell for you. I'm having this baby, and I don't need anything from you. My life will be just fine once you're out of it." She lowered her hand and placed the fake, frozen smile back on her face. "I hope you do well in L.A. Goodbye, Jared."

He reached out as she walked away, then closed his hand and pulled it back. There was nothing left to say. She denied it so sincerely he almost believed her. He *wanted* to believe her. The Tasha he thought he knew wouldn't have deceived him, but he'd seen the evidence himself. He didn't know Tasha at all.

He walked back toward the doors leading into the fellowship hall. Tasha was standing inside. When he entered, she passed him a bulletin and fan. She smiled as if he was any other late arriving parishioner, but her eyes didn't meet his.

Monica waved at him from one of the back pews, and with an inward sigh, he walked over to join her.

CHAPTER 32

Tasha didn't hear a word of her father's sermon. She spent the entire service staring at the cross above the pulpit. The struggle to ignore Jared seemed physical. It was as if she could feel him in the same room, breathing the same air and hearing the same things. A few times during the service, her skin would tighten and tingle, and she knew he was looking at her. During those times, she read the words on the cross over and over, to avoid meeting his gaze.

She wouldn't talk to him as long as he accused her of deliberately getting pregnant. She'd always wanted to have kids, but if given a choice she wouldn't have had his child. Or at least, the child of the Jared she knew now. She'd been afraid, but she'd admit hopeful, when she'd first learned of her pregnancy. But Jared's accusations killed all of that hope, and turned the light happiness she'd had in her heart into a cold, dead weight in her chest.

The final chords of the benediction played and Tasha gave up her cross gazing vigil to prepare for everyone's departure. Her gaze traveled to Jared and an electric shock went through her when their eyes met. She quickly looked away and smiled as she watched her dad and his deacons descend from the pulpit to walk down the aisle. She stepped to the side to give her dad room at the door.

"Are you okay, Tasha?" her dad asked. "You looked as if you were daydreaming through my sermon."

Tasha patted her dad on his shoulder. "I'm fine, Daddy. You did a great job."

He didn't look as if he believed her, but couldn't say more as church members began to exit. Her dad shook everyone's hand on the way out and Tasha stood beside him, smiling and nodding. She was about to leave her dad's side to join her mom and sister and the front of the church when Kevis approached.

Her eyes widened when her dad shook his hand and turned to smile broadly at Tasha. "Tasha, I'm sure you're glad to see our newest visitor. I'd hoped you would have gotten here earlier to sit with him. He came to bible study earlier just to see you, although I hope he enjoyed the lesson and my sermon."

Kevis smiled at her dad. "I did, sir." He turned to smile at her. "Good morning, Tasha. You look wonderful."

Her dad beamed. "You two go on and talk." He ushered Kevis around him toward Tasha then turned to the next people exiting.

She took Kevis's hand and pulled him down the aisle away from her dad and the exiting congregation. Jared and Monica were shaking hands with her father now. Jared smiled cordially to her dad, before quickly moving on. He glared at her over his shoulder as he walked through the door.

She ignored the pain of that look and instead gave Kevis her practiced smile. "What are you doing here?"

"It's been two weeks since our date, and not a word out of you. I've played basketball at the Rec Commission almost every night, and I haven't seen you there. I remembered you saying your father preached here, so I thought I'd take a chance." He raised his eyebrows and shrugged. "I hope my persistence is wanted. I thought we had a great time."

Tasha nodded, but looked toward the front of the church. Her mom and sister were watching her and Kevis with unconcealed interest. "I did have a great time. I've just had some things come up. It's kept me busy."

"Is that your nice way of saying you're not interested?"

She shook her head, but still avoided his eyes. "No, I was interested. I am interested. I just don't know if the time is right. Or if you'll stay interested."

He gently took her chin in his hand and turned her to face him. "I was interested the first time I saw you. Nothing has changed."

She sighed and really smiled for the first time in weeks. "You say that now."

"And I'll continue to say that. I meant what I said on our date. I'm not into playing games, I'm looking for something real."

Tasha reached up and pulled his hand from her face. She didn't let go, but held his hand in hers. "Why couldn't I have met you two months ago?"

He frowned, but her dad walked up before he could question her. "Tasha, why don't you invite Kevis to dinner?"

Tasha looked between her dad and Kevis. "I didn't know you were so close."

Her dad shook his head. "Just met him today." He grinned at Tasha. "I guessed you were dating someone, I'm glad you finally decided to introduce him to the family."

"Daddy…"

"It's okay, Tasha," Kevis cut in. "I would love to join your family for dinner."

Tasha sighed. It would be easier to get this over with than try to explain to her dad she and Kevis had only had one date. A part of her realized by doing this, her parents may assume Kevis was the father of her child. She had no intentions of telling them who the real dad was. Angie would know, but she wouldn't tarnish her parent's good thoughts about Malcolm by admitting what an ass his brother was. But, she'd be sure to clear Kevis's name.

Her dad's eyes shined with pride. "Good. Good. Tasha, why don't you and Kevis go on to our house? Angie and Jonathan will be there shortly with the girls. Your mother and I have to talk to Georgia Brown. She's got a…situation she wants to discuss with us."

Tasha frowned. "Is she okay?"

Her dad nodded. "She's fine. We'll talk about it later." He turned to Kevis. "I look forward to dinner with you, son. Tasha is our baby girl, so I want to make sure you're taking good care of her."

"My plans are to take good care of her," Kevis said, smiling at Tasha.

Her dad laughed. "I like him already." He patted Kevis on the shoulder and walked away.

Tasha raised an eyebrow. "What on earth did you do to win him over so quickly? My dad usually gives the men I date the third degree."

Kevis chuckled. "Nothing crazy, I swear. I just introduced myself, told him that we'd been out, and that I really liked his daughter. Oh, and I might have mentioned that I was a doctor."

She laughed. It felt good to really laugh. She hadn't thought she'd laugh again. "You might have?"

"Hey, my goal was to impress. Father *and* daughter." His full lips curled into a seductive smile.

There were probably many women who'd thrill over that smile, but it didn't affect her in the least. The slight attraction she'd felt for him before was gone. Jared's accusations had killed more than her happiness and hope; it had killed her faith in men.

She shook her head to rid herself of that thought and took Kevis's hand. "You have impressed me. Come on, I'll introduce you to my sister and you can follow us to my parents' house."

They met up with Angie and Jonathan at the front of the church. Angie grinned at Tasha when Kevis introduced himself as Dr. Kevis Flynn. Apparently dropping the doctor bomb impressed sisters as well. Kevis stayed with them as they gathered up Angie's girls and headed to her parents' house.

Thirty minutes later, Angie and Tasha began prepping for dinner. Her mom already had a pot roast ready so they busied themselves with making sides. Jonathan and Kevis got along easily as they talked about sports, but when Kevis mentioned that he'd volunteered on the campaign for a local democrat who'd run for county council, the same underdog that Jonathan had supported, they quickly got into a discussion about the upcoming election year.

Tasha and Angie came out of the kitchen every once in a while to check on the men. When she brought Kevis some tea, he took her hand and thanked her before turning back to his conversation with Jonathan. Angie didn't ask Tasha again what was wrong, as she smiled happily between her and Kevis.

An hour after they arrived at her parents' home, Tasha realized she was enjoying herself. It was the life she'd wanted, the life she would have had, if she hadn't fallen for Jared and gotten pregnant. When Angie's girls came in and insisted their dad participate in a tea party, Kevis didn't hesitate to join.

Tasha laughed as her oldest niece took Kevis by the hand and dragged him to the tea set they'd put up in the playroom. He grinned and shrugged as he passed her, then pulled back to place a quick kiss on her cheek.

"I couldn't help it, you look so beautiful," he said before following her niece down the hall.

Dammit, Jared, dammit! she thought. *Why did I have to fall in love with you? Why don't you want me, or our child? I would have been happy with this life. I wanted this life, now I don't. I want you.*

But she didn't have Jared and never would. He thought she'd gotten pregnant on purpose. He didn't want her or the baby, and only offered to help if she admitted she was wrong. It wouldn't be fair to Kevis to continue to act as if they could be together. In a few months, he and the rest of the world would know what had happened.

Tears filled her eyes and she rushed back into the kitchen, her hands resting over her abdomen. Angie was beating mashed potatoes. She turned when Tasha walked in and the smile on her face withered away.

"What's wrong?"

Tasha went around Angie and took a dishtowel out of the cabinet. She dabbed her eyes and tried to smile. "Nothing, I'm—"

"If you say you're fine one more time I'll choke you." Angie marched over to Tasha and took her shoulders in her hands. "I should have known it was wishful thinking to see you and Kevis together. Kenyatta told me something happened in Atlanta, but you and Jared won't talk about it. Tell me. I'm your sister. I love you."

Tasha looked at Angie. The concern in her sister's eyes was comforting. "Angie, I messed up."

Angie frowned. "How?"

"I'm…"

"Hey, girls." Their mother breezed into the kitchen with a huge smile on her face. "Is dinner almost ready? Your father is starving. That was all he talked about on the way home. Eating dinner, and Georgia Brown."

Tasha turned away from Angie. She picked up a spoon and stirred the mashed potatoes. Her mom began looking in the pots on the stove, oblivious to the tension in the room.

Tasha could feel Angie's gaze on her back, but didn't turn around. She was grateful when her sister answered their mom.

"Everything is ready, Mom. We just need to set the table."

"Good, good. You know, I'm so glad you two are my girls."

"Oh, really, Mom? Why?" Tasha asked. She didn't turn around, but if she didn't contribute to the conversation, her mom would ask what was wrong.

Her mom stirred the gravy on the stove. She nodded, satisfied, before answering. "It's that Georgia. She's gone and got into trouble."

"What kind of trouble?" Angie asked. She moved to stand beside Tasha, who continued stirring the potatoes.

"I know it's the new millennium, and things aren't the way they used to be," their mom said, "but I still don't like the way people accept women getting pregnant outside of marriage." Tasha's hand slowed. "She doesn't even know who the father is. Apparently she was seeing two guys at once. It's awful, when you think about it. Sleeping with two guys without protection. Anyway, neither of them want her or the baby. She came to me and your dad for advice."

Tasha stopped stirring, but didn't face her mom. "What did you tell her?"

"To give it up for adoption. What else would we tell her? That baby would be better off with a mother and a father, instead of growing up with a mother who doesn't have the good sense to know not to get pregnant by a man who doesn't want her."

Tasha gasped. From the corner of her eye, she saw Angie turn to look at her. She turned to face her sister. Angie's eyes were full of dread as she shook her head.

"Is that what you'd tell me, Mom? To give up my baby?" Tasha said, still looking at Angie.

Angie shook her head again. "No, Tasha."

Their mom looked between the two. "Don't be silly. Your dad and I both know you wouldn't do something so stupid." Her mom giggled. "If things work out, you'll marry that doctor in the other room and give us some legitimate grandchildren."

Tasha whipped around to face her mom. She held the spoon she'd used to stir the potatoes in front of her like a knife. "But what if I was that stupid? Would you want me to give up your grandchild?"

Her mom scowled. "Tasha, stop. You don't speak those things into existence."

Her dad came into the kitchen. He walked over to the crockpot to look at the pot roast inside. "Is it time to eat?" When no one answered, he looked around and took in the scene. "What's going on?"

Her mom shook her head. "I was telling the girls about the situation with Georgia, and apparently Tasha doesn't like our advice."

Her dad frowned at her. "What's wrong with our advice? She and the baby will be better off if she gives it to a loving home."

Her mom snorted. "Tasha was asking if we'd give the same advice to her."

Her dad laughed. "Really, Tasha. I only know of one immaculate conception, and until you get married, I don't think we'll be saying your name and baby in the same sentence." He turned back to the crockpot, dismissing the subject.

Rage, white and hot, flowed through Tasha. No one wanted her child. Not Jared, or her parents. It wasn't her baby's fault she'd made a mistake. A few months ago, she would have agreed with her parents' advice. But now that she was a soon to be single mother, it wasn't so easy to just give up the child she'd created.

She lowered her hand and placed it over her midsection. Angie gasped. Her dad turned around and looked at the two of them.

Tasha raised her head and met her dad's eye. "It wasn't immaculate conception. I had sex with a man who made no secret that he never wanted to marry me. I thought I knew what I was doing, but apparently I didn't."

Her mom reached for her dad, who glowered at Tasha. "What are you saying, girl?"

Tasha took a deep breath. "I'm pregnant, Daddy."

Her mom cried out and her dad's face fell. "This isn't funny," he said in a hard voice.

"Tell me about it," Tasha said. "He doesn't want me or the baby. He thinks I did this on purpose, but I didn't. I can't change what happened, but I can do what I think is right for the future. I'm having this baby."

"Baby?"

Tasha turned to Kevis standing in the door of the kitchen. He looked as if he'd just seen a ghost. She nodded. "I'm sorry, Kevis. I should have told you that I...I'm pregnant."

He frowned. "But I thought you were a virgin."

"What?"

He shook his head. "Never mind."

She quickly put the pieces together. "Charles told you I was a virgin. Is that why you asked me out?"

He sighed before meeting her eyes. "I told you I don't play games, so there's no need to lie. Yes, when Charles told me you were saving yourself for marriage, I was curious. When I met you, I wanted to go out with you regardless of what Charles said. But I won't play second to another man." He looked at Tasha's dad. "It was nice meeting you all, but I think it's time for me to go."

Tasha glared at him. "You were only interested in me because I was a virgin?"

He shook his head. "And you used me to make your jock jealous. Goodbye, Tasha." He left the kitchen and a few seconds later the front door closed.

"Tasha, tell me this is a joke. Tell me you didn't really go and get yourself in trouble," her dad said.

Tasha swallowed her surprise over Kevis's confession and faced her dad. "I can't tell you that, Daddy. I swear to God I wish I could, but I can't."

He slammed his fist on the counter, making their mother jump. "How could you do this? I thought you had more sense. You and Angie were my pride and joy. I bragged to everyone about my daughters and how they were waiting for their husbands."

"That's your fault, Daddy, not mine. I never said—"

"Yes, you did!" he cut in. His face was balled up in anger and he pointed at her. "You promised your mother and me you'd wait. You said you'd keep yourself pure. Instead, you bring disgrace down on you and me."

"I didn't plan for this to happen."

"What did you think would happen? Sinning with some man who doesn't want to marry you?" He slapped his hand on the counter again and she flinched. "Good Lord, Tasha, you're about to bring a bastard into my house."

Angie stepped up. "Daddy, don't say that."

215

Her dad looked at Angie. "Why not? It's the truth. She's having a bastard, by some bastard that doesn't want her or the baby. And now she's expecting me and your mother to step in and help her. No, I don't want anything to do with it."

"I don't need anything from you," Tasha said. "I'll raise this child on my own."

Her dad waved a hand and walked out of the kitchen. Tasha ran behind him. He went up the stairs and Tasha yelled after him. "I don't need anyone's help! I'll do this on my own!" The door to her parents' room slammed.

The sound was the final blow to her heart. She bit back a sob as she stared up the stairs, waiting for her dad to come back, knowing he wouldn't. When she turned around her mom and sister stood in the door of the kitchen watching. Her mom looked at her with disappointment in her eyes. Angie's eyes were filled with pity and sadness. Unable to take it, Tasha grabbed her purse by the door and fled.

CHAPTER 33

Jared hopped in his car and sped up I-20 east toward Helena. The morning sun was quickly burning off the fog, the only reminder of the previous night's rain. The traffic was light on the interstate and he made good time. He'd skipped his morning workout—something he hadn't done without reason in weeks—in his haste. When he pulled up in front of the small brick office building he breathed a sigh of relief. Devin's Ford F-150 was parked in the side lot.

It was too early for the front door to be opened, so he walked around to the building's side entrance. A nurse was slowly getting out of her car as he rounded the corner. He gave her his best heart-breaker smile. "I'm here to see Dr. Jones."

The nurse didn't smile back. She looked at her watch. "Sir, it's seven. Our office doesn't open until eight."

Jared kept smiling as he walked over to help her out of the car. "I realize that, but I'm a friend of his and I really need to see him."

She frowned at him, shook off the hand he had on her arm, and walked to the side entrance. "Like I haven't heard that before."

Jared rushed up behind her. "Just tell him Jared Patterson is out here." When she rolled her eyes he reached out and took her hand. She glared and he immediately dropped his hands. "Please."

"Mmmhmm," she said and disappeared behind the solid brown door.

Jared tapped his foot and checked his watch. He wanted to catch Devin before he was bogged down with his patients. Plus, he had a plane to catch. He checked his watch again—only two minutes had passed, but it felt like two hours.

He turned toward the door and raised his hand to knock when it opened. Devin stepped back when he saw Jared's raised fist. "I know you didn't come all the way up here just to hit me."

Jared dropped his fist. "Nah, man, I was about to knock."

Devin stepped out and eyed Jared curiously. "What's going on? Malcolm and I have been trying to reach you."

Jared ran a hand over his face. "I know. He even came by the house last night. I pretended I wasn't there."

Devin crossed his arms. "You want to tell me why?"

"Because I didn't want to see him."

"I know you have a tendency to avoid difficult situations, but there's no need to do that with Malcolm. He's your brother."

Jared shook his head. "And he's a choir boy. I didn't want to listen to him preach."

"Preach about what? How you treated Tasha? Because if that's the case you'll hear it from me instead."

"You two need to preach to Tasha about how she treated me."

"Jared, that girl loved you."

"Yeah, she loved me enough to sneak and get pregnant." The words didn't feel right. But what else could he say? He'd seen the evidence.

Devin unfolded his arms and put them on his hips. "Tasha's pregnant?"

Jared rubbed his jaw and began to pace. "Yes. She told me in Atlanta."

Devin reached out to grab Jared's arm. "And you kicked her out after she told you that?" He glared at Jared.

Jared pulled away. "You don't understand. I found a condom in my bag with holes in it. She was poking holes in my condoms, Devin." He shrugged. "She tricked me."

Devin frowned. "Tasha poked holes in your condoms? You've got to be mistaken."

Jared shook his head. "I don't want to believe it. I swear I don't, but what other explanation is there? I caught her going through my bag in Charleston. It was one of the same condoms we'd had down there. She even told me how much she wanted to get married and have kids. I just didn't think she would do that."

"Did she confess?"

"No. She says she didn't do it."

"Maybe she didn't."

"I wasn't sleeping with anyone else when we were together. Who else had access?"

Devin held up his hands. "I don't know, but she doesn't seem the type."

"I didn't think Tasha would do something so low either." Jared sighed and leaned against the nurse's car. "You were right in Atlanta. I did love her. Shit, sometimes I feel like I still love her. But I can't be with her knowing she did that to me."

If Devin was surprised he didn't show it. "Jared, she's having your baby. Regardless of the circumstances, you've got to make things work."

"I can't. I'm leaving for L.A. today."

Devin scowled. "You're leaving? What about Tasha?"

His stomach clenched. "Look, she chose to get pregnant without telling me. I don't owe her anything."

Devin stalked over to Jared. "I don't condone what she did, but you can't just up and forget your child like that."

"I know, but I need some time...away from her. When I'm around her, I forget how messed up she treated me. I can't deal with that."

"So you're gonna run. Just like you always do."

Jared stood. "Look, the plan to go to L.A. came long before Tasha got pregnant. It's Cassandra's birthday, I go every year."

Devin looked skeptical. "When are you coming back?"

Jared shrugged. "I don't know, Malcolm's wedding."

Devin pointed his finger. "That's September."

"I know."

Devin raised another finger. "It's June. You're going to forget the woman who's having your baby for the entire summer?"

Jared sighed. "That's why I'm here. I want you...no, I *need* you to check in on Tasha for me. Make sure she and the baby are okay. If she needs anything let me know. I'll get it."

Devin's brown furled. "Why aren't you telling her this?"

Jared balled his fists. "Because I can't look at her right now." He took a deep breath. "As much as I want to turn my back on her and the baby, I can't. I wouldn't make a good father on my own, and I don't have to be in their lives to take care of them."

"Just like you weren't in your mother's life, but took care of her," Devin said.

"Yeah, something like that." Jared looked at his watch. "I've got a flight to catch."

"Are you going to tell Malcolm about the baby?"

Jared's lips rose in a twisted sad smile. "I'll call him from L.A. If I told him in person, he'd try to kill me."

Devin drew his lips in. "You're probably right. Look, man, don't stay out there that long. I guess I can understand your need to get away after that kind of betrayal, but come back and work things out with Tasha. You two are having a kid together."

"I'll see what I can do." Jared reached out his hand. Devin looked at him for a second before taking it. "Thanks, Devin. Just keep an eye out on her."

"How am I supposed to do that from Helena?"

Jared smiled. "Kenyatta will tell Malcolm everything, and he'll come running to you complaining about how pissed he is at me. Don't you know that's why you're our friend? You keep us sane."

Devin grimaced. "Well who's going to keep me sane?"

Jared laughed. "You got it all together, man."

Devin joined in but the smile didn't reach his eyes. "I do, I guess."

Jared turned to go back to his car, but paused. "Oh, and keep an eye on that doctor Kevis whatever. I don't want him sniffing around trying to claim my baby."

Devin's brows rose. "Is he still trying to see Tasha?"

220

"He was at her dad's church this weekend, and they looked all chummy."

"Why do you care, if you don't want her?"

"I never said I didn't want her. I just don't want to want her," Jared said. He turned and got in his car.

He checked the clock on his dashboard. It was seven twenty. His plane didn't leave until nine. He pulled out of the parking lot and drove through the small town toward the interstate. He didn't need to go back home—his bags were in the car and anything else he might need his assistant could send later. But he wasn't in the mood to sit around the airport for hours. Columbia airport was nowhere near as busy as Atlanta or Charlotte, so arriving early wasn't a necessity. He wouldn't give in to the urge for what he wanted to do. He'd done that on Sunday, and that had blown up in his face.

His mind ran over the conversation he'd had with Tasha on Sunday. She was adamant she hadn't gotten pregnant on purpose, and he wanted to believe her. He wanted to believe her so badly he was almost willing to say to hell with it and try to get back what they'd had. Or, what they'd started to have. He couldn't hate her. He hadn't lied when he told Devin the love wouldn't go away. She'd buried herself deep inside of him in a place that no other woman had ever accessed. Because of that, he didn't trust himself around her. Seeing her get sick on Sunday was like a knife in his chest. He wanted to take care of her the same way he'd done when she'd had the allergic reaction. Watching her stand for the rest of the church service had annoyed him more than he cared to admit. She should have been sitting down, not wearing herself out.

He gripped the steering wheel and cursed in frustration. But he couldn't ignore what he'd seen. His mistrust in women went too far back, it was so much a part of him it overruled his need to have her in his life. Even though he now knew the misunderstanding behind his father's death, it didn't change the fact that he'd spent the last fifteen years believing women were untrustworthy. One revelation couldn't take away years of having women pursue him for money, sex, or fame. He didn't want to see her and he didn't want to talk to her. Asking Devin to let him know if she needed anything was better than most men would do in this situation.

Yet his hand still grabbed his cell phone resting in the cup holder and pressed the preset number for the Rec Commission. His immediate need to make sure she was okay before he left town outweighed his desire to forget her.

Feeling sick with himself for calling after admitting to Devin he couldn't handle seeing her, he started to hang up but the receptionist answered on the second ring.

He cleared his throat. "Is Tasha Smith in?"

"No, she called in sick today. Is there anything I can help you with?"

Jared squeezed the phone. "No thank you. I'll try later." He tossed the phone in the passenger seat. He'd reached the outer edges of town and increased his speed as he approached the interstate. Ignoring the voice in his head calling him a fool for caring, and the knowledge that going to her took him on the opposite side of town from the airport, Jared drove toward Tasha's home.

CHAPTER 34

Tasha walked out of her doctor's office in a daze. It was confirmed by a professional. She was pregnant with Jared's child. She barely noticed her surroundings as she got on the elevator and pressed the button. It wasn't as if she hadn't known what the doctor confirmed, but before coming she could almost ignore it. She could say to herself the tests she'd had were faulty or she'd misread the result. But when her doctor came back and said "Congratulations" there was no way to ignore that.

The surprise on her doctor's face was almost comical. To have a patient go from being a virgin at their January visit to pregnant in June must be unusual. Tasha liked Dr. Robinson, and usually found it easy to open up to her about anything regarding her health, but when she'd hinted about the father, she'd clammed up. She knew Angie, Kenyatta, and Malcolm would guess who the father was, but the truth wouldn't come from her lips. If Jared didn't want her, then she didn't want to even mention his name.

"Excuse me, miss. Isn't this your floor?"

Tasha blinked several times and turned to the man in the elevator with her. He had a frown on his face and was holding the door open.

"Thank you, it is," she said and got off the elevator. She looked down the hall toward the parking garage, before turning in the opposite direction and entering the walkway that crossed Taylor Street and connected her doctor's office and Baptist Medical Center. She walked onto the walkway and stared at the people on the street below. She didn't want to go home. There was too much stuff there to remind her of her stupidity. Her bookshelf filled with romance novels and romantic comedy DVDs. All of them were going to Goodwill. They were full of lies. Life didn't work like that; life wasn't full of happy endings and romantic men who loved you forever. Life was full of men who didn't trust women and fathers who abandoned daughters in their time of need. The box under her bed with her life goals, including the plans for her future wedding, would go in the trash. That plan had been shot to hell the minute she'd asked Jared to take her virginity.

How stupid and naïve she'd been. The main reason she'd kept her distance from Jared after meeting him years ago was because she knew his reputation. She'd heard the gossip about him, followed some of it actually. She was fully aware women threw themselves at him. It was foolish to have thought she would be immune to what other women craved. She could have moved on if he'd treated their situation like any of his other affairs. But she'd asked him not to treat her that way. She opened her heart and he'd crashed in, setting himself so fully inside of her that even when she'd known it was time to move on she hadn't.

She pressed her head against the glass of the crosswalk and sighed. Her eyelids fluttered down as she remembered the way they were. How he'd talked to her about his problems. The way he'd held her on the beach in Charleston. How much fun they had watching basketball together. How he'd come to her after her date with Kevis and said he loved her. Her heart lurched painfully and she squeezed her eyes tighter. It was all a lie. He'd admitted it in Atlanta. In the end he had treated her like the rest of the women in his life, and that hurt as much as him accusing her of planning this pregnancy to trap him.

"The time for pity parties is over," she whispered. Taking a deep breath, Tasha pushed away from the glass and stared at her reflection. She may have been stupid, foolish, and naïve before, but she couldn't afford to be now. She had to be smart, strong, and capable for the child she carried.

"Tasha?"

She froze, before whipping around and facing Kevis. He was in scrubs, carrying a cup of coffee in his hands. When she didn't speak, he came closer.

"Are you okay?"

She blinked and nodded stiffly. "I'm fine."

He looked around. "Where's your jock?"

Tasha glared at him. "That's none of your business."

He scoffed. "He's no longer in the picture is he?"

Anger snapped up her spine. "What does it matter to you? It's not as if you're much better. You only asked me out because you thought I was a virgin."

"I was curious about you because of that. What man wouldn't be, but I asked you out because I was attracted to you. I showed up at your dad's church because I thought there was something between us."

She crossed her arms. "Well, you were wrong."

"I wasn't wrong. I just didn't realize the thing between us was another man."

She shook her head. "Forget this."

When she tried to walk away, he sighed and placed a hand on her elbow. "I'm sorry I was out of line."

She snatched her arm away and crossed them. "Yes, you are."

He looked down, shuffled his feet, then met her eye. "Just tell me if he's still in the picture."

"Why?"

"Because, if he's not…I'd like us to try and be friends."

Holy crap. Her palms became sweaty and her heartbeat picked up. A solution. She wouldn't be a ruined woman. She shook her head to rid herself of the thought. Kevis was not a solution. "You can't be serious."

He nodded. "I'm not saying let's start dating or anything, I'd just like us to be friends. I like you Tasha, and I don't want us to part on bad terms." He held out his hand. "Friends."

She stared at his hand before finally taking it. "Associates."

He smiled. "Whatever you want to call it." He lifted an eyebrow. "We would have been good, huh?"

Her lips curved into a reluctant smile. "We might have been."

"Fair enough." He squeezed her hand. "Promise you'll take care of yourself."

She nodded. "I will."

He dropped her hand. "Good."

She turned back toward the parking garage and her car and he crossed the walkway into the hospital. Sure they'd said they would be friends, but would they really. She wasn't sure if she'd ever be able to trust Kevis, and the look in his eyes told her he'd been hurt by her pregnancy. As much as she wanted to regret sleeping with Jared, she wouldn't have this child if she'd never had, and despite the circumstances behind its conception, she wanted this baby. She also wanted Jared, now more than ever. Which was stupid.

On the way home she stopped at Dollar General and bought four storage containers for the books, magazines, and everything else she needed to clear out of her house. Angie called her when she was in the store, but she didn't answer her phone. She hadn't talked to Angie since the disaster that should have been Sunday dinner. From her sister's messages, she'd gathered her parents were still upset, but her mom was begging her dad to apologize. It was a small comfort to know her mom was taking her side in this. But she couldn't face her family until she got her feelings straightened out.

She turned the corner onto her street and gasped. Jared's silver sports car sat in her driveway. The very small amount of fortification she'd built since leaving the doctor's office nearly shattered. She pulled in beside his car and stared at him sitting on her porch step.

She allowed herself one second to let her feelings for him warm her insides. He was dressed as usual, basketball shorts and a sleeveless t-shirt, and as always, her heart did a silly flip flop when his eyes met hers. He stood and she had to remind herself to breathe he walked toward the car. His gait was unhurried, but tense.

He came and opened the door. She swallowed hard before getting out. He didn't speak as he looked over her face and body. Feeling his gaze as much as a touch she took a step back.

"Are you okay?" he asked.

She nodded and turned away to get the storage containers from the back of her car. "I'm fine, but why do you care?"

He took the containers from her. "I called your job, and they said you called in sick. I came to make sure you were okay."

Tasha looked at the roses growing along her porch, the tree in the yard, and the sky. Anything was better than looking in his eyes. "You've already told me how you feel. You think I'm a lying, scheming, conniving bitch that's trying to trap you into... something by having this baby. You don't want me or this baby and you're moving back to L.A. where I can't expect to get anything from you." Her voice grew shaky as she spoke and she had to stop and take a deep breath. She wouldn't cry in front of him. "So again, I ask why you care."

Jared groaned. "Dammit, Tasha, I can't just shut off what I feel for you. Regardless of what happened."

Her eyes flew to meet his and her lip twisted in anger. "You don't feel anything for me. You said it in Atlanta, you only told me you loved me so I'd come with you."

He put the containers on top of her car. "No, that's what I let Malcolm believe. I'm the one who always said I'd never fall in love. I'm the one who doesn't trust women. I was going to be a bachelor forever. I couldn't say out loud to everyone something I'd only just admitted to myself."

She crossed her arms. "So you were too proud to admit you loved me. I wasn't thrilled about falling for you either, Jared. But

I admitted it to Kenyatta. I took the sad pitiful way she looked at me because I believed what we had was real."

He stepped toward her. "It was real until you..." He sighed, looked away, then turned back to her. "Can we talk about this inside?"

She shook her head. "Shouldn't you be training or somewhere? I've got a lot to do today, and I don't have time to beg you to believe me."

She reached for the containers on her car, but he was faster and grabbed them before her. "Look, I've already missed my flight waiting on you."

She froze. "You're leaving today?" She'd known he was going back, he'd even told her it would be this week. But that didn't make it hurt less to know he was really leaving her in a matter of hours.

He nodded. "We need to talk before I go."

She walked around him toward her front door. His footsteps followed. What was left to say? Even though he said he'd really loved her, he couldn't have. You trusted those you loved, and it was obvious he hadn't trusted her.

He followed her into the living room and placed the containers on the couch. The couch had too many good memories. Pushing back her anxiety, she turned to go into the kitchen. He followed.

"Were you sleeping with Monica when you were sleeping with me?" She blurted out the first thing she wanted to know. Someone had to have ruined his condoms other than her.

"No. I did sleep with Monica, but it was a few weeks before you and I hooked up."

"Were the condoms messed up when you bought them?"

He ran his hand over his face. "No, the package was sealed."

"How many women did you sleep with while using those condoms?"

Jared cringed and looked away. "Tasha, stop it."

"No, I won't stop it. I didn't do this, but you're determined to think I did. You said you really did love me, but you couldn't have. If you did you would know this isn't something I would do."

He rushed over and took her hands in his. "Don't you understand that because I loved you I don't want to believe it?"

Pain sliced through her when he said "loved." He didn't love her anymore, and, idiotically, she still loved him. "Then believe it. Believe me."

She stared in his eyes, begging him to trust her. It didn't take long for her to become aware of the heat from his body and the intoxicating smell of him. Her eyes traveled to his lips and memories of them together flooded her system. She leaned closer to him and his head lowered. She tried to ignore the hot frenzy within her, but his eyes became soft and she licked her lips in anticipation. He dropped her hands and stepped away.

He put his back to her and she watched his shoulders rise and fall as he took several deep breaths. "I can't think straight when I'm around you. I never could, otherwise I would have turned down your offer in the first place." He slowly turned to face her. "I've got to get away and going to L.A. is what I need. Regardless of how it happened, it happened. You're pregnant, and because I care about you, I take back what I said earlier. I'll help with the baby."

Anger shot through her like a lightning rod. "Don't give me that crap. You don't care."

He tensed. "Obviously I do or I wouldn't offer to help after what happened."

"Either you love me or you don't. Either you believe me or you don't. I don't want some half assed attempt to do what's right."

"I can't do that right now."

"Do it now, or don't do it at all. Don't come back into my life if you don't believe me. We don't need that."

He flinched. "Tasha, I will take care of my child."

"As far as I'm concerned this isn't your child. Unless you admit right now that you believe me, I don't want anything to do with you."

"It's not that simple."

"It is for me."

She stared at him and silently prayed he would believe her. It was reverting back to her foolish ways to hope for love to conquer all. That he would look in his heart and realize the Tasha he loved would never do something so awful to him. He walked toward her and reached out to brush his hand lightly over her cheek. He splayed his hands in her hair and pulled her close. Happiness washed over her when he pressed his lips against hers. It was a brief, fleeting kiss. He buried his nose in her hair before inhaling deeply.

"I'm sorry, Tasha, but I can't. Not right now." He stepped away. "If you need anything, let Malcolm or Devin know. They'll be sure to tell me." He turned and walked out of the kitchen.

She didn't know how long she stood there after her front door closed. He couldn't trust her. No. He wouldn't allow himself to trust her. She saw it in his eyes.

She slowly walked from the kitchen to the living room. She picked up one of the storage containers and walked over to her bookshelf. One swift stroke of her hand and one shelf was empty. Then the next, and the next. She dumped everything into the box until the shelf was clear. She marched into her room, pulled the box from underneath her bed, and carried it out the back door. She didn't look through it before she dumped first the contents, then the box directly into the trash. She was tired of letting Jared Patterson break her heart. She would clear her mind of him and everything that reminded her of love, happiness, and fairy tales. It was all a lie. Love didn't conquer a damn thing.

CHAPTER 35

The acrid smell of strong coffee woke Jared. He groaned as he pulled a pillow over his head and rolled over, burying his face in the satin sheets on the bed. There was a dull ache behind his ears and his stomach rolled from the coffee scent he couldn't muffle. He knew Cassandra liked her coffee strong, but that didn't make it any easier getting used to waking up to the smell. He'd avoided looking for a place to stay in the three weeks he'd been in Los Angeles, but after suffering this particular wakeup call for too long it was time to make a decision. Either find a place in L.A., or go home.

He peeked from beneath the pillow at the clock beside the bed. The red numbers glowed, announcing that it was eight a.m. He swore and jumped from the bed, but paid for it with another wave of queasiness. Cassandra's birthday party was today, but the celebration had started the night before. Her ex-boyfriend insisted on throwing a party in her honor at a club. Jared had known he'd pay for the tequila shots he'd drowned like Kool-Aid, and his sick stomach was testimony to that.

Ignoring the urge to lie back in bed, he pulled on a pair basketball shorts and a t-shirt before leaving the bedroom. Cassandra hadn't asked why he'd insisted on coming early for her birthday and he hadn't offered. He'd thought about Tasha and the baby constantly since leaving Columbia.

The look in her eyes when she'd begged him to believe her that day in her kitchen haunted him. He had believed her, and that scared him more than anything. He'd felt his suspicion slipping away when she'd insisted yet again that she hadn't tricked him. Her sincerity pierced through all his defenses and cut him in the gut.

His love for her said she wasn't lying, but logic said she was. He wasn't used to trusting emotions when it came to relationships. What if his love for her was clouding his judgment? He'd never been in love before. It was scary to think love would have him trust her so deeply. So he'd run. Malcolm, Devin, his mom, they all were right. When he didn't know how to handle things he took off. That was why he'd taken tequila shots like a frat boy on spring break—he knew he'd run from Tasha and he wanted to drown his shame.

Bright sunlight bombarded his senses when he opened the door to the bedroom. Cassandra's apartment could only be described as bright. Everything was white: the walls, the carpet, her furniture. The monochrome theme was broken up by bright splashes of red, orange, green, or yellow in the form of pillows, throw rugs, or paintings. Floor to ceiling windows let sunlight in and the effect on his senses was overwhelming.

He squinted as he jogged down the stairs into the kitchen. Cassandra sat at the bar with a white coffee mug in her hand. She was another blotch of color in her all white paradise in a hot pink camisole and shorts pajama set. She had on full make up, which meant she'd already showered but planned to lounge around all day before her party that evening. Despite his annoyance with the coffee, he smiled inwardly. Cassandra couldn't even be comfortable in her own apartment without looking as if she'd stepped out of a makeup studio.

Her perfectly arched eyebrows rose when he entered the kitchen. "Well, I see you finally decided to climb out of bed."

Jared opened the fridge and pulled out a glass pitcher of orange juice. "Eight in the morning isn't late."

"Maybe for some, but it is for you. You've gotten up at four every morning since you've been here to go jogging before working out. I thought you were training for something, or trying to kill yourself."

He poured juice into a glass. "I work out every morning."

"But you also work out for a few hours in the afternoon."

He shrugged. "I'm a trainer."

She cupped the mug in her hand and placed her elbows on the bar. "But you're not training anyone."

He downed the juice. "I'm back in L.A. If I want clients out here then I need to make sure my body is tight."

The corner of her mouth lifted in a smile. "Your body looks pretty tight to me."

She winked and he laughed. "I think the tequila is still in your system." He walked over to sit across from her at the bar.

She laughed. "It's in everybody's system. Ramon knows how to throw a party."

Jared groaned. "Please tell me tonight won't be as wild as last night."

She bit the tip of her tongue and grinned. "Tonight's going to be wilder than last night. It's my birthday. We have to celebrate it in style."

Jared dropped his head to the bar. "I'm too old for this."

Cassandra sucked her teeth. Her hand, still warm from holding the coffee mug, rubbed the back of his head. "Poor baby, you stayed in the country too long. Now you can't hang with us city folks."

Jared lifted his head and glared. "You're getting too old for this too, Cassandra."

She tossed her head. "You must be crazy, I'm twenty-four."

Jared laughed. "Okay, keep telling yourself that." He stood. "I'm going to jog off some of this alcohol." He went back over to the fridge and pulled out a Gatorade and one of his protein bars.

She took a sip of her coffee. "Come on, lova, take today off. Whip up one of your hangover remedies and lounge on the couch with me."

"If I don't run this morning I'll be jumpy all day. I have a lot of built up energy I need to get out."

Her eyes narrowed. "Are you running to get in shape, or are you running from something?"

"That's foolishness." He ripped open the protein bar and took a bite.

"When are you going to tell me about the woman that drove you back here? Don't look so surprised—you ran to South Carolina when I hinted at us getting back together, it only makes sense that a woman made you run back to California." She drank the last of her coffee, stood, and walked over to put the mug in the sink. When she turned to face him her arms were crossed. "What happened?"

Jared shook his head. "Nothing happened."

"Jared, don't play me for a fool. What's going on? I know you promised to come out for my birthday, but showing up three weeks early for it and having no solid plans for when you'll return is a bit much."

He grinned. "What, a guy can't spend some time with his homegirl?"

She raised an eyebrow. "Jared."

He sighed. He might as well tell her, although he hated to hear the different ways she would curse him out for running. He'd been cursing himself out since walking out of Tasha's door. He opened his mouth when his cell phone rang.

Cassandra sighed and pointed at him. "I'm not forgetting this," she said as she walked out of the kitchen.

Jared picked up his phone from the counter and checked the caller ID. It was Devin. "How is she?"

"She looked the same, but you'd know that if you were here." Disappointment colored Devin's tone. Devin was updating him as best he could, but he only saw her during his Wednesday night games.

Guilt pressed down on Jared. "I know. Look, I'm coming back next week."

"When did you decide that?"

Jared could hear the surprise in Devin's voice. Hell, he'd surprised himself. He couldn't keep this up much longer. Cassandra was right, he was working out like a crazy person. But it wasn't for clients, it was to pound out his guilt for leaving Tasha. It was time to go home and face this situation.

"I've been out here busting my ass working out or drinking trying to forget this situation with Tasha and I'm tired of doing it. It's time to come home and work things out."

"Can you really handle knowing what she did to you?"

Jared pinched the bridge of his nose. "I don't know if I believe she really did it. I mean, I saw her in my bag that night, but Tasha wouldn't poke holes in my condoms."

"Are you sure?"

Jared remembered the devastation in her eyes when he said he couldn't trust her. "I'm sure. She's having my child. We can work something out."

He heard Devin sigh on his end. "Well, it may be harder than you think."

Jared gripped the phone. "What do you mean?"

"Kevis is still in the picture. He's coming to games early and helping her get the equipment set up. It's obvious he's still feeling her. If you don't want someone else calling your kid Daddy, you better get back here quick."

Crazy thoughts invaded his mind: Tasha sleeping with Kevis, passing her pregnancy off on him, Kevis doing the honorable thing and marrying her. Him watching another man live a life with the woman and child he'd left behind because like a fool he'd run to L.A. He didn't need to wait to get back to Columbia, he needed to go home today. "That baby's not calling anyone Daddy but me. Thanks for looking out, man."

"No problem. I'll see you soon."

"All right, bye."

He ended the call and stared at the phone. "Cassandra!" he yelled. He spun around and was startled to see her ducking behind the door. "I saw you."

She came around the corner and eyed him guiltily. He wasn't upset about her eavesdropping—she was his friend and she wanted to know why he'd run. But, she had the same deer in the headlights look Monica wore. Right after he'd caught her ruffling through his nightstand for a condom and then stepped on a pin.

"Monica."

Cassandra scowled. "I'm Cassandra."

He shook his head. "No, Monica did it. She was in my nightstand. She poked the holes in my condoms." He balled his hands into fists. "That bitch. It was right in front of me and I accused Tasha."

It came to him as simply as if he'd always known. The reason he'd thrown Monica out in the first place was because of her snooping in his nightstand. The same nightstand where he kept his condoms. It was so obvious, but he'd only considered Monica a nuisance after he'd fallen for Tasha. Her constant popping up now made sense. She'd been trying to trick him. Shame and guilt brewed nastily in his gut. He'd blamed Tasha when the answer had been right in front of his face.

Cassandra took a tentative step toward him. "What's going on? Is Monica the pregnant one?"

"No, Tasha's pregnant. Monica poked the holes."

"You were sleeping with both of them?"

"No, Monica did it before I started with Tasha. Tasha didn't do it."

Cassandra gave a weak smile. "But she's still pregnant."

"I don't care. I love her," he said. Cassandra's eyes grew wide as saucers. He waited for the regret to hit him for saying it out loud. But it didn't come. It was liberating to say it and not be afraid to admit it. He'd been afraid to accept how much he trusted her.

Afraid to admit he believed her when she said she hadn't tricked him based on her word alone. Now that he realized the truth had been staring him in the face the entire time he felt like a royal idiot.

He grabbed Cassandra by the arms. "How do I fix this?"

"Fix what? I don't know. I'm still trying to comprehend you saying you love her," Cassandra said.

"I accused her of tricking me. I left her even after she begged me to stay. You're a woman—how do I fix it?"

Cassandra shrugged. "I really don't know, Jared. Like they say, when a woman's fed up there's nothing you can do about it."

He let her go and ran his hands over his face. "I fucked up. I left her. She won't forgive me." His head snapped up and he looked at Cassandra. "I'm not good at this stuff. I don't know how to tell her I messed up and I'm sorry."

Cassandra leaned against the counter. "You can't tell her, you'll have to show her."

Jared rubbed the back of his neck. "For how long?"

"As long as it takes."

He tried to imagine how long it would take for Tasha to forgive him. He couldn't blame her if she never forgave him. For him to accuse her of deceiving him after refusing to admit his feelings for her in front of his family was bad enough, but the fact that he'd walked away after she'd begged him not to made his task seem as possible as moonwalking to Mars.

He turned his back to Cassandra and dialed Tasha's number. It went straight to voice mail and he wanted to throw the phone against the wall. He was going back today and would stick so close to her during this pregnancy people would think they were joined at the hip. He'd show her every day until this baby came and beyond that, he loved her until she finally realized they belonged together.

He turned back to Cassandra. She held up her hand. "I know, you're going back tonight."

He nodded. "I have to. I need to check on her and my baby."

Cassandra took a deep breath. "I can't believe this. You'll probably marry her too?" When he cringed, she rolled her eyes. "I'll look for flights and pack my bags."

He stopped her as she tried to walk past him. "Wait a second. You're skipping your birthday celebration?"

She raised an eyebrow. "I wouldn't miss seeing you crawl after a woman for anything. Just remember that you owe me a huge party next year."

He pulled her into a bear hug. "I don't deserve you."

"No, you don't," she said with a smile before pulling away and going upstairs.

CHAPTER 36

Jared rubbed his jaw and took a deep breath to calm his racing heart. He stared at Tasha's front door and reached for the doorbell for the third time. The afternoon sun burned his back and sweat beaded along his brow. But even if it were cloudy he'd still be sweating bullets. He wasn't used to begging forgiveness from a woman and he wanted Tasha's forgiveness more than anything.

Once he'd landed the first thing he did was call Monica and confront her. To his amazement she hadn't lied, but thankfully confirmed that she wasn't pregnant. He would have dragged her to every court in America if she were. Instead of calling her every dirty name in the book he'd ended the call and deleted her number. From the defeated sound of her voice, he didn't expect to see her again.

He wiped the sweat off his hands on his khaki pants. The second thing he'd done was shower and change into what he hoped was a responsible looking outfit before coming to beg Tasha to forgive him. With a sigh he pressed the doorbell.

She opened the door and his breath caught. She was dressed in her pink Rec Commission t-shirt and khaki skirt, her hair hung loosely around her shoulders and there was a glow to her caramel skin. She was breathtaking. He held out the bouquet of roses he'd brought.

Her cold gaze went from the roses to his face before she lifted her chin. "What do you want?"

He swallowed his guilt and called on his pride. "I'm sorry. I never should have doubted you."

She crossed her arms and narrowed her eyes. "What do you want?"

He dropped the flowers to his side. "I know you didn't poke the holes in the condoms."

Her lips twisted. "Really, what brought on this epiphany?"

"I realized you wouldn't do something like that. I trust you."

Anger flashed in her eyes. "You trust me? You *trust* me! After I begged you to believe me and you still ran off to L.A., you have the audacity to come here and think flowers and saying you trust me will make it all go away? You don't trust me, Jared. If you did you wouldn't have left."

He reached out and she stepped back. "I know, and I'm sorry. Tasha, I didn't know how to handle it, okay? I'd just found out about my dad—"

Her brow furled. "What about your dad?"

"There was more to the story. Drugs caused his heart attack. My mom wasn't having an affair."

Concern replaced the anger in her eyes. "I'm so sorry."

He stepped forward. "I've wanted to talk to you about it since finding out. My mind was so screwed up after learning what happened. Then Malcolm was digging on me for misleading you," he sighed heavily, "When I saw the condom, it was easier to believe you would do that than trust my instincts."

Her face hardened and she raised her chin. "That's supposed to make me feel better? You were a coward and you ran. You didn't want to face what was real. You didn't want to make what we had real and you took the easy way out."

"It wasn't easy, Tasha. I've thought about you every minute since Atlanta."

She scowled. "Really? Were you thinking of me while hooking up with Cassandra? I saw the reports of you two partying it up. I also know you stayed with her in L.A."

He closed his eyes and dropped his head, mentally cursing the media. "I didn't sleep with Cassandra." He lifted his head and looked at her.

Tasha made a noise that sounded a lot like a growl and tried to slam the door. He caught it before she could close it and pushed his way in. "Nothing happened."

"You expect me to believe that? You had to sleep with me almost every night."

He reached for her again but she stepped away. "You, Tasha, only you. I don't want another woman the way I want you. I haven't loved a woman the way I love you. I don't want to sleep with Cassandra, or Monica, or anyone else. I only want you."

Her eyes softened slightly but she turned away. "It doesn't matter, Jared. I told you before if you couldn't believe me then it was over. I meant what I said."

He stepped up behind her and put a hand on her shoulder. He wanted to draw her close, but instead took comfort that she hadn't pulled away. "I know you meant what you said. I know coming here and saying I'm sorry won't erase what I did. You offered me love and trust and I didn't know how to handle it. I've spent so much of my life mistrusting women and second-guessing every gesture they made. I know it's not a good excuse for what I did, but it's the only excuse I have. I love you, Tasha. And I love this baby." She tried to pull away but he increased the pressure on her shoulder. "I won't ask you to forgive me today. I haven't done anything to make you trust me again, but I will. I will show you that I mean what I'm saying until you believe me."

He pulled her against him. She relaxed into his embrace. He leaned down to place a kiss on the top of her head and breathed in her fresh scent.

The moment was fleeting and she jerked away. She turned to face him but didn't meet his eyes. "Please leave."

He stiffened. "Are you and the baby okay?"

She nodded, still avoiding his gaze. "We're fine."

"I'll come back tomorrow to check on you."

Her eyes snapped up, frustration and desire clearly evident in her glare. "Don't. It's over, Jared. It should have been over a long time ago, but now it's truly over." She opened the door and pointed. "Just go."

He walked over to stand before her. When he spoke, his voice was like steel. "It's not over. You're carrying my child. I will be a part of this baby's life and I will fight every day to be a part of yours. I meant what I said—I love you."

"Love doesn't mean a thing if you don't trust me." She looked into his eyes. "And you don't trust me. If you did, you wouldn't have left. If you did, you wouldn't be ashamed to let your family know. You would have believed me." Her voice broke on the last words and his heart constricted. He reached out to touch her, but she slapped his hand away. "Go."

He wanted to argue, to beg her forgiveness, but he wouldn't. Right now actions would speak louder than words. Regardless of what she said, he would show up tomorrow and every day after that to check on her and the baby. Even if she never forgave him, he'd make sure she understood that he wouldn't leave her again. He'd show her constantly how sorry he was and how much he loved her. Without another word, he turned and walked out.

CHAPTER 37

Tasha twisted in the seat in her obstetrician's waiting room. She studied the other occupants in the large waiting area. There were couples smiling and holding hands. Mothers and daughters sitting around talking, even a grandfather sat with his wife and granddaughter. Some women were alone reading magazines or e-readers or playing with cell phones. Of the women who were alone, two were obviously pregnant. She caught the eye of one and they both gave the small awkward smile of strangers caught staring. Before she looked away, Tasha noticed the wedding ring on the other woman's hand.

Her eyes lowered to her naked ring finger. She absently rubbed the spot where a ring would fit. In the two and a half months since Jared returned he'd pushed his way back into her life. He called to check on her daily. He volunteered to set up for the Wednesday night basketball games, and reminded her to leave early on animal adoption day. He popped up at her house at least once a week with a new item for the baby. Last week it was a crib he'd insisted on putting together. Watching him in her developing nursery as he smiled and talked about the baby caused her heart to yearn for him so badly she'd fled. His determination to show her how much he cared was frustrating, infuriating, and killing her resolve to fall out of love with him.

He didn't pressure her to forgive him as he'd done the day he returned. Instead he said, "I love you" at the end of each phone call, which she refused to repeat. He constantly touched her. The back of her neck, her lower back, her hand. It was maddening. It was heaven.

He shifted in the seat next to her. She looked at him and bit back a smile as he drummed his hands on his knees and tapped his toes. Her appointment was at eight on Friday morning. He'd missed his morning workout to come, which meant he was bursting with restless energy. As endearing as his fidgeting was, she didn't want him there. He'd insisted on coming after she'd mentioned a doctor's appointment. To her surprise, he knew the twenty-week visit was the one where she'd learn the baby's sex. He'd read *What to Expect When You're Expecting*. Her resolution not to love him almost completely dissolved when he'd mentioned that.

The problem with not loving him was twofold: one, she did love him, and two, he was showing her daily he still loved her.

Whenever she felt herself slipping she remembered his accusation, how he left her, and the way he'd rather his family believe he didn't love her than tell them. But it was harder and harder to remember the bad when he was working so hard to show her he cared. She knew he'd told Malcolm and his mother about the baby. Kenyatta called Angie to tell how Malcolm went ballistic when Jared explained what happened before he left for L.A. The only thing that kept the brothers from fighting was Jared admitting he was wrong and taking responsibility for his actions. Between that, and Malcolm's happiness about his approaching wedding, the brothers remained on speaking terms.

Despite all his efforts, Jared never mentioned the word marriage. He said he loved her, he wanted to be in her life, he wanted to take care of the baby, but that was all. Realizing it was better for her child to have a father in its life, she'd grudgingly accepted his assistance, but she wouldn't let Jared back into her heart. She wouldn't be happy as his girlfriend for the rest of her life. If there was even the smallest chance for her to meet someone else, she couldn't afford to fall back into the easy relationship she'd had with him before.

She turned away from him. He reached over and placed his hand over hers. Heat shot through her and she stiffened. She began to pull her away but he held on. When he rubbed her ring finger the same way she'd done before, her eyes shot up to his. He wasn't looking at her. He stared at her hand.

She gazed at his face, taking in his smooth brown skin, full lips, and shiny black hair. He wasn't in his usual workout uniform, instead wearing a green golf shirt and slacks. He didn't wear the cutoff shirts and basketball shorts everywhere anymore. She liked the more mature look, but missed seeing the tattoo on his upper arm and those marvelous legs. The desire to reach out and touch him hit her hard and fast. Her breathing quickened and the blood felt thick in her veins.

She closed her eyes and looked away from him in a weak attempt to break the spell. "Are you nervous?"

He continued to hold her hand. "Isn't it obvious? I can't sit still."

She glanced back at him; the corner of his mouth lifted in a smile. He still wasn't looking at her so she let herself stare longingly at his lips as he spoke. "I hope it's a boy. I know what to do with a boy. I'd have no clue with a girl. But I guess it would be perfect payback for me to have a girl after the way I treated women." His eyes rose to meet hers so quickly she wasn't able to hide her longing. She wanted to look away. She wanted to forget Jared had a chokehold on her heart, but when he smiled, she let out a staggered breath. His smile melted away. Longing and desire swirled in the depths of his chocolate eyes. "Let me back in, Tasha." His voice was low but passionate. "You know we're good together, and you want it as much as I do."

Yes, yes, yes! is what clamored through her heart, but her mind pulled her back. She wanted it all, not part of the story. "What I want hasn't changed. I still want to get married someday."

He closed his eyes and sighed before looking back at her. "Tasha, we don't need a piece of paper to make this real."

"I want it all, Jared, and I'll have it one day. It'll be harder with the baby…and you around, but one day I will meet someone else and he'll want to marry me."

He leaned closer. "But we…"

"We used to sleep together and got pregnant. Nothing more." She pulled her hand away and sat back. It hurt to say those words, but they were necessary. She had to be strong for her child.

The waiting room door opened before Jared could answer and Tasha's mother burst into the room. She looked around until she spotted Tasha. The bright smile on her face dimmed a bit when she saw Jared, but it didn't go away as she walked over.

Her mom had gone against her dad's will and insisted on being at her side. It was a small comfort, but her dad's refusal to talk to her still hurt. She'd missed every Sunday dinner since their fight. She was willing to keep up the silent treatment until her child attended college, and hated that she'd be forced to come back to his church because of Kenyatta and Malcolm's wedding.

Inevitably, her mom had learned Jared was the father after he'd returned and made such an effort to be in her life. Although her mom had pressured her into accepting his help—he was the baby's father, after all—it didn't stop her from asking if Kevis was still an option. Tasha knew her mom secretly hoped she and Kevis would work out. Their tentative friendship was working, although he stopped coming to the Rec Commission to play after Jared returned.

Her mom sat in the empty seat next to Tasha. "Angie told me you had your appointment this morning. Why didn't you call me? This is a big occasion." She didn't acknowledge Jared.

"Mom, I don't need you to come to every visit."

Her mom waved her hand. "Yes, you do. The more I report back to your dad, the closer he is to coming around. Last night he asked if we knew the sex of the baby yet. I think he's looking forward to seeing you at the wedding tomorrow."

"He could have visited me long before Kenyatta and Malcolm's wedding," Tasha said.

Her mom patted her hand. "He wants to see you, baby. He's

just stubborn. You know how he feels about appearances before his church. Maybe if you brought a date to the wedding…"

"A date?" Jared cut in. "Tasha doesn't need a date, she's carrying my child."

Her mom rolled her eyes. "But you two aren't together. She can date whomever she chooses. What about that doctor? Aren't you two still taking on the phone?"

Tasha closed her eyes and groaned. Jared sat up in his seat. "What? You're still seeing the good doctor?"

Tasha shook her head and cut her eyes at her mom before turning to Jared. "No. We're just friends. He just calls to check and see how I'm doing."

Jared scowled. "It's none of his business how you're doing. If you need anything you tell me, not him."

Tasha stiffened. "We're friends, Jared. Besides, I haven't said anything about Cassandra living with you."

He narrowed his eyes. "She stayed with me for a week after I came back from L.A. You know there's nothing between us."

"Do I really?" He opened his mouth to reply but she held up a hand. "It doesn't matter. We are not together."

His dark eyes flashed fire. "Is he the guy you're hoping to marry? The reason we can't be together?"

She rolled her eyes and grunted. "You're the reason we can't be together."

The ultrasound technician came into the waiting area and called Tasha's name. But she and Jared just glared at each other. His jaw was tense. His eyes clouded with anger. The sparks between them were so thick she was surprised the air didn't crackle. His eyes dropped briefly to her lips and despite herself, she licked them. It was enough to ignite the desire that always lingered when he was near.

"Come on, Tasha, let's go back," her mom said. She jumped up and pulled on Tasha's arm.

Tasha slowly stood and Jared popped up behind her. They headed toward the ultrasound technician, who held up a hand. "Only one other person can come with you."

Tasha turned to tell Jared to wait, but he took her elbow and pulled her forward. He turned to her mom with a determined look in his eye. "Wait here."

Her mom's mouth fell open before she snapped it closed. Tasha expected her to argue. Instead Virginia nodded stiffly and sat back down.

Tasha snatched her elbow out of Jared's hand and turned toward the ultrasound tech, who smiled nervously and looked from Tasha to Jared. "I'm Jane, I'll be doing your ultrasound. You can follow me."

Tasha nodded and followed Jane from the waiting room. She didn't have to turn to know he followed. As always, she sensed him behind her. Jane led them into a small room with a bed and an ultrasound. Pictures of the various stages of pregnancy lined the wall and a few hand drawn pictures, presumably from Jane's children, were on the cabinets.

"If you'll go in the bathroom and empty your bladder. Leave off your bottoms and wrap in one of the hospital gowns when you come back out," Jane said.

Tasha nodded and followed her instructions. When she finished she avoided looking at Jared who stood stiffly beside the door. Jane smiled when she came out and motioned for her to sit on the bed. Anxiety crept up her spine. What if something was wrong with the baby?

Jared rushed over and took her hand. Her eyes met his and he smiled reassuringly. When he squeezed her hand, her anxiety fled. She forgot about their earlier argument and all of the reasons why she shouldn't love him. If her mom had insisted on coming back, she would have wished Jared were there instead.

They didn't speak as Jane squeezed the cold jelly on Tasha's slightly rounded stomach. She tensed when Jane put the ultrasound on her belly. A relieved sigh rushed out of her lungs when the sound of the heartbeat filled the room.

Jared looked around. "What's that?"

Jane smiled. "Your baby's heartbeat."

A goofy grin split his face. He looked at Tasha's stomach in wonder before meeting her eyes. "You hear that?"

She smiled. "I do."

He squeezed her hand again and looked at the screen. "What's that?"

Jane explained what she looked for on the screen, how she checked the baby's skeletal system and took measurements, and the blood flow in the heart. Jared was enraptured and asked a lot of questions. Jane smiled and answered his questions in stride. Tasha's heart melted with each one of Jared's grins, gasps of wonder, and swellings of pride.

Jane looked at them both with a grin. "Are you ready to know what you're having?"

Tasha gulped. "I guess so."

Jane turned to the screen and pointed. "It's a girl!"

Happiness and love swelled within her. A girl. Her mom would be disappointed that she'd have to wait on a grandson, but she would easily get over it. Tasha hadn't cared either way, as long as she was healthy.

Jared clutched her hand and she turned to him. "She'll be as beautiful as her mother," he said. He leaned over to kiss her forehead.

Tasha bit her lip and squeezed her eyes shut. She wanted too much, she wanted him too much. She pulled away and turned to Jane. "Does everything look okay?" She took her hand from Jared's. His body stiffened beside her, but she didn't look his way. She was getting sucked into feeling this was a real relationship when it wasn't.

"She looks beautiful," Jane said. She printed out the pictures and made notes on her chart. Jared reached over to touch Tasha's shoulder but she shifted away. Jane looked back at them oblivious to the tension. "I'll take your chart to the nurse while you get dressed, then come back and take you out for your regular visit."

Tasha smiled and nodded at Jane. "That sounds great, thanks."

When Jane walked out, Tasha began to slide off the table but Jared moved to stand in front of her. He placed his hand on the ends of the bed, making it impossible for her to get up. "What's wrong? I thought you'd be happy to find out it's a girl."

She avoided his gaze. "I am happy."

"Then why did you pull away from me? I'm ecstatic and you're stiff." He grinned at her. "We're having a girl."

She sighed and met his eyes. "No, I'm having a girl."

His smile twisted into a scowl. "Tasha, we are in this together."

"No, we're not. We aren't together and we won't be together."

"That's because you won't let me back in. What else do you want me to do? I've apologized. I've told you over and over how much I love you. I've tried to learn everything I can about babies so I can help when she's here." He straightened and pulled the golf shirt from his pants. "Hell, I'm even dressing like a choir boy to prove I'm ready to be with you. But you keep pushing me away."

"I never asked you to change."

"I know. I want to change. I'm doing all of this because I want you to forgive me and take me back. Shit, Tasha, I'm not this guy. I don't *chase* women and beg them to come back, but I'm willing to do that for you. I know I messed up. I know I didn't believe you when I should have, but can't you see how much I regret that? Can't you see how much I love you?"

"You don't love me enough, Jared."

He looked at her as if she'd sprouted another head. "What the hell is that supposed to mean?"

"You want a relationship on your terms. You don't want to step out of *your* comfort zone. I have to compromise. I have to give up my wish to get married. I'll have to face my parents' disapproval about our *relationship* every Sunday. I'll have to trust that your love, which is so fickle, will be strong enough to keep you with me without a commitment." She pounded her chest with each statement. Tears burned the back of her eyes, and for the first time she was afraid she would actually spill them in front of him.

He scowled and put his hands back on the ends of the bed. "Do you think marriage is going to make me more committed to you? Married people cheat, get divorced, and leave. I know married guys who are far less committed to their wives than I am to you. I can't jump off the deep end and change who I am in the blink of an eye. I'm offering you commitment, love, and security for as long as we want it."

"But I want it forever."

He spun away. "A piece of paper doesn't equal forever, dammit!" He slammed his hand on the counter.

She slid off the table. "It's more than a piece of paper, Jared."

"Maybe to you, but not to me."

She lifted her chin. "And that's why we can't be together."

He clenched his jaw, rubbed his hand over his face, and took a deep breath. "I'll let your mom finish this visit with you."

Her throat constricted. Afraid to speak without crying she nodded. He looked at her once more before stalking out.

CHAPTER 38

"Jared, you ain't finished with that tie yet?"

Jared turned from the mirror in the church basement and faced his brother. Malcolm looked comfortable and polished in his traditional tuxedo. Devin and Uncle Bruce were sitting on a couch in a corner laughing, while Mr. Carter sat nearby smiling. They were all fully dressed, while Jared was still trying to figure out the intricacies of a bowtie.

Malcolm had the same goofy grin on his face he'd sported when Jared had picked him up for the bachelor party the night before. Surprisingly, he'd enjoyed himself just sitting at a bar laughing and drinking with Malcolm, Devin, Uncle Bruce, and even Mr. Carter. Months ago, he would have bemoaned the lack of naked women involved. Now, the only woman he wanted to see naked asked for something he wasn't sure he could give.

Jared scowled at Malcolm. "Who knows how to tie a damn bowtie?"

Malcolm laughed and walked over. "Most men who wear more than workout clothes every day." He pushed Jared's hands out of the way and took over.

"You would pick a bowtie instead of a regular tie. I know how to tie that," he grumbled.

Malcolm shrugged. "Kenyatta and I wanted a simple and straightforward wedding. No frills, no extras. A traditional tux is as simple as you can get." Malcolm finished and stepped back smiling.

Jared rolled his eyes. "Are you gonna grin like that all day? It's sickening." He turned back to the mirror. The tie was perfect, but he still tugged at it.

Malcolm laughed and sat on the arm of the couch next to the mirror. "Why shouldn't I smile all day? I'm finally marrying the woman I love. After two years of waiting, I'm not ashamed to be happy."

Jared looked over to make sure the other guys weren't listening before turning to face Malcolm. "Why get married? Why does the piece of paper make what you two have real? I mean, you were perfect before and committed to each other. Marriage doesn't change that."

Malcolm rubbed his goatee and considered Jared. "I know marriage doesn't mean much to you, but it does to me. I saw what Mom and Dad had before he got all messed up, and I want that. Kenyatta does too. She's always wanted the same type of relationship her parents have."

Jared shook his head. "But you can have that without being married. You can still be committed to each other without going through the pomp and circumstance of a wedding."

"You could, but it's more than that. When I almost lost Kenyatta, I knew I wanted to be with her forever. I can tell her every day, but I want to make it official. I want to stand before God, our family, and friends, and tell her I love her and will be there forever. No matter what comes our way, I want the world to know I'm with her until the end. I want to introduce her as my wife, not just my girl or my lady." Malcolm stood and continued to grin. "I know it sounds crazy to you, bruh, but that's just me. You'll just have to permanently revoke my player card." Malcolm hit Jared's arm and walked over to join the rest of the guys.

Jared watched Malcolm as he joined the conversation with Devin and Uncle Bruce. Malcolm laughed and joked around a lot more. Before Kenyatta, it was always work; now he seemed happier, freer. There wasn't a hint of anxiety or stress in his stance.

Jared looked at himself in the mirror. His shoulders were stiff. His jaw clenched. There was tension around his eyes. The only time he'd felt as relaxed and comfortable in life as Malcolm appeared was when he was with Tasha. She eased his fears about success, she made his burdens more bearable, she made his days brighter. He'd been tense and edgy since they'd parted ways. Even before her, he'd never been completely relaxed. It was always some sort of hustle: hustling to get client, hustling to start his line of food products, hustling to avoid relationships. That was what his life would go back to without Tasha.

He imagined life without her and his neck tightened. She deserved to have it all: husband, kids, the whole nine. But could he give her everything? He didn't know if he was the type of man who could make her happy forever. She wanted the perfect life he'd never believed existed. Except it had for the months they were together.

He wanted that perfect life when he was with her. He wanted the sweet, honest, dependable woman who'd be there for him at the end of the day. He wanted to take care of her and make things easier when her job brought her down. That was why he couldn't give her up—he had the perfect life with her, and he wanted it back.

Jared's hands got clammy and his heart beat erratically. *Damn, I can't really be considering this.*

"Jared, you all right? You look like you've seen a ghost," Devin said from across the room.

Jared cleared his throat and wiped the sweat from his brow. "I'm good," he said in a tight voice.

Malcolm and Uncle Bruce both looked over. He would have taken pleasure that the smile finally left Malcolm's face when their eyes met, but Tasha's dad came downstairs. Jared recognized the stern jaw and commanding posture from the pictures in Tasha's house. Reverend Smith glanced briefly at Jared before going over to Malcolm.

"I hope you're ready, son. The ladies have arrived and we'll be starting soon."

Malcolm's smile returned full force. "I've been ready for years, Reverend Smith."

Jared would have rolled his eyes if he weren't so shaken by the realization that he wanted to marry Tasha.

Reverend Smith laughed and patted Malcolm's shoulder. "That's what I like to hear. Who's your best man? I'd like to go over some things before the wedding."

Malcolm called Jared over. Reverend Smith frowned at Jared before turning back to Malcolm with a smile. Jared barely heard the instructions, but it didn't matter. Stand beside Malcolm, hand him the ring, walk down the aisle behind him and Kenyatta. It was pretty straightforward. The hard part would be not rushing over to Tasha the moment he saw her and telling her he thought he could handle marriage. They could elope, go somewhere just the two of them, and say simple vows. No big deal, no big fuss.

But he knew she'd want the church wedding with their family and friends surrounding them. A band, a large reception, and all the trimmings. He cleared his throat and tugged at his bowtie. He'd have to do it. Eloping would be her caving in to his terms again.

"Did you have something to add, Jared?" Devin asked.

Jared looked up. Everyone stared at him. He shook his head and wiped his hands on his pants. "Nah, just something in my throat. Is that all?"

Reverend Smith nodded. "That's all for the wedding, but I would like to have a word with you."

Jared looked at Malcolm, who gave him a warning look. They hadn't discussed Tasha's pregnancy as part of the pre-wedding peace agreement. It would have been too much to ask for the wedding day to go by without it coming up.

"Sure, where do you want to talk?"

Reverend Smith held up his hand. "There's no need to sneak off for this discussion. We all know that my youngest daughter is…pregnant with your child."

Devin and Uncle Bruce made faces and turned away. Mr. Carter sighed and sat on the couch. Malcolm didn't move.

Jared nodded. "She is."

"And we all know you two aren't together. I've heard about you, and I know you're not the type to make an honest woman out of her. So I'm asking you to step aside and let her be happy."

Jared's eyebrows shot together. "Excuse me?"

"It'll be harder for her to find a husband with a baby, but times have changed and since it's just one child it's still possible for her to be happy. If you cared a little, step aside."

"But sir…"

Reverend Smith raised a hand. "I found the number of the guy who was interested in Tasha. He knows she's pregnant and still offered to help. I believe he can make her happy, so I invited him to the wedding. Let's make this day go smoothly, okay? No antics, no, as you kids say, *blocking*. Let her be happy."

Jared's eyes narrowed. Hitting the reverend before the wedding could only delay things by a half hour tops. "I can make her happy."

Reverend Smith shook his head. "Please, she's not here to see your dramatics. Just step aside." He turned to Malcolm and smiled. "We'll use the back stairs to go up so we don't see the ladies." He turned and strolled toward the stairs.

Jared pointed and started after him, but Malcolm stopped him with a hand to the chest. "Not today, man."

"But he just told me to step aside and let another man have Tasha and my baby." Jared tried to push away but Malcolm pressed hard.

"Jared, this isn't a competition. It's real life. If she'd be happier with someone else…"

"She loves me, she'd be happier with me."

Malcolm rolled his eyes. "Don't ruin this day, okay? Just let it go. You can fight this out later."

Devin stood and walked over. "It's time to go up."

Jared and Malcolm stared at each other. He wanted to fight this battle now. He wanted everyone to know he was the right choice for Tasha. But Malcolm was right, today wasn't the day. He nodded stiffly and Malcolm relaxed. Jared tried to control his breathing as Malcolm, Devin, and Mr. Carter followed Reverend Smith up the stairs.

Uncle Bruce came over. He narrowed his eyes and stared at Jared. "Do you love her?"

He straightened his shoulders and looked his uncle in the eye. "I do."

Uncle Bruce smiled. "Then to hell with them. Make all the ruckus you want today, that's what family does—ruin other people's occasions." He winked before turning to go up the stairs.

Jared followed slowly. He appreciated Uncle Bruce's advice, but he wouldn't ruin Malcolm's day. He'd pull Tasha to the side, explain how he felt, and covertly work to keep this guy her dad mentioned—he'd bet money it was the good doctor—away from her.

All that was shot to hell when he entered the sanctuary. Tasha stood at the back of the church. Her tan skin glowed in the silver dress and her full lips were curved into a smile. His heart lightened and his crotch tightened. His gaze traveled over her still thin figure, lingering on her stomach. The roundness of her pregnancy was only slightly visible beneath the dress. Their child was there. His mouth curved into the same goofy grin Malcolm had worn all day.

The doors of the sanctuary opened and Jared's grin fell as Dr. Kevis Flynn entered. If Tasha was surprised to see him, she didn't show it. They shook hands, and Kevis leaned over to kiss her cheek. White-hot jealousy shot through Jared. He took a step forward, but Malcolm grabbed his arm.

He turned to Malcolm who shook his head. Pushing back the need to rip every appendage from the good doctor's body he stepped back. Tasha turned away from Kevis and caught his eye. Her lips parted and her eyes softened for the briefest second before she looked away.

Almost instantly, she was moving to the side and the bridal recession music began to play. He noticed nothing as the wedding party entered. He kept his eyes on Tasha. She'd sat beside Kevis. He willed her to look at him, but she avoided his gaze. She looked at everything except him. He wanted her to see the look in his eyes, to see he wanted the same things she wanted. He wanted everyone to know he loved her.

Reverend Smith began to talk. The wedding had started. He looked at Malcolm and Kenyatta. They looked as if it were only the two of them in the church. Love and happiness shone in both of their eyes. He looked back at Tasha and his heart constricted when their eyes met. He would marry her. Today if she wanted. He mouthed the words *I love you* and hoped she would do the same.

Instead, she closed her eyes and for the first time since he'd known her, he saw tears go down her face. She stood and turned to walk out. Kevis looked between her and him before standing too.

Without thinking, Jared did the first thing that came to his mind.

"Stop!" he called out.

*

Tasha froze at the door. The murmurs and rustling of the people in the church proved her imagination wasn't running wild. Turning slowly, she faced the front of the church. Her eyes met Jared's, hers questioning, his pleading.

"Are you stopping my wedding?" Kenyatta screeched.

Jared looked between Kenyatta and Malcolm. "No."

"Then why did you yell stop?" Malcolm said, scowling.

Jared turned back to Tasha. "Tasha, don't leave. Please, don't leave."

She looked around the church. Everyone looked eagerly between her and Jared. It was too much. The entire day had been too much. Seeing him at the altar, feeling his gaze on her so keenly it could've been a caress. The pain of knowing it would never be them at the altar was worse than she could imagine.

"No, you stop, Jared. This is your brother's wedding. Please stop the games." She turned to leave.

"No more games. Tasha, I love you. Do you hear me? I love you and I don't care if everyone hears it."

She turned back. He moved away and came to the front of the aisle. "You were right. I wanted our relationship on my terms. I was uncomfortable with people knowing how I felt, so I only shared my feelings with you. I was ashamed to let people know that I love you more than anything. I didn't know how to trust what I felt. I didn't know how to trust in general, and because of that, I hurt you. I am sorry, and I'll show you that I'm sorry for the rest of my life."

"But it's not enough," she said. "I want more than that."

He walked toward her. "I want more than that too. Marry me, Tasha." She staggered and he rushed forward. "Marry me today. Be my wife, let me take care of you, our child…our children. Please, Tasha, please marry me."

Warmth spread from the tips of her toes to the roots of her hair. Tears welled in her eyes and for the first time she didn't care who saw her crying. Jared Patterson had proposed to her in the most dramatic fashion possible, and she was ecstatic.

He reached for her, but she hesitated. "But you said marriage doesn't matter."

"It matters when you realize you've waited forever for your soul mate."

Unwilling to fight her feelings, Tasha flung herself into his arms. His lips came down on hers and she clung tighter. He kissed his way to her ear and repeating over and over that he loved her. She didn't know how long they stood there, before the sound of people clapping broke through her haze.

Jared pulled away but held her hand. He rushed back down the aisle and pulled her along with him. He turned to Kenyatta. "I'm sorry."

Kenyatta grinned and shook her head. "I can't believe it."

He pulled Tasha to his side and joy fluttered through her.

Jared looked at her dad. "Reverend Smith, I know we'll need a license later, but will you marry us after you marry them?"

Tasha reluctantly met her father's gaze and was surprised to see satisfaction in his eyes. They hadn't spoken in weeks, but apparently the tidy ending to her pregnancy pleased him. It hurt a little to know that's what it took for him to accept her, but her happiness was too great to make room for pain.

Her dad smiled. "If you promise no more outbursts." There was laughter from the pews and her dad's smile broadened.

Jared looked back at her. "Is this okay? I know you probably had your perfect wedding planned out."

Tasha looked at her sister, standing as a bridesmaid, smiling at her. Her mom sitting in the front pew with tears in her eyes. Her dad at the pulpit with a self-satisfied look. Then she looked at Jared, smiling at her with love and affection.

"This is the perfect wedding."

ABOUT THE AUTHOR

Synithia Williams has loved romance novels since reading her first one at the age of 13. It was only natural that she would begin penning her own romances soon after. It wasn't until 2010 that she began to actively pursue her publishing dreams. Her first novel, *You Can't Plan Love* was published by Crimson Romance in 2012. When she isn't writing, this Green Queen, as dubbed by South Carolina's State Newspaper, works to improve air and water quality, while balancing the needs of her husband and two sons. You can keep up with Synithia by visiting her website, *www.synithiawilliams.com*, where she blogs about writing, life and relationships, on Facebook (*www.facebook.com/synithiarwilliams*) or on Twitter *@synithiaw*.

In the mood for more Crimson Romance? Check out *Secrets of the Heart* by Patti Shenberger at *CrimsonRomance.com*.

.